THE LINE OF FIRE . . .

Doberman cursed himself as he whacked the Hog up to maximum power. Diversionary flares shot out of the wing tips, bursting in the path of the shoulder-launched missile. It kept coming. He'd been caught flat-footed, at low altitude with no speed to help him get out. He just hadn't expected someone to be sitting down there with a damned heat-seeker. He checked—it was still hunting his trail.

Stupid!!! Worse—arrogance. He'd flown as though he was invincible, and now he had to pay the piper. The only question was whether he'd pay in sweat or blood. He concentrated on pushing the Hog into a series of hard, swaggering turns, lighting off flares like mad as he went.

He might have prayed or wished for luck, but there really wasn't time.

Don't miss the other explosive novels in the HOGS series:

HOGS

GOING DEEP

HOG DOWN

FORT APACHE

SNAKE EATERS

HOGS #5
TARGET: SADDAM

James Ferro

BERKLEY BOOKS, NEW YORK

This is a work of fiction. Names, characters, places, and incidents are either the product of the author's imagination or are used fictitiously, and any resemblance to actual persons, living or dead, business establishments, events, or locales is entirely coincidental.

HOGS: TARGET: SADDAM

A Berkley Book / published by arrangement with the author

PRINTING HISTORY
Berkley edition / July 2001

The Penguin Putnam Inc. World Wide Web site address is
www.penguinputnam.com

ISBN: 0-425-18073-5

BERKLEY®
Berkley Books are published by The Berkley Publishing Group,
a division of Penguin Putnam Inc.,
375 Hudson Street, New York, New York 10014.
BERKLEY and the "B" design
are trademarks belonging to Penguin Putnam Inc.

PRINTED IN THE UNITED STATES OF AMERICA

10 9 8 7 6 5 4 3 2 1

Shotgun's Hog Rules

1. Never leave base without your wing mate.
2. You can never be too ugly, too low, or too slow.
3. Pay attention to the plane, not the explosion.
4. If God wanted you to fly higher than five hundred feet, he'd have given you an F-15.
5. For every action by the enemy, there is an opposite and disproportionate reaction—be sure to administer it harshly.
6. The hotter the target, the better the bang.
7. If you can't read the sign, you're not close enough to smoke it.
8. Never fire your cannon when taking off unless absolutely necessary.
9. Under no circumstances should you attempt to eat anything with pits during a bombing run.

PART ONE

VOLUNTEERS & MANIACS

1

Lieutenant Colonel Michael "Skull" Knowlington stepped out from his office in the ramshackle trailer building known as "Hog Heaven," headquarters for the 535th Tactical Fighter Squadron at King Fahd Royal Air Base in eastern Saudi Arabia. The cold air of the desert night stung his eyes closed; the Devil Squadron commander had to stop and rub them open. He began to walk again, ignoring the soft glow of the moon above, pretending he didn't hear the uneasy murmur that came from the nearby hangar area where his A-10A Thunderbolt II "Warthog" fighter-bombers were resting after a long day of bombing Iraq. A few mechanics tended to battle damage; here an engine was being overhauled, there a wing was being patched. The workers might account for some of the noise, but not all of it—the A-10A had always seemed more animal than machine, and tonight a distinct murmur rose from the parked planes, as if they were rehashing their missions in a late-night bull session. In a few short hours, the planes would be back at it, loaded with missiles and bombs and bullets, jet fuel packed into their arms and bellies. They waited now in the shadows, metal bones shrugging off fatigue, green skins still sparking with the electricity of the day. If any warplane could be said to be more than a simple machine, it was the Hog, a two-engined stubby-winged dirt-mover so ugly most pilots argued she *had* to have a soul—aeronautics alone would never have gotten anything that ungainly off the ground.

Knowlington ignored the Hogs and he ignored the moon and he ignored the cold. He ignored the acknowledgment of the security detail. Like the planes and their pilots, he was due a few hours in the sack. More—he'd been strapping planes around his narrow frame for just about thirty years now, and if it weren't for the fact that he was a bona fide, decorated war hero with tons of friends in high places, and could be a serious SOB besides, Michael Knowlington would be more than retired by now. He was due a long, long rest, the kind of rest where the most important thing you did all day was check the obits to make sure you were alive, then went back to bed.

Some people wanted him to take that rest. There were reasons beyond length of service, the same reasons that kept him a lieutenant colonel when most of his peers were either long gone or wore stars on their uniforms. But Skull had never been good at resting, much less reading obituaries. He wasn't even very good at sleeping, especially not when there was a war on, especially not when he had an enemy on his ass and gravity was pinching his face and chest from all directions.

Which was how he felt now.

Which was good.

Something flashed in the sky behind him. The muscles in his neck snapped taut but didn't flinch. He walked on, moving his legs stiffly through the shadows, pushing toward a large parking garage at the other end of the base, skirting the edge of Tent City, a mass of tents and temporary housing units where many of the base personnel—and all of Devil Squadron—lived. He walked quickly and with purpose but without fear, and more importantly, without desire.

For Michael Knowlington, fear and desire had often walked together. Not fear of the enemy, not desire for glory. It would be wrong to say that he wasn't afraid of dying, or that he didn't like the honor of recognition. But from the very first day in Thailand aeons ago when he had wedged himself into the cockpit of a Thud and taken off for Vietnam, neither the enemy nor glory had haunted him. The fear he felt was much more basic. He'd been afraid of letting others down. And he *had* let others down: as a wingman, when his mate nearly got shot down by a trailing MiG Knowlington should have handled; as a leader, when his flight got nailed by a battery he should have scoped out before the mission; as a squadron commander, when one of his boys had gotten in over his head.

The last had happened three times, once in Vietnam, once in the States, and once last week.

Fear—and its guilt—fueled a deep, unquenchable desire. It was mundane, it was ordinary, but it was very real. For much of his Air Force career, Michael Knowlington desired, thirsted, for alcohol. It had tugged at his athletic frame and dulled his reflexes; it had rounded the sharp edges of his brain. Worst of all, the thirst had fueled the fear, which in turn increased the thirst.

But it was gone now. He'd been sober for only twenty-two days, and had come perilously close twelve hours before to falling back. But as he walked across the darkened base, ignoring the moon, ignoring the planes, his nose stinging with sweat and jet fuel, he realized he didn't want a drink.

And that was good, though nothing to bank on.

A Hummer carrying two Air Force MPs shot out of the darkness as he finally neared his destination. As the Humvee pulled up alongside him, a sergeant leaned out and spoke in a pseudo-whisper, as if raising his voice would wake some sleeping giant nearby.

"Colonel, excuse me," he said, "but there's a Scud alert. Sir, I have to ask you to take shelter."

Knowlington nodded but said nothing, continuing to walk. The MP started to repeat himself, but his words were drowned out by a loud shriek in the distance.

Skull kept walking. The ground rumbled. It was an explosion, but nothing that threatened him. He knew that from experience.

During his first tour in Vietnam, Knowlington had manned a machine-gun post with a frightened E-5 whose specialty was developing recon photos. Guerrillas had attacked the small base Skull was visiting on a liaison mission; he and the sergeant had worked through ten belts of ammo while ducking at least five grenade attacks. During his second tour in Vietnam, Skull had spent two nights at the Marine base in Da Nang when it came under rocket attack—as sure a glimpse into the bowels of hell as ever was offered a live human being. Distant explosions didn't impress him. He kept his pace, aiming toward a nearby parking garage, and ignored the comments from the Hummer, which vanished back into the darkness.

The two Delta troopers standing guard at the entrance to the parking garage wore the blank expressions of stone statues as he approached. Though both sergeants instantly recognized the Air Force officer, they challenged him as fiercely as if he were an Iraqi infiltrator. For the humble parking garage was the Saudi home of the Special Operations Command; its officers were running a variety of top-secret operations north of the border. And while Lieutenant Colonel Michael Knowlington was one of the handful of men permitted access to the "Bat Cave" inside, even General Schwartzkopf himself would have had to withstand the ritual humiliation of passing the Delta boys' sentry post.

Not that Schwartzkopf would have done so as quietly— nor as quickly—as Skull. But then, Skull tended to hold the D boys in higher esteem, and the feeling was mutual.

Cleared through, Knowlington proceeded to the operational headquarters, a collection of sandbags, filing cabinets, and desks in an area that had once housed the car collection of a minor prince. Skull got about as far as the former parking spot of a yellow MG roadster when one of the general's aides accosted him.

"Colonel, General's not available, sir," said the lieutenant, who despite the hour and locale could have cut himself on the creases in his uniform.

"Shit-yeah, he is." Skull made sure his gravely voice carried well through the complex. "I talked to him a half hour ago. He's either on the cot over there or sitting at his desk."

"God, Mikey, what the hell is it now?" growled the general from beyond the makeshift walls.

The lieutenant stepped back apologetically. Skull passed into the operations room, where the general was indeed sacked out on his cot. The general had come over to the joint Special Operations command from the Air Force; he and Knowlington went back far enough for Skull not to wince when he called him "Mikey."

Which he did again, adding in a few more succinct Anglo-Saxon words.

"Sorry to disturb you," said Knowlington, standing near the table.

"Fuck you, you are. What's up? You still pissed about your girl Rosen going north?"

"My technical sergeant is a woman," said Knowlington, emphasizing each syllable because he was indeed still pissed. "But we've gone over that."

"I shipped Klee out. Bang, he's gone. He should have come to me and he didn't. That problem is taken care of."

Klee was the colonel who was responsible for sending the Devil Squadron's top electronics whiz north into Iraq. Rosen had returned a few hours before to Al Jouf, a forward operating area in western Iraq where she had been overseeing maintenance on a pair of Devil Squadron A-10As. Needless to say, Rosen had volunteered for the duty north in the combat zone, a direct violation of all sorts of laws, policies, and orders, not to mention common sense. Which merely proved Devil Squadron enlisted personnel were as crazy as the officers.

"Rosen's not why I'm here," said Skull.

"Okay. Shit. I don't think I've had ten minutes of sleep since I came to this stinkin' country." The general sighed and sat up. He glanced at Skull, then followed his gaze over toward the sandbags that marked the entrance to the room. "Lieutenant, make yourself scarce."

"Sir, yes, sir," snapped the lieutenant.

"Love 'em when they're still wet, don't you?" said the general as the nugget lieutenant's steps echoed smartly across the smooth concrete. Skull, for all his love of the service—and he truly did love the Air Force—had never really cared for the snap and starch, nor did he like hazing new officers, so he didn't answer. He stood stoically as the general hauled himself off the cot and went to the desk, where he turned on a small lamp and sat. He'd been sleeping in his fatigue uniform. He reached under the desk for his shoes. "What's up?"

"The intelligence officer who went north with your boys has a theory."

"Wong?"

"Yes, Captain Wong. There was a special unit of Iraqis in the village where the Scuds were hidden. They weren't part of the Republican Guard. They weren't Muslim either. Which he thinks means they were part of an elite unit, probably all related to each other. Those sorts of units typically have very special missions."

"I'm not catching the drift here, Mike." The general stretched his shoulders backward; his body was so stiff the cracks echoed loudly. "Schwartzkopf is on my butt—on everybody's butt—about the Scuds. One hit Tel Aviv last night. We have to nail those suckers."

"This is bigger than Scuds."

"How?"

"Wong thinks Saddam's going to be in that village twenty-four hours from now. I want to put together a team to get him."

2

At roughly the same time Colonel Knowlington was making his way to the Spec Ops Bat Cave, the man whose report had sent him there was setting out on a perilous journey to the dark side of the international army's "occupation" of Saudi Arabia. Captain Bristol Wong, late of the Pentagon, most recently assigned as an "observer" to assist Scud-hunting operations, knew that time would be of essence if Saddam was to be targeted. He had therefore decided to hunt down the one Westerner who, in his considered opinion, knew everything worth knowing about the Iraqi leader. This was itself a mission wracked by difficulties and fraught with dangers and a thousand contingencies, not the least of which was commandeering a helicopter that could deliver him to Riyadh at this ungodly hour. A short if expensive private limo ride took Wong from the relative safety of the sophisticated Islamic capital to a fiery wasteland some miles to the south, where he was dutifully deposited in front of a ten-million-dollar suburban castle replete with neon flamingos and female car hops tastefully clad from the waist down, and from the top not at all.

Wong administered the customary bribes to the Pakistani doorman and his hulking assistant, withstood a rather physical and inefficient weapons check, and passed into the lobby of the club. There he was met by two women whose midsections had recently been graced by staples in major men's publications; their present attire revealed no evidence of fasteners, though their smiles suggested they were ready to bend any metal Wong offered. He made the tactical mistake of telling them that he was simply there on business; they cooed and clucked, and he had almost to force his way past to the short, marble staircase that led down to the gaming room.

The man he had come to see, Sir Peter Paddington, was surrounded by a phalanx of women and gamblers as he held court at the thousand-dollar-minimum craps table. Paddington—he worked officially for British MI-6, was attached to at least one other ministry, and did contract work for unspecified "exterior interests"—held his right hand high over his head, rattling the dice like a wary cobra shaking its tail. With a flick of his wrist he struck, the crisply tailored cuff of his white shirt flashing from his blazer sleeve as his hand jerked above the table, unleashing a pair of threes.

"Six the hard way," said the croupier from the side of the table. A salsa band added a flourish in the background.

Wong snaked through the crowd as the bets were placed. Before he managed to draw alongside Sir Peter, nearly a hundred thousand dollars had been laid out on the table, covering his next throw.

"Bristol, you have returned," said Paddington, sipping his martini. He had not rethrown the dice, believing that the karma of the moment had to be specially chosen.

He also wanted to make sure all of the betting was complete, as the establishment paid him a discreet commission on the house take.

"I have a matter to discuss with you," said Wong. "Business."

Paddington frowned ever so slightly, then turned back to the table. His hand flashed, the ivory cubes rolled.

"Seven," said the croupier, honestly surprised.

Despite the bust, there was audible disappointment as Paddington put down the dice and led Wong toward a side room. Four young women accompanied him, nipples poking at the taut silk of their dresses.

"You want?" Paddington asked Wong, pausing at the draped doorway and gesturing toward the women.

Wong rolled his eyes.

"Sorry, girls," said Sir Peter, waving his hand. "I'll be with you presently."

Wong followed Paddington through the thick brown drapes into a room made up like a private London club. Dark leather chairs sat in small clusters in front of hunter green walls lit by soft lamps and barrister's bookcases stacked with hunting guides and royal lineages. But the most impressive element of decor was the smell, a kind of tweedy dankness surely imported direct from Cambridge. A man stood before a portable bar at the far end of the room, looking at them expectantly. Behind him stood a pair of imposing portraits of unimposing kings.

"Spell yourself, my good man," Paddington told him expansively, "after you supply me with a martini, of course."

The bartender nodded. "And you, sir?" he asked Wong.

"My American friend doesn't drink when he's working," said Paddington. "And as he is always working, he doesn't drink."

"A slight exaggeration," said Wong. "But I do not wish a drink."

The bartender mixed a martini, very light on vermouth, two olives, a sliver of lemon, then removed himself through a door somewhat disguised as a panel at the side of the room.

"So what brings the world expert on Russian weapons to the notorious Club Habanas Saudi?" Paddington asked after the waiter had left.

"I need to confirm a theory," said Wong.

"About Saddam, I suppose."

"Perhaps," said Wong cautiously. "We're dealing with code-word material."

"Naturally." Paddington sniffed the air, as if the dampness had suddenly run out.

"Speculative code-word material," added Wong.

"Quite."

Wong knew that the British intelligence expert had all of the necessary clearances to receive Pentagon and Cent-Com briefings on every aspect of the war. He was also well aware that mentioning that the material was classified would insult Paddington somewhat, as it vaguely called into question his ability to keep a secret. But that was his point. In Wong's experience, Sir Peter worked at his peak only when mildly insulted.

The summary Wong proceeded with left out many details—including the existence of Fort Apache, the behind-the-lines support base recently abandoned by U.S. Special Operations troops. He was also vague about the exact location of Al Kajuk, the village in Iraq where he had been just a few hours before, noting only that it was near the Euphrates and within "a fifty-mile parabola" west of Baghdad.

"You still like those big words," said Paddington. "Why can't you say 'circle'?"

"That would not be precise," said Wong. "I was referring to the intersection of—"

"Yes, quite. I remember my grammar-school geometry." He swept his hand contemptuously. "You want to know if it's within the area he uses to hide? Of course it is."

Wong nodded and told him about the Iraqis he had come across outside the village. The men had been Christians and seemingly related—they looked like cousins if not brothers. The commander had been carrying documents that indicated someone or something named Straw would be at the site at midnight January 26.

At the word "Straw," Paddington put down his drink. "I see. Yes."

"I thought it was one of their code words."

"I didn't say it was," noted Paddington.

"Of course not," said Wong.

"This couldn't have been a very elite unit if you escaped, eh, Bristol?" Sir Peter laughed and put down his martini glass on the bar. "Christians. Well, they are undoubtedly one of the small special groups Saddam uses, beyond doubt. Yes. You have unit identification?"

"They had sanitized uniforms."

"Oh, quite interesting. Yes. But their purpose could be one of several. Not least of which would be guarding the Scuds which I presume you had actually been sent to investigate."

"There was a regular unit and a Republican Guard attachment handling that," said Wong.

"Eh," said Paddington with a noncommittal swagger of his head. "The more the merrier, eh?"

"There's been a marked pickup in coded radio transmissions from the area in the past twenty-four hours," said Wong, who had checked before delivering his report to Knowlington. "And one with the word 'straw' in it."

"Humph," said Paddington.

"My question is this: If Saddam were planning on staying at the village, would an attack on the Scud missiles there deter him?"

"A reasonable question," admitted Paddington. He stared at the wall, as if visualizing the Iraqi leader. Then he reached to the bar and took up his drink, draining it. "Let me tell you something about this area of Iraq." Paddington frowned at the empty glass. "Saddam has had trouble ensuring the loyalty of some of his—shall we call them lesser government ministers? And so he has taken to holding some of their families hostage. And in other cases, not bothering to hold them hostage. He has also had revolts among his Shiite brethren, and is treating them with even less delicacy."

"I saw no signs of a slaughter," said Wong.

"You wouldn't, would you? Unless you knew what to look for. And in any event, I suspect you were occupied with other matters. He uses units from diverse areas, basically as far away and as uninvolved as possible. He is not, as you Americans would put it, a schmuck. That would be my first suspicion here. Though I admit the area, so close to Baghdad, makes me suspicious. Most of the Shiites are located elsewhere, and the ministers are in Baghdad and to the north. But, of course, generalities. From the intercept and these notes, yes, it is possible."

"How likely?"

"Always looking for your percentages, eh?"

"You're the one who calculates the odds."

"Fifty-fifty. Perhaps higher in your favor. But—I would say it is also possible that it is a decoy. He has several and the procedures are exactly the same."

"What would you look for?"

"His Mercedes," said Paddington. "And then, if you find it—I would look in exactly the opposite direction. He doesn't use the official car outside the capital. Except when he does. No schmuck, as I say." Paddington got up and went over to the bar, where he retrieved a bottle of dry vermouth, a tray of olives and lemon twists, and a pint of gin. He opened the vermouth and set it down on the bar top, then carefully ran the overturned martini glass around the mouth of the bottle to catch the fumes. Satisfied, he plopped in two olives and filled the glass to the rim with gin. He waved the lemon peel over it and then held the glass to his lips.

"Cheers," he told Wong.

"Your health."

"Nothing like a martini," Paddington said after a long sip. "I would look for a station wagon with a red crescent, an international aid vehicle, inside a small military convoy. That will be where he is ordinarily. No tanks, perhaps an armored car or two. Mostly he fears a single assassin or a demonstration, an attack that would be best handled by foot soldiers traveling in trucks. He has experience." Paddington took a delicate sip from his glass, not quite finishing it. "He might travel with no more than a company's worth of men. He does not want to draw too much attention to himself, of course. On the other hand, there would be forces where he was going."

"Would he avoid a place that had just been bombed?"

Paddington smiled. "The key question."

"And the key answer?"

"You don't mean that as a joke, do you, Bristol?"

"No," said Wong.

"Pity." Sir Peter finished his martini. "My estimation is that Saddam would think that was just the place to be. He is very superstitious. And, I must say, the pattern of your bombing so far bears him out, except in Baghdad itself. The more you attack a place, the safer he feels it is. Logical, in a way."

"What about the ambush of his advance people?"

"That is trickier." Paddington stepped back to the bar. "The Iraqis seem to be aware that there are commandos operating in their territory, but their responses are a puzzle. Unfortunately, one of the consequences of bombing the C-3 network so efficiently is that there are fewer broadcasts to intercept. Human intelligence is worthless. I'm honestly not sure. He might think it a good sign, he might not. It would depend on whether the Iraqis felt it was related. If they thought it was part of an earlier attack, it might not change things."

"To the best of my knowledge we wiped out the unit. They don't know who attacked."

"Even the Iraqis would realize it wasn't Mickey Mouse," said Paddington.

"You've told me in the past that these units have their own enemies," Wong said. "An attack on them might be classified as an uprising."

Sir Peter was unimpressed. As he began mixing a fresh drink, he detailed more of Saddam's highly variable routine. Despite all of the efforts being made to track him—and the British as well as the Americans had devoted a great deal of resources to the project—Saddam disappeared for long stretches. He was maddeningly unpredictable.

"My personal suspicion is that he is as apt to turn up at

a spot like your village as anywhere. I can tell you, greater odds have been tried." Paddington took another sip. "But that is not an official estimate."

"Understood," said Wong.

"I'll have to pass some of this along," said Sir Peter. "I'm afraid the chaps above me will feel it interesting."

Wong nodded. "Would you like to be involved?"

"What? Go over the border?" Paddington blanched. "Do you think I'm mad?"

"Just wanted to make sure."

"I'm not like you, Bristol. I purged my system of that sort of silliness years ago. Years ago."

"If we had a briefing, would you be available?"

Paddington sighed. "You know how I detest meetings."

"There is another wrinkle," said Wong.

"Being?"

"An American is on the ground near the village."

"You left one of your men?"

"No. He's officially listed as KIA. But I believe he's alive."

"That isn't like you, Bristol," said Paddington. "Leaving a man behind?"

"He wasn't in my unit," said Wong, realizing this was a rather lame excuse. "He had been in action several miles away the day before. His team was overrun and he was seen dead from a helicopter."

"Lazarus."

"I believe the initial report was exaggerated."

"And he just materialized at Al Killjoy? Quite a story, Bristol."

"Kajuk," said Wong. "He could have walked from the area where he was last seen. It's less than ten miles and along a highway. I did not actually see him; I surmised his presence from some unaccounted-for gunfire."

Sir Peter's eyes flashed. "You want an excuse to look for him."

"No," said Wong. "Saddam is the primary mission."

"Already declared dead?" Paddington pursed his lips, thinking. "A Lieutenant Dixon, I believe. Working with one of your Delta Force teams. Oh, now I understand—he was with your A-10A squadron. Ah. Very sentimental of you, Bristol. Uncharacteristic. Hmmm. Happens in a war zone, I suppose."

"If the opportunity presents itself, I will look for him," said Wong. "But that would not be the focus of the mission."

Paddington shook his head and concentrated on his martini. This time he merely passed the glass in front of the vermouth bottle.

"Will you participate in a planning session with Cent-Com?" asked Wong.

"Surely I don't owe you that, do I?"

"There was Romania."

Paddington sighed. "If my commander orders it."

"He already has," said Wong.

"As I feared." He eyed his freshly poured drink, then took a sip. "Pity," he said, addressing the glass. "I seem to have put in a touch too much vermouth."

"Happens in a war zone," said Wong.

"Quite."

3

Captain John "Doberman" Glenon stepped back from the nose of his A-10A Thunderbolt II fighter-bomber, preparing to administer a preflight up-and-at-'em good-luck slap to the business end of its 30mm Avenger Gatling gun. Before he could do so, however, he was thrown off balance by a blow to his shoulder blades so severe it could only have come from a concussion grenade.

Or his wing mate and best friend, Captain Thomas "Shotgun" O'Rourke.

"Yo, Dog Man, you ready to kick this dump or what?" demanded Shotgun, grinning behind a steaming cup of Dunkin' Donuts coffee.

And it definitely was Dunkin' Donuts, since it was in an oversized Big Gulp cup.

"Don't sneak up on me like that, especially this early in the morning," said Doberman, shaking off Shotgun's chuck.

"Touchy," said Shotgun, gurgling his coffee. "Gotchya good-luck charm, I see," he added, nodding at the small silver cross Doberman had pinned to the chest of his flight suit.

Doberman felt his face flush. Until a few days ago, he wouldn't have been caught dead believing in good-luck charms, let alone pinning one to his chest. But the last few days had taught him not to spit Fate—or superstition—in the eye.

Still, he didn't like to admit that he might actually believe in luck or good fortune, not even to Shotgun.

"Ain't nothing," Doberman said.

"Shit, Tinman says it's voodoo. Or whatever the hell he says in that accent of his. Own personal language."

"Yeah, well, maybe it's good luck and maybe it's not," said Doberman. "I'm not taking any chances."

"What I'm talkin' about," said Shotgun.

"Looks good to go, yes, sirs?" said Tech Sergeant Rebecca Rosen, ducking out from under the wing on the other side of the plane. Sergeant Rosen, a technical wizard and crew chief of considerable standing, posed the question as a stated and accepted matter of fact. Indeed, though Rosen was operating with a minimal support team—and even less sleep—she had thoroughly examined the aircraft prior to the pilots' arrival at the maintenance pit, which amounted to a small piece of tarmac nudged against the sand at the forward operating area in northwestern Saudi Arabia. "We're going to schedule that right engine for a complete overhaul when you get back to the Home Drome," she added to Doberman. "But it's fine for now, assuming you don't do something stupid like suck some sand through it. You won't, will you?"

Coming from the mouth of any other sergeant in the Air Force, the words would have seemed like an insult to Doberman, whose temper was even shorter than his five-four (on tiptoe) frame. But the captain was hopelessly in love with this sergeant, though he hadn't been able to tell her yet. And in fact, he was increasingly tongue-tied around her—which explained why all he could do was stare at her very delicious, if tired, eyes.

"I'll set up the maintenance on it myself," added Rosen.

"I'm supposed to be catching a flight back to Home Drome in a few hours. Assuming I can't talk the Capo out of it."

"Capo" was Chief Master Sergeant, First Sergeant, capo di tutti capi, Wizard of Wizards, Allen Clyston, who ran Devil Squadron. The unit was commanded by Colonel Knowlington and staffed by a fine collection of officers, but like any efficient military organization, the sergeants ran things. And the Capo was the sergeants' sergeant, the squadron's master of fate and minder of souls.

Rosen smiled, and Doberman felt his knees starting to tremble.

No shit.

"Relax, Captain. I'm just being cautious," she said. "Plane can go at least another hundred hours without fiddling with the motor or anything else. I promise. Honest. It's showroom-pretty."

"Planes look weird," said Shotgun.

"Captain?" asked Rosen.

"No bombs. No Mavs," said Shotgun, shaking his head sadly. "No rockets. Nothing. Naked. What I'm talking about here is nude. Out of uniform. Obscene. Got to be a reg against it."

"We're flying straight to Fahd," snapped Doberman. "What do you want to do, bomb Riyadh?"

"If it needs bombing, I'm up for it," said Shotgun. He slapped the front of Doberman's Hog. "Even the Gat's empty."

"Begging your pardon, but your cannon has been reloaded," said Rosen in a tone that suggested she wasn't begging anything. "As is Captain Glenon's. And he has fresh Sidewinders."

Her voice softened ever so slightly when she mentioned the air-to-air missiles, and she glanced back at Glenon. Last night, Doberman had made Hog history by using the Sidewinder in a dogfight—even better, he had managed to nail an MiG in what had to rate as the most lopsided battle since open-cockpit P-26's tangled with Japanese Zeroes at Pearl Harbor in 1941. Doberman had, in fact, saved

Rosen's life—as well as the lives of three other people aboard a small AH-6 fleeing Iraqi airspace.

But as far as the world was concerned, Doberman's exploit hadn't occurred. Command had declared that the need to keep ground operations north of the border secret extended to the aircraft supporting those operations. In other words, Doberman's flight hadn't happened, and therefore the shoot-down hadn't happened.

Officially. Unofficially, every member of the A-10 community either knew about the shoot-down or would shortly. Glenon wouldn't get a medal or headlines, but he'd be stood plenty of beers. And knowing he'd save Rosen felt loads better to Doberman than taking salutes from a dozen dumb-ass generals.

As for kissing her . . .

That would have to wait. Doberman sighed as the sergeant turned her attention back to Shotgun, who was whining about not getting a full complement of Mavericks, or at least cluster bombs, beneath his wings for the routine ferry flight home. The tech sergeant demonstrated her experience in grade by restricting herself to a single smirk as she walked away, leaving the two jocks to saddle up and get on with the morning flight.

From a pilot's point of view, flying the Warthog was a relatively straightforward operation. The A-10A personified the concept of no-frills flying. Its cockpit would have been familiar to the P-26 pilot.

Well, some of it, at least. No P-26 pilot ever dreamed of a heads-up display, and even though the Hog was slightly underpowered and agonizingly slow by contemporary standards, its twin turbos pumped Doberman into the sky at a pace that would have left the P-26 pilot gasping. Glenon eased his stick back gently, the Hog's fuel-filled wings lifting the plane easily into the sky. Unlike nearly every other jet designed after the 1940's, the A-10A's wings were not swept back, part of a design strategy to enhance low-speed/low-altitude maneuverability. The fuselage's rather odd shape—it looked like a beached whaleboat with wings—was the result of two other design strategies: survivability and maximum firepower. A good hunk of the front-end weight came from a ring of titanium that protected the pilot's sides and fanny from artillery fire. The rest came from the Avenger 30mm cannon, arguably the most important feature of the plane. The Gatling-style cannon spat a mixture of incendiary and uranium-tipped slugs custom-designed to unzip heavy armor—and not incidentally, obliterate everything else.

Airborne, gear stowed, Doberman walked his eyes across the wall of gauges in front of him, checking his sense of the plane against the cold data of the indicators. A small TV screen used to target Maverick air-to-ground missiles sat in the upper right-hand corner of the dash; without any AGMs aboard, it would remain blank the entire flight. Below the screen were two sets of gauges monitoring the General Electric turbofans that hung in front of the tail. Relatively quiet as well as efficient, the TF-34's hummed at spec, propelling the A-10A toward its 387-nautical-miles-per-hour cruising speed, which Doberman would achieve at five thousand feet, give or take an inch.

"Devil One, this is Two. I have your six," said Shotgun, drawing his plane into trail position behind Doberman.

"One," acknowledged Doberman over the short-range Fox Mike or FM radio.

"Kick-butt sun," said Shotgun.

Doberman grunted at the scenery and checked his INS guidance system. Preprogrammed way-points helped the pilots make sure they were on course as they flew. Hog drivers also carried old-fashioned paper maps, though by now Doberman and Shotgun had so much experience flying over northern Saudi Arabia and Iraq that they could almost tell where they were by looking at the dunes.

Almost.

"So, Dog Man, what's the first thing you're going to do as squadron DO?"

"Who says I'm going to be squadron DO? I'm only a captain."

"You're a high-time Hog driver, the squadron's longest

in-service pilot, and all-around peachy-keen guy," answered Shotgun. "Besides, Skull loves your ass."

"They'll probably bring somebody in from the outside."

"Nah. You da man."

"I don't want the headaches." Doberman snapped off the mike button and rechecked his instruments. DO stood for Director of Operations. Traditionally, the DO rated as the number two man behind the squadron commander. Devil Squadron wasn't particularly traditional—it had been thrown together from a bunch of discarded planes, its pilots shanghaied and "volunteered" from other units. It had an extremely bare support structure, with a short chain of command and a relatively thin roster of fliers. But it also had an amazingly high sortie rate, and had already dropped more than one million pounds of bombs, missiles, and curses on the enemy. A lot of bang for the buck, as Shotgun would put it.

All of which meant Devil Squadron's DO worked twice as hard as he would in another unit. The last DO, Major James "Mongoose" Johnson, had been sent home after being shot down, injured, and rescued. Doberman had never gotten along with him; from Doberman's point of view, Johnson tended to be a bit of a prig and was always on his butt for little bullshit things. It wasn't just Doberman either. Johnson seemed to think he had to be everywhere, looking over everything. He rode the maintenance people especially hard; Glenon couldn't go near the hangars without hearing somebody bitch about him. But Goose hadn't been the worst DO Glenon had ever served with, and Doberman could have put up with the jerk for as long as necessary, especially if it meant he didn't get tagged with the gig.

"Ah, you're bullshitting me," said Shotgun. "Once you're DO, you're on your way. Stepping-stone to general. Shit, with that shoot-down, you'll be wearing stars next week. Just remember me when you're in the Pentagon. Score some tickets for a 'Skins game, okay?"

"*Seeing* stars maybe."

"General Dog Face. Probably have your own box at RFK, right?"

"Who the hell said I ever, ever wanted to be a general?" blustered Doberman. "And I thought we were flying silent com."

"Silent com? Can you do that in a Hog?"

A call from the AWACS controller monitoring their sector ended the banter.

"Devil Flight, this is Coyote," said the controller, who was aboard the Boeing E-3 Sentry aircraft orbiting to the south.

Doberman acknowledged, verifying their course and status.

"Can you handle a detour?" asked the controller. "Army unit near the border has a situation and needs some support. You're the closest flight."

"Give us the coordinates," answered Doberman, touching Tinman's medal with his thumb before nudging the Hog northward.

4

Captain Lars Warren took a deep breath—his fifth in perhaps the last twenty seconds—and fixed his glare on the runway in the distance. It was his second approach to King Fahd; he'd aborted his first landing attempt when he realized he was going too fast to land safely.

That was an excuse. He'd aborted it because he'd panicked. And it was happening again. Even worse than before,

His pinkie began to quiver. Lars glanced at his hands on the steering yoke of the big four-engined plane. His fingers' light-brown flesh had turned violet from the pressure he was exerting. Lars pushed his right elbow further into his stomach, trying to keep the tremor from extending to the rest of his fingers. It was terrible flying posture—it was terrible posture, period—but he wasn't thinking about that; all he was trying to do was land his Hercules C-130 in one piece.

The thing was, he'd landed Herks maybe a thousand times before. He'd landed this very plane at least twenty times, including twice on this long, sturdy, and accommodating strip. It wasn't difficult—the high-winged transport was an extremely stable and generally forgiving aircraft. In many respects it was actually easier to fly than the 737 he had been flying two weeks ago when his Air National Guard Unit was ordered into the Gulf to spell other units.

Lars was a good pilot. In fact, he was better than good; he'd been up for an assignment as a training supervisor at the airline before the Gulf War complicated things. He had had flown 707's and Dash-8's and C-141's and a KC-10 and so many C-130's he could do it all in his sleep.

But he was having trouble landing. He was having trouble flying. And everyone on the flight deck knew it.

"Gear set," said his copilot. His tone was gentle, but part of Warren bristled as if the man had cursed him for being a failure and a coward.

The rest of him trembled, just afraid.

Afraid of what?

Afraid of flying.

Hell, no. No way. Flying was walking, with a checklist. Shit. He could fly in his sleep.

Afraid of being shot down?

He was flying a cargo plane, for christsake. He was behind the lines—he always flew behind the lines. Way, way, way behind the lines. No one was going to shoot at him. He'd been here for two whole days and last night's random Scud attack was the closest he'd come to anything remotely warlike.

But that had unnerved him. He'd been preparing to take off when the alert came in.

The warhead had landed on the other side of the country, but it had shaken him up. Still, when the all-clear came they went ahead with the mission, a routine supply hop. He'd done okay, though little things had bothered him. He'd forgotten to ask the copilot for the crosswind correction—not a big deal. He'd bounced a little on takeoff to come back—something he never, ever did, but no big deal.

Now, though, this was a big deal. Lars felt his legs turn to water as the edge of the runway loomed ahead. Hot air rose in waves from the concrete. In just a few seconds it would be buffeting his wings.

If he let it.

Shit. All he had to do was skim in. Everything was perfect. Let the plane land.

Give it to his copilot.

No!

His copilot was talking to him. The tower was talking to him. A plane—a loaded Warthog—was on the runway, on the runway.

In the way.

What the hell?

Abort.

Abort!

"Captain?"

Lars snapped his head toward his copilot. As he did, he realized the A-10A wasn't moving on the runway. It was well off to the side in the maintenance area, being prepared for a morning mission.

Nothing was in his way. His brain had done a mind flip, constructing boogies to spook him.

God, help me, he thought to himself. I'm losing it.

A pain shot through his chest, striking so hard he lost his breath mid-gulp.

Heart attack.

It's just panic, he told himself.

"Captain?"

"Yeah, I'm landing," Warren said, not caring how ludicrous it sounded. He pushed his elbows in and closed his eyes—actually closed his eyes—as the wheels skipped and screeched but finally rolled smooth against the tarmac. For a second his entire world turned black; for a second his addled mind completely lost its grip, furling and swirling in a darkness filled with bullets and missiles, Scuds and MiGs and SAMs. Then slowly, very, very slowly, the fog lifted. He was able to open his eyes; he realized he had already begun applying brakes. His copilot was busy on his side of the console; they had landed in òne piece.

"No offense, Lars," said the copilot as they found their

way toward the hangar where they were assigned, "but, uh, you okay?"

Warren bit back the impulse to ask if the man—a young, white captain whom he didn't know very well—was going to report him.

What would he report? That he came in too fast? That he seemed to hesitate at the last second?

That he closed his eyes?

That Lars Warren was petrified, twenty-three years after his first solo. That Lars Warren, who as a fourteen-year-old had single-handedly broken up an armed bank robbery by tackling a robber, had suddenly become a coward at forty-three. All because of a random Scud attack that had been thwarted by Patriot missiles miles and miles away.

Or because he'd always been a coward, deep down.

Lars said nothing, blowing air out through his clenched teeth and nodding instead.

5

Doberman scanned the ripples in the sand, mechanically moving his eyes back and forth across the terrain as he pushed Devil One toward the trouble spot just over the Saudi border. Intelligence and the mission planners divided the desert into neat kill boxes, subdividing Iraq into a precise checkerboard that could be measured to the meter. But the nice clean lines got wavy as soon as you pushed your plane low enough to actually see anything. Distances blurred, coordinates began to jumble. For all the high-tech paraphernalia, war in the desert still came down to eyeballs and pilot sense. Glenon had a healthy helping of both—but he wasn't Superman, and he felt himself starting to get pissed as he stared down at the area where the American troops should have been. The pilot had a notoriously short fuse, but even he knew he was in a particularly bad mood all of a sudden. Maybe it was because he hadn't had that much sleep; maybe he was angry with himself for getting tongue-tied with Rosen.

Or maybe it was what Shotgun would call PBS—Pre-Blowup-Syndrome.

The ladder on the HUD altimeter display notched steadily downward as Doberman hunted for the slightest sign of the conflict the AWACS had sent them to contain. He kicked below three thousand feet without any sign of the unit that had called for air support—without, in fact, seeing anything but yellowish blurs of sand. Finally, a thick scar edged against the earth in the right quadrant of his windshield. Doberman nudged his stick, steadying the A-10 toward what he thought was the thick trench that marked the Saudi-Iraqi border for much of its length. But the man-made trench was actually a British Army position two miles back from the border and not precisely parallel to it; when he realized his mistake he cursed over the open mike.

"My eyes are screwing me this morning," he told Shotgun.

"Sun's wicked. I got dust bunnies northwest, uh, off your nose at eleven o'clock—no, let's call it five degrees on the compass. Could be our friends."

Shotgun was behind him by a mile and at least two thousand feet higher. But sure enough, when Doberman looked in the proper direction he found a small bubble of dust.

"How the hell did you see that?" he asked, snapping onto course.

"Carrot cake," said Shotgun. "No better source of Vitamin A. Enhances your vision rods. As a matter of fact, I was thinking of grabbing another bite, so long as I'm playing Tonto back here."

"You're eatin' carrot cake?"

"Hey, man's got to have breakfast," replied Shotgun. "I figured the bacon would have been cold by the time I got a chance to eat it. One of these days, I'm figuring out how to get a microwave in here. Course, nuked bacon tastes like cardboard. What I really need is a deep fryer. Could slot it in over the radio gear, if I can get one of Clyston's techies to order the parts."

Anybody else would have been kidding.

Doberman reached to the armament panel, readying the cannon. He could now see two distinct smudges on the ground. One seemed to consist of a dozen ants surrounding a small pickle they'd stolen from a picnic. The second, behind them by about a mile, looked like two large and angry bees.

He nudged toward the bees, setting up for a straight-in dive across their path. They were tanks, moving at a fair clip.

"Rat Patrol to Devil Flight, Rat Patrol at frequency ten-niner looking for Devil Flight. Understand you are in our box. Please acknowledge."

"Devil Flight," answered Doberman. "I have two enemy vehicles in sight. I'll be on them in about ten seconds. Keep running."

"Negative, negative. We're stationary. We see you. We're southeast of you, a mile directly south of the truck and the men," said the soldier. "They're not the problem. Repeat, they're not the problem. Don't hit them."

Before Doberman could ask what the hell was going on, the tanks stopped moving. A large mushroom appeared near the truck and its attendant ants. They veered off to the right, followed by another mushroom.

"T-72's or maybe Chinese 69's in that second group," announced Shotgun. "What's the deal, Dog Man?"

"I don't know. I see the tanks but I don't have Rat Patrol. Let's take a turn while we sort this out. Cover my butt."

"Butt's cleaner than the floor of the Route 17K diner in Monroe, New York," said Shotgun.

Doberman took that for a compliment.

"Rat Patrol," added Shotgun. "I like that. Nothing like taking your inspiration from a sixties TV show."

"Yeah, right."

"Better than *Ozzie and Harriet.* Or *My Mother the Car.*"

As Doberman swung the Hog around, he nudged the GAU to its high setting, the preferred choice for breaking serious armor; roughly sixty-five slugs a second would pour from the nose when he pressed the trigger. Though it allowed for a more potent burst with less time on target, the higher rate also increased the amount of gas expelled by the powerful cannon, not insignificant at low altitude because it was possible to choke the engines. Besides, the high rate was overkill for soft targets, where the normal thirty bullets a second were more than enough to guarantee obliteration.

"Devil One to Rat Patrol. I see tanks firing on a truck. Are these both Iraqis? Explain to me what the hell's going on," he told the ground unit.

"They're both Iraqis, yes. The first group is trying to surrender to us," the ground unit's com specialist explained. "Tank or something's trying to stop them. We're not sure exactly what's after them. They started out talking to us on the radio but we've lost contact. They're about to get nailed."

"I don't have your position," Doberman warned.

The last thing he wanted to do was whack good guys. But the coordinates the soldier started feeding him only made him more confused, and there wasn't time to pull out the paper map and sort the whole damn thing out. He had dropped through 1,500 feet and was lined up perfectly to cross the path of the lead tank—he had to go for it now or bank around, let the tanks get off another four or five shots.

Doberman pushed his stick, putting the Hog into a shallow dive. He saw something on his left, a U with dots in the sand, a mile and a half away, closer to the tanks than the truck.

Had to be Rat Patrol.

Balls.

A pair of mushrooms erupted on the ground about two hundred yards from the truck. It veered to the right, then stopped moving.

"Okay, Rat Patrol. Hang tight. I got ya," said Doberman. "Gun, the Ural is surrendering to our guys, so leave him alone. I got the tank."

Shotgun's acknowledgment was lost in the fuzz of another transmission overriding the squadron frequency.

Doberman wouldn't have heard it anyway—he was all cannon now, the targeting bull's-eye centered on the front end of the Russian-made T-72. While not to be taken lightly, the forty-ton tank was at a severe disadvantage against the Hog; having stopped to get a better shot at the fleeing deserters, it was an easy target. Doberman nudged his stick gently to the right, then squeezed the trigger. The first shells, fired at just under 750 meters away, missed low, but that was merely a technicality—the stream moved up, following Doberman's stare and the plane's momentum, uranium and high explosive dancing through the steel plates as if they were paper. The T-72's gun retracted, then burst apart, choking on its own charge. The turret opened like a rose bursting to meet the morning sun.

Doberman jammed his pedals, swinging his tail hard to the left as he tried to yank the Hog around and line up on the other tank. He'd come all the way down to five hundred feet, still descending, but wanted the other T-72. He was so close he could see the gunner at the top cursing as he splayed shells from the twin 7.62mm machine gun in his direction. Something plinked against the Hog's armored windscreen as Doberman pushed his trigger to fire. He flinched, then tightened his grip on the stick, nailing down the trigger. The bullets spat off to the right, drifting with his momentum. Doberman worked the rudder pedals, giving a little body English with his shoulder as he tried to walk the cannon fire onto the target. He got a few rounds near the front fender, but then just had to give up, the desert yawning up at him.

Doberman pulled back, jerking four g's as the Hog angled her wings upward. He cleared the ground by about fifty feet—too close for comfort, but not as close as he thought he'd cut it.

He was just starting to climb when Shotgun shouted a warning in his ear.

"Missile launch! Missile launch from the Ural! Those fuckers weren't giving up, Dog Man!"

6

He woke up thirsty, his throat hard, his mouth hot.

Lieutenant William "BJ" Dixon stared for a minute more, at the hazy blue sky. He was sore, cold, tired, but more than anything else thirsty. He remembered the small canteen of water on his belt and reached for it, his arm and shoulder joints cracking. The bottle felt like ice, and he realized he too must be freezing, though all he could feel was his thirst and the scorching heat in his mouth. Fingers fumbling, he rolled himself onto his stomach and got on his knees, then finally managed a drink. The water fell across his teeth to his tongue and into the back of his mouth; he began to choke. His body wanted water and it wanted air as well—he choked and he gasped and he tried to drink, and the only thing he could manage was to fall forward against the rock-strewn side of the ditch where he'd spent the night, stomach heaving, body retching. He had nothing to give, nothing to puke except mucus and viscera, the scrapings of his soul. He curled in the dust, muscles spasming, chest and stomach wrenching against the hard Iraqi soil. A metallic taste mixed with the vaguely bloody flavor of vomit in his mouth.

When it was over, Dixon lay against the rocks. He stayed there a long while. His knee hurt and his shoulder had been whacked out of joint and maybe he'd broken a rib, and his head felt like it had been squeezed into a sardine tin, but considering the other possibilities, it wasn't that bad. Two hundred miles inside of enemy territory, without hope of getting out, it wasn't that bad.

He stayed there awhile longer.

Not bad at all.

"When did I begin lying to myself?" he asked finally, speaking the words in a whisper. He pushed himself upright and took a tiny sip of the water, then another, then a third.

There was a sound in the distance. Trucks.

Dixon recapped the water and reached down to grab his campaign hat, a "present" from the Delta unit he'd parachuted into Iraq with as a ground FAC helping coordinate strikes on Scuds. BJ grabbed the AK-47 he'd taken yesterday from a dead Iraqi and clambered up the side of the dry streambed, staring across the scratchy terrain toward the highway.

Two Iraqi troop trucks approached from the west. The trucks moved steadily though not quickly, traveling in the direction of a missile-launching site American fighter-bombers had attacked yesterday. The highway swerved southward, toward Dixon, to skirt a hill. There were no houses or other buildings in sight; the area was apparently used as farmland, crisscrossed with irrigation ditches, though BJ guessed it wasn't particularly productive. The local population seemed confined to a small village on the other side of the hill; there had been Iraqi troops there yesterday, and he hadn't gotten close enough to see more than the minaret of a mosque.

As the trucks followed the highway, turning in his direction, Dixon flopped against the ditch, ducking from view. But as he lay against the rocks he asked himself why. Hiding just delayed the inevitable.

He wasn't going to surrender, nor was he going to allow himself to be captured. But it was senseless to think he might somehow make it back to allied lines. A huge desert lay between him and Saudi Arabia.

So there were two choices. Kill himself, or make the Iraqis kill him.

Better to make the Iraqis do it. At least he might take a few of them with him.

BJ stood, pulling the rifle up, cocking it under his arm. But by now the trucks were past him. He swept his aim to follow, squeezed the trigger—a bullet sailed from the rifle, skipping into the dirt less than fifty feet away.

The trucks kept moving, oblivious. The highway was nearly a mile away; if the drivers heard the crack of the gun over their engines, they chose to ignore it. Dust billowed in a thin swirl behind them, funneling over a shallow rise as they disappeared. There was another highway as well as a turnoff for a village somewhere beyond the rise, but it seemed as if the trucks had been swallowed by the blue fringe at the edge of the universe.

As Dixon stared at the disappearing film of dust, he realized he was yelling, screaming at the Iraqis to come back and fight. He pointed the AK-47 upward and kicked off a short burst, then let the gun hang down. Slowly, he craned his head left and right, twisting it nearly 360 degrees. He was alone.

His stomach reminded him of his hunger with a low rumble, a gurgle that sounded more like a gasp for help. With nothing to eat, he took another swig from the canteen instead, then another. He had about half the bottle left, a few ounces—it would be gone before noon.

So that was his deadline.

Better to take a few of them out when he went.

Slowly, Dixon looked left and right, turning his whole body this time. Satisfied that he was truly alone, he began to walk toward the left side of the hill, heading in the direction of a ramshackle road that led to the village.

7

Major Horace Gordon "Hack" Preston hopped out of the small C-12 Huron that had ferried him across from Tabuk to his new squadron. After flying F-15's, anything was likely to seem slow, but the bare-bones two-engined Beech—essentially a Model 200 with Air Force insignia—had trudged across the Saudi peninsula, its three-pronged propellers huffing and puffing the whole way. He was a terrible passenger to begin with, but sitting in the C-12 was like rolling a heavy rock up Purgatory Hill.

An apt transition to his new assignment, Preston thought as he stepped away from the plane and got his bearings.

Yesterday, Hack had nailed an Iraqi MiG and damaged another. His reward came swiftly: a long-awaited promotion to squadron commander.

Except, not quite. Because the hotshot pointy-nose fast-mover zipper-suit jock had been made only second in command—director of operations—not squadron commander.

Worse, far far far worse, he had *somehow* been placed with an A-10A squadron.

Preston bit back his bile and asked an enlisted man near the parking area where the 535th was located. The man pointed toward an A-10 maintenance area on the other side of the base, and said the trailer unit that served as its headquarters was located just beyond it.

"They call it Hog Heaven," said the airman enthusiastically, as if he were pointing out Old Faithful.

Hack grunted and began walking in that direction. He had his gear in a small overnight bag—the rest was to follow him to the base.

His new assignment offered two consolations. One was the fact that, on paper, the squadron was actually listed as a wing. While at present this didn't fool anyone—Saddam especially—he had been told more A-10's were expected to be added in the near future, in essence creating a new squadron; he'd be in line for that command.

The other consolation was a rumor that the present commander wasn't cutting the mustard, in which case Hack would get his slot. In fact, a friendly general had hinted that was the whole reason for his appointment. Of course, the general worked in Washington, so there was no telling what if anything the hint was worth.

But why would Preston want to command a unit of Hogs?

He wouldn't. Preston had flown A-10's for two of the worst years of his life. He had angled and pleaded and connived the whole time to get out of them to a *real* airplane. And now he was back.

A Humvee sat near a short fence beyond a low-slung building on his left. Two airmen sat inside, their backs turned away from the ramp area. Preston went to the Hummer, opened the rear door, and hoisted himself and his small bag inside.

"Uh, excuse me," said the driver sharply.

"Take me over to the headquarters for the 535th," he said, settling into his seat.

"Uh, sir?" said the other airman.

"That would be Major. Come on, let's go."

The men—clearly not there for him—stared at him from the front of the vehicle. Preston returned their glare, confident that they would comply with his order without further instruction.

And so they did. The driver slapped the vehicle into motion, smashing the gas pedal and wheeling it around sharply, obviously trying to call attention to the fact that he wasn't happy. But then again Preston wasn't either, and so he ignored the bumpy ride.

Hack had never been to King Fahd before, and after the relative order of his Eagle base at Tabuk, the place looked cluttered and confused. Besides hosting every Warthog in the Gulf, Fahd was home port to an assortment of Spec Ops and SAR craft—C-130's, Pave Low helicopters, and the like. An odd assortment of support craft and stragglers had also found their way here: a Navy A-6 that had suffered battle damage and couldn't make it back to its carrier, a pair of OA-6 Broncos training with Delta troops as advanced scouts, even an ancient civilian Constellation that had taken refuge after escaping from Kuwait. Preston stared at the planes, unimpressed; slow movers all, they reinforced his sense of exile. The ride took him through the area where the 535th's Hogs were stored and maintained— it was easy to spot, with a large banner across the top of the largest metal building declaring it "Oz: Home of the 535th 'Devil' Squadron."

A slightly smaller banner hung beneath it: "Eat This, Saddam."

Preston shook his head. That would have to go.

"Hog Heaven, sir," announced the driver as the Humvee skidded to a stop a few yards from a patched-together trailer complex off the side of the main area of the base. Closer to the planes and the Spec Ops areas than the other A-10A commands, the ramshackle building looked like a carny camp without the charm.

Preston pulled himself out of the Humvee, which jerked away before he could properly close the door. Hack walked across the patched concrete and climbed up the rickety stairs. Inside, the building seemed to sway as he passed down the hallway.

In the civilian world, seven o'clock in the morning was relatively early; most people would still be making their way to work. The Hog squadron was experiencing a lull as well—but only because most of its planes had already left on the morning missions assigned to it by the "frag" or fragment of the Air Tasking Order that laid out the allied game plan for the air war. The squadron shared quarters with an Intelligence group at the far end of the hallway; Preston, with no signs on the doors to guide him, walked toward the buzz. As he passed a room on the right, he stopped short—it was a large lounge dominated by a massive projection-screen TV. The set was tuned to CNN, where Bernard Shaw flashed his impressive eyebrows as he spoke into a microphone.

The CNN screen changed. It was night. Hoses of red tracers filled the sky. Preston stepped into the room as words appeared in the lower right. "Downtown Baghdad." Suddenly light flashed in the lower right corner of the screen—a bomb or missile hitting. The camera jumped. More explosions, secondaries most likely. Fire filled the sky.

The scene changed. It was morning. "Live," according to the words at the bottom.

Buildings. "An Iraqi Baby Food Factory," claimed the words.

Undoubtedly a lie, Hack thought.

"Excuse me," said a gravelly voice behind him.

Preston stepped to the side to get out of the way. The other man walked inside, past the large, overstuffed couches to the side of the room. Three large refrigerators and bins of junk-food snacks sat along the wall, next to a long wooden table. There was a coffee machine there—next to a bean-grinder. The officer poured himself a cup without glancing at him.

It was Michael Knowlington. Hack had worked with him, briefly, during an assignment at the Pentagon about a year before. They hadn't gotten along particularly well.

"You're early," said Knowlington without looking up. "Good."

Before Preston could answer, the colonel had replaced the coffeepot and begun striding from the room. All Hack could do was follow down the hall to a small office on the right. The colonel took no notice of him, and in fact had reached to close the door behind him when Preston pushed himself into the doorway.

"Colonel, I—"

"Come in if you're coming," said Knowlington.

In contrast to the room with the TV, the squadron commander's officer was as spartan as a porta-john on a remote work site. There were exactly three pieces of furniture—a three-drawer metal desk pushed against the wall and two metal folding chairs, neither of which had any padding. The walls were blank; a set of blinds hung down over the window. Knowlington sat in the chair behind the desk, turning it to face the other seat, which was against the wall near the door.

Guy was so low on the totem pole, Preston thought to himself, he couldn't even get furniture. Obviously the rumors must be true; he must be on his way out.

"I understand you helped out near Apache yesterday evening," said Knowlington. "Thanks."

"Apache? You mean the MiG that attacked the helicopter?"

Knowlington nodded. Preston and his wing mate had actually been involved—though at the last minute, and then largely as spectators to the main event. While they tangled with several MiGs that had apparently been launched as decoys, two Hogs had somehow managed to fight off a Fishbed closing in on a Spec Ops helo.

More than fight it off—one of the Hogs had nailed the SOB, an incredible feat in the slow-moving A-10.

"Those were your planes?" Preston asked.

"Two of my best pilots. They should be back soon. They'll be here for your coming-out party."

Anyone else would have said the last words with a

smile. Knowlington said them as if he were reading off a list of numbers on an engineering chart.

Hack nodded. On the flight out he'd considered whether he ought to say something about burying the hatchet or getting along or letting bygones be bygones—make some reference, at least, to their "disagreement" in D.C. But now that he was here, sitting two feet from Knowlington, he didn't know what to say.

At least the man didn't smell like booze.

"I'd like to get to work," Hack told him. "First thing, I think, is review the duty roster, then look over the maintenance. I want to make sure the planes are ready to go. Right off, I thought I would—"

"I believe you'll find that Sergeant Clyston has everything under control."

"*Sergeant* Clyston?"

"You know Allen?"

"No. But who's the officer in charge of—"

"If there's a readiness problem with the planes, it comes straight to me," said Knowlington. "Clyston oversees the maintenance sections. He reports directly to me."

"Ordinarily—"

"We're not fully staffed," said Knowlington. His voice remained as neutral as ever. "That's an advantage, because it means we don't have a lot of bullshit and red tape. We have just enough people to get our job done. Most days."

Not a laugh, not a hint of humor.

"Well, I'm not in favor of bullshit either," started Hack. His "but" never got out of his mouth.

"Good. I'm due in Riyadh in two hours and I have some details to look after," said Skull, standing and opening the door for him. "We'll introduce you formally at 1300 or thereabouts. Bernie'll get you situated. He's down the hall with the Intelligence people; we share resources."

There was just the hint of irony in Knowlington's voice. Angry at being brushed off but not exactly sure what to do or say, Preston got up as deliberately as he could, only just managing not to slam the door behind him.

8

NORTH OF THE SAUDI BORDER
26 JANUARY 1991
0710

Doberman cursed himself as he whacked the Hog engines to maximum power, goosing the throttle for all he was worth. Diversionary flares shot out of their wing-tip dispensers, bursting in the path of the shoulder-fired missile.

Truth was, he'd been caught flat-footed, at very low altitude without a lot of flight energy or momentum to help him escape. He hadn't expected someone to be sitting down there behind him with a heat seeker.

Stupidity.

No, worse: pilot arrogance, one of the seven deadly sins. He'd flown as though he was invincible, and now had to pay the piper. The only question was whether he'd pay with sweat or blood.

The SA-7 the Iraqi soldier had launched at him was a relatively primitive heat-seeking missile. Its nearest Western equivalent was the Redeye missile, a 1960's man-portable weapon outclassed by contemporary SAMs like the Stinger and the Russian SA-16, to say nothing of systems like the British Blowpipe or the Swedish RBS 70.

Still, the SA-7 flew at just under one thousand miles an hour and had a range of two miles; the Hog was well within its lethal envelope. About the only thing Doberman had going for him was its fuse—a direct-action device that required the missile to actually hit something before detonating the RDX/AP explosive.

Of course, Doberman had no way of knowing exactly what had been launched at him. Nor did he do much in the way of analyzing the odds. He concentrated on pushing the Hog into a series of hard, swaggering turns, lighting off flares as he went.

He might have prayed or wished for luck, but there wasn't time.

9

As Shotgun shouted his warning, Doberman ducked left and tossed flares, obviously in control of the situation. So O'Rourke turned his attention toward meting out the only acceptable punishment for firing on a Hog.

Death. With extreme prejudice.

The fact that the Iraqis who had fired on his wing mate might have other SAMs at their disposal was irrelevant.

"What I'm talking about here," said Shotgun, as if he had a set of loudspeakers to harangue the Iraqis with, "is basic Hog etiquette. You have to learn how to be polite."

Rumor had it that Miss Manners was planning on devoting an entire chapter in her next book to the proper use of thirty-millimeter cannon fire at dinner parties. If so, she could have used Shotgun's first run as a textbook example—he pushed his nose nearly straight down on the spot where the lingering smoke fingered the guilty party.

The cannon was not really an effective weapon against individual soldiers, who presented a difficult target for an aircraft moving at four hundred miles an hour. Cluster bombs or even old-fashioned iron would have clearly been the weapon of choice, as Miss Manners would undoubtedly note in a well-worded aside at the start of her chapter.

The Iraqis, however, could not afford to wait for the book. The soldiers disappeared in a percolating steam of sand and explosive as Shotgun rode the trigger for an extra-long burst, the gun's recoil actually slowing the A-10A's descent. He worked his rudder pedals to walk the torrent of bullets into the troop truck that had accompanied the men, slicing a neat line roughly along the drive shaft, not to mention the rest of the chassis.

There was a bit too much smoke to see the vehicle split in half, and besides, the flames got in the way. Nonetheless, Shotgun gave himself an attaboy as his crosshairs slipped toward one last knot of soldiers lying in the sand. These men had the audacity to actually fire at him—or at least that seemed to be the implication of the tiny flashes of red coming from their position.

"Definitely not polite," said Shotgun, squeezing his trigger. "You gentlemen are going to have to learn not to shoot out of turn. I'm afraid you fall under the jurisdiction of Hog Rule Number 5. For every action there is an opposite and disproportionate reaction."

10

Doberman held the plane steady as a white arrow shot past his canopy. It began to veer across his path, but then wobbled and exploded, detonated by its self-destruct mechanism as its fuel gave out. The pilot ducked, though the warhead was too far away to do any damage. He brought the stick back and started to climb, turning around toward the battlefield to get back in the game.

Doberman caught a glimpse of Devil Two diving nearly straight down on the Iraqi truck, smoke pouring from the Gatling gun in its chin. Between the smoke and the glinting sun, the Hog's dark green skin looked as if she were bathed in perspiration, a magnificent winged beast meting out justice to a parcel of demons escaped from the underworld.

Doberman got back to three thousand feet as he reassessed the battlefield. Shotgun began recovering at very low altitude, pulling off to the southwest. The Iraqis were either all dead or out of SAMs; Devil Two flew off unscathed.

Which left the T-72 he'd been homing in on when he was so rudely interrupted. The tank commander had taken the course of all intelligent Iraqis—he was turning tail and running away. Dust and sand spewed out behind him.

Doberman eyed his flanks cautiously before attacking. He put the plane into a long but shallow dive, a surfer riding the last wave toward shore. It was a peaceful, gentle maneuver, a glide rather than a plunge, the Thunderbolt II seeming to float downward on a summer breeze.

Then he blasted the hell out of the bastard with two quick squeezes of the trigger.

The first pack of bullets caught the edge of the tank's turret like the sharp edge of a crowbar, wedging in and lifting, tossing it off like a discarded bottle cap. The massive sewer cover scraped briefly against the side then plopped into the sand.

The second burst finished off the work, igniting the insides of the Russian-made tank. The heavy slugs of depleted uranium that made up the bulk of the combat mix bounced back and forth in the tank's interior, but the heavy lifting had already been done by the very first HE round to slap into the open hull; the three members of the tank crew were incinerated as it ignited a fuel line at the edge of the engine compartment.

Doberman let go of the trigger, shoving his right wing down and pirouetting sharply in the air, turning back toward the border. The other tank sat on his right, the truck to his left. Men lay on the ground around both vehicles. Nothing moved.

The dark shape of Shotgun's plane appeared a mile and a half ahead, climbing above him.

"Devil Two, this is One," Doberman said. "You have anything else moving down there?"

"Neg-a-tivo," said his wing mate. "Clean slate."

Doberman tensed as he flew toward the position of the soldiers who had called in support. He suspected they were part of the Iraqi plot.

"Rat Patrol to Devil Flight. Shit, man, we are sorry about that. Jesus, we're sorry."

"Yeah," said Doberman. He spotted their ditch, or what he thought was their ditch, about a half mile out at ten o'clock, between his nose and left wing. "Gun, you think these guys are legitimate?" he asked over the short-range frequency, which linked him only to his wing mate.

"AWACS woulda authenticated 'em," said Shotgun.

"Yeah."

"Got to go with it, Dog," said Shotgun.

Glenon scowled beneath his mask but didn't reply. He hated it when Shotgun used his serious voice. But his wingman was right—they had to accept that Rat Patrol was authentic.

In theory.

"You got me?" he asked his wing mate.

"I have your lovely effigy within my fierce gaze."

"What the fuck does that mean?"

"I'm on your ass."

"Cover me while I buzz these suckers."

"Dog."

"Just watch my butt. I'm not going to do anything stupid." Doberman pumped the throttle and dove the A-10A down, zooming over the American position at all of ten feet AGL. Two round shapes popped up, then hunkered down.

"Shit. What gives, Devil flight?" demanded the soldier.

"Just saying hello," said Doberman, still not convinced that the soldiers were friends.

Shotgun, in the meantime, had hailed the AWACS, filling them in on everything that had happened. The controller assured him that the unit was a legitimate one.

"But what's that mean really?" Doberman said to him over the short-range radio as they climbed away from the border. "They have a legitimate frequency and passwords, but that's it, right? I mean, the controller is sitting in an airplane—he doesn't know."

"You're getting paranoid, Dog Man. You got to lighten up. Anybody can make a mistake."

"Maybe." Doberman studied his map and position on the INS. He plotted a new course for home.

"Yeah," said Shotgun after he relayed the data. "Looks good." His voice was nearly drowned out by the strains of "Rocket Queen," the last song on Guns 'n' Roses' *Appetite for Destruction* CD.

"I thought you were laying off the heavy metal," said Doberman, putting his nose on the new bearings.

"You can't get enough of the classics," replied Shotgun, who had to be the only combat pilot in the world with a flight suit customized with a full-blown stereo. "I'm thinking of broadening my outlook, though," added Shotgun. "I mean, a man has to be open to new experiences. You have to move forward."

"What do you mean? Rap? More grunge rock?"

"Early Beatles."

"Yeah, yeah, yeah," sang Doberman, as if they'd rehearsed it.

11

Skull shifted on the hard metal chair, sipping the dark black liquid the CentCom staff claimed was coffee and trying to keep himself from bitching out loud. He'd caught a total of three hours sleep last night, including the ten minutes on the Huey hustling here for the high-level briefing session on the "Straw" mission. But fatigue didn't bother him—war was a twenty-four-hour, do-it-yourself operation, and this particular product had a serious freshness date on it, due to expire in less than fourteen hours. Which meant it was exactly the sort of situation he liked; it kicked his pulse up and tightened his muscles, got his eyes into sharp focus. If anything, he was too awake.

What irked him was the attitude of the CinC staff running the show. It wasn't just that the Army people had started frowning the second Wong opened his mouth to begin the briefing. It was the way they frowned—as if Air Force people had no ability to analyze anything below ten thousand feet, let alone propose and organize a combined ground-air covert operation.

Not that they treated the Delta folks any better.

Maybe it was just an Army thing, but Skull got the impression that they saw the whole thing more as an annoyance than an opportunity. They called it "Strawman" rather than Straw, hinting at the implication that the intelligence was bogus or perhaps even planted. Even the conference area that had been assigned—a basement room in a Saudi government building with two large folding tables for everyone to crowd around—seemed to signal that the mission had something less than top priority.

Officially, the allies weren't supposed to be targeting Saddam. President Bush had even said they wouldn't during a press conference. But that was BS and everybody knew it. So why were they getting the sneers and knowing glances?

Wong, Knowlington, and the Spec Ops staff had put together a plan for four six-man teams of Delta troopers to make a high-altitude, low-opening parachute drop at 2000 hours about three miles southwest of the target area. The troopers would coordinate with a flight of F-111's, visually IDing the target before clearing the strike. The fighter-bombers would use laser-guided smart bombs to destroy the convoy. The ground teams would then escape in a pair of Pave Lows an hour after the attack, covered by four planes from Devil Squadron.

Technically, the A-10's were ill-suited to night-support missions; they'd have to use special Maverick AGMs as night-vision equipment if things got heavy. But it was a kludge Skull had made do with a few days before when he'd gone north to rescue one of his men.

He expected an argument. He also anticipated that with a target like Saddam in the offing, the brass might want something a little flashier than the earth pigs—aka Aardvarks, Varks, and One-Elevens—handling the action.

What he wasn't prepared for was the flat-out statement that the Delta teams couldn't be made available.

"We're not risking that many men on this," said Major Booker, an infantry officer from the CinC staff who was running the meeting. "It means taking away from Scud-hunting and that can't be done. The Scuds are job one."

"These teams are currently in Riyadh. They're not even technically reserves," said Captain Leterri, who was presenting the Delta perspective at the briefing. Leterri looked like he wanted to say something along the lines of, "All they're doing is jerking off." The highly trained soldiers in question were, in fact, acting as a bodyguard pool for Cent-Com and the CinC—glorified rent-a-cops far from the action. It wasn't exactly what they wanted to be doing.

Booker raised his shoulders and lowered his head, as if he were an eagle looking down from a craggy perch. The veins popped in his long, sinewy neck. "If the men are available," he said, "then they should be hunting Scuds."

Leterri was not to be cowed. "They can conduct that mission immediately after this. The Pave Lows—"

"We're not risking helicopters that far north."

"We had Pave Lows there last night," snapped Leterri, exasperated.

"Actually, the helicopter in question was a Pave Hawk," said Wong. "While operating at the extreme end of its range, it accomplished its mission with typical efficiency."

"Irrelevant," snapped Booker. "Antiaircraft defenses have picked up in the area. We are not risking either Pave Lows or Pave Hawks there. The assets are too precious."

"Aw, bullshit, Major," said Leterri, no longer able to control his frustration. "What the fuck do we have them for if we don't put them to use? Shit, they got in last night, they'll get in tonight, they'll get in tomorrow."

"We have fresh satellite data," said Booker. He sounded almost triumphant and waved to a sergeant near the door, who stepped forward and put the photos on the long table. Wong took them and began studying them. Paddington, one of the two British representatives at the session, leaned over his shoulder and whispered something.

It seemed clear to Skull that Booker's job was to rain on the parade, scuttling the mission if possible. Skull couldn't let that happen—not because he wanted to nail Saddam, but because he saw the mission as the only chance to search for Dixon. Officially, his lieutenant had been listed as KIA; nobody was going to send a search team looking for him, especially that far north, without very solid evidence that he was alive. This was their best—maybe only—shot at getting him back.

So it was time to take over the meeting.

"Here's the thing," he said, speaking in the deceptively soft tone that he had honed through years of maneuvering with the brass, "and with all due respect to the other services represented, we have a serious opportunity here, based as much on luck as good intelligence. We only get one shot. The ground team is important, because the planes may need to be directed in at the last minute, depending on what's going on. We considered using a Pave Penny TSL system, lazing the specific vehicle, and we can still do that if that's what you'd prefer. But the F-111's can do the targeting on their own if we have the ground team directing—"

"We can't spare F-111's," said Booker.

"Why don't we let Tommy tell us that?" said Skull. He kept his contempt veiled as he motioned to the Black Hole planner officially representing the Air Force theater commander at the session. Black Hole ran the air war, assigning hit lists to squadrons in a daily briefing or task order known as the ATO, for air tasking order. Knowlington was well connected with the planners and their bosses, and would never have included the planes in the game plan without having checked to see if they were indeed available.

"We can have a flight of F-111's on target whenever you want," said the captain, Tom Marks.

"What are they tasked for now?" said Booker.

"There are two flights. One is going after bridges north of Baghdad, and the other has a generic Scud-hunting mission down near—"

"There are no generic Scud missions," said Booker. "Every damn Scud in the Gulf has to be eliminated."

"With all due respect," said Skull, "don't you feel nailing Saddam is more important than going after the Scuds? Hell, the damn things can't hit the broadside of a barn."

"Tell that to the people in Tel Aviv," said Booker.

"Eliminate Saddam and the war ends."

"I doubt it. In any event, assassinating world leaders is not one of our war aims."

"Right," said Skull, laughing derisively. Even he had his limits. "What priority do we have exactly?"

"You have no priority," said Booker. "This is a high-risk mission."

"You're vetoing it?"

"I didn't say that."

Booker, finally called out, physically stepped back. He glanced at his two aides and gave his shoulders another heave. "The CinC wants it to proceed, if feasible, but with minimal resources. The Scuds must remain a priority. We can't divert from any other missions."

"Minimal resources means what?" said Skull.

"No diminishment of the Scud mission. No diminishment of other priorities," said Booker.

They might have taken a few more turns around that circle had Wong not interrupted.

"The air defenses have definitely been increased," he said. "And in a most interesting way. Possibly with SA-11's. Very interesting."

"SA-11's?" said Marks.

"What's the significance?" asked Booker.

"SA-11's are not known to have been deployed in Iraq since experimental use at the behest of the Soviets during the so-called Iran-Iraq War," said Wong. He slid the pictures to the center of table and identified three revetments obviously prepared for missile launchers; he explained as an aside that there should be a fourth, though it was not discernible. He then zeroed in on one of the vehicles in the revetments, showing the circumstantial evidence that had led him to conclude it was an SA-11 battery.

"These are clearly placements for two vehicles." He pointed at the small wedge that represented a parking spot. "Typically, an SA-11 battery would consist of two vehicles, one a radar van located here, the other a four-missile turntable providing 360-degree coverage. The wide envelope would also make sense given this configuration, for the parameters of the acquisition radars would be covered, as you can see."

Wong quickly traced squiggly circles extending out from his wedges, forming a neat hedge completely covering the approaches to Al Kajuk. A wedge of open space covered the right northwestern corner—obviously where the other battery must be.

"I don't see a van," said Tommy.

"Yes, precisely," said Wong. "It hasn't been moved in yet. This vehicle here, obscured by the tarp as it moves along the area, is most likely the radar unit. But we can't be sure. That is why my conclusion is tentative. There is the possibility that they are bluffing. There is also the possibility that this has been established for different missile defenses." Wong began a dissertation on the amount of space typically cleared for radar trucks and support vehicles, concentrating on the one site that had been worked over by a bulldozer or some other earthmover. He could not rule out SA-6's or SA-8's, or even other potentially portable defenses. Skull kept nodding and signaling to him to wrap it up; as usual, Wong was delivering much more detail than necessary.

"No matter what they put there," said Knowlington finally, cutting him off, "we should prepare for the more capable missiles."

"Getting Weasels might be a problem," said Marks, referring to SAM-killing Phantoms. "But there's a flight of Tornados available."

"The Tornados would be appropriate," said Wong. "Their ALARM missiles could accommodate the threat."

"I agree with Bristol," said Paddington. "Quite."

Knowlington had caught a sniff of gin on the British intelligence expert's breath when they were introduced. Even if he hadn't, he recognized the pale eyes, twitchy gestures, and most of all the sweat as characteristics he used to have when he went too long without a drink. Shaking Paddington's hand, he'd stared briefly into his eyes. He hadn't seen himself there; a good sign.

Nonetheless, the British agent knew his stuff. He added a few comments about how the defenses were likely to be arrayed, Wong nodding along in the background. He also noted that the British ALARM missiles, designed to be used against advanced antiaircraft systems like the SA-11, could linger above the battlefield until the radar was activated—a distinct advantage compared to the HARM missiles carried by the Phantoms.

To the Army people, the discussion of the missile types was clearly academic. To Skull, it was anything but. The SA-11 was more capable than the SA-6 it was designed to replace. And the SA-6 was, in the words a Hog driver might use, a real son of a bitch.

Wong, on the other hand, seemed absolutely elated.

"It would be reasonable to expect that SA-11 would be deployed as point defense weapons guarding a high-priority asset," he noted, "such as Saddam."

"That doesn't change the mission's priority," insisted Booker. "This is still speculative."

"It does change the targeting," said Tommy. "We have to take out those batteries if we're going to fly up there."

"If the attack were carried out at low altitude, I believe we could make do with one or two, at least at the start," said Wong. "This corridor would provide access to the roadway south of the village. Hitting just one several hours prior to Straw's arrival would lessen the likelihood that he would seek other quarters."

"Possibly," said Paddington.

"If he's going to go somewhere else, why even bother?" asked Booker.

"A logical question," said Paddington. "The answer is that our friend is very superstitious. He has also taken the time to study allied bombing plans. His conclusion is that you never strike the same place twice."

"That's an exaggeration."

Paddington shrugged.

"This seems like an even longer shot than I thought," said Booker.

Skull listened vaguely as the Delta representatives argued with Booker, the discussion threatening to degenerate into a shouting match. To be honest, Booker did have a point—the mission was a long shot, even if the payoff was astronomical. Assuming the information was correct, assuming the profiles of Saddam were correct, assuming, assuming, assuming—the odds of actually nailing a moving vehicle in the middle of the night were very high.

"All right, so it's a long shot," Knowlington said finally. "What's the largest ground force we can authorize?"

Booker turned and looked at him. "The smallest force necessary to identify the vehicle. Two men. That's all I'm authorized to approve. That's all the chief will approve."

"That's way too little," said Leterri.

"That's two men who may be dead in the morning," said Booker.

"Sure, if that's all we send."

"What about searching for my pilot?" said Skull. "We need a full team."

"With all due respect," said Booker sharply, pointedly repeating Knowlington's own phrase, "Lieutenant Dixon has been declared KIA."

"But he's not."

"The speculation put forth by Captain Wong is unpersuasive."

"Bullshit, Major," said Skull. "Bullshit."

"Two men," said Booker. "There is still the problem of inserting and retrieving the team."

"C-141 high-altitude jump," said Leterri.

"The SA-11's make that problematic," said Wong. "Better to use an MC-130 infiltrating at low altitude and making the drop in the clean corridor once the missiles hit. The mission can be accomplished with three men, two to handle the vehicle and another to act as scout. I, of course, will take the latter role."

Knowlington stared at Booker, silently fuming. He expected Booker or someone to argue with Wong, but apparently everyone in the room knew of the Intelligence officer's extensive background with covert operations.

"How do you get back?" asked Marks.

"If helicopters are not permitted north, a STAR-Fulton pickup would be the only logical option," said Wong.

"At night?" asked Booker.

"We can do it if we have to," said Leterri.

STAR stood for surface-to-air recovery; Fulton was the name of the man who had pioneered it. A Hercules flying at just under a hundred knots snagged a line suspended from a balloon at five hundred feet. The line propelled the man, or in some cases two, upward, streaming him behind the airplane. He was then winched into the rear of the plane.

Not pretty, but doable. In theory, at least.

"There's one thing I want to get clear," said Knowlington. "Dixon has to be a priority."

"Neither Strawman nor Dixon is a priority, Colonel," said Paddington dryly. "Obviously, His Cincship sees this as a mission for volunteers and maniacs."

"Screw off," Knowlington told the British agent.

Paddington shrugged. No one else spoke.

"We're getting Dixon back," Skull said, standing and pointing at Booker.

"If he's there," said the major. "And if you find him, within the other parameters of the mission. And if we can arrange a package. And if the commander in chief approves it." He glanced menacingly at Paddington, who merely smiled, obviously secure in the knowledge that he could not be touched. Booker nearly spat at him as he continued. "Frankly, my opinion on this whole escapade is lower than the general's, I can assure you."

"And I can assure you we're getting Dixon back," said Knowlington. He crossed his arms and glared at the rest of them before slowly retaking his seat.

12

The corpse lay in a rut a few steps up the hill, arms thrown over the back of its head as if Death had held the body prisoner before taking the soul.

Dixon stared at him for a moment. The Iraqi soldier had been killed by the Delta team yesterday as they escaped after finding the missile-launch area and calling in A-10's and F-16's to strike it.

Or maybe he'd shot him himself. Dixon couldn't remember.

BJ felt as if a dark cloud had descended around his neck, dread trying to strangle him from behind. He felt something like compassion, something like sorrow, and even guilt as he looked at the man.

But the soldier was an enemy.

More importantly, there was a weapon near his body; that meant more ammunition, bullets to replenish the ones Dixon had foolishly wasted earlier.

Bullets that would mean he could kill more men.

More enemies.

He lowered himself on wobbly knees, reaching to take the dead man's AK-47. The rifle lay less than twelve inches from the Iraqi's face. As Dixon grabbed its barrel he felt something on his knuckles, a breath—he jerked his hand away, snapping upright, swinging his own rifle down to aim at the Iraqi.

Impossible. The soldier couldn't be deader. The back of his shirt and his pants down to his thighs were caked solid with blood.

BJ lowered himself more quickly this time, then closed his eyes when he took the gun.

The clip, the rifle, was empty.

A thick web belt circled the dead man's waist.

A cartridge holder.

The heavy, pungent odor of rotting meat drifted up from the corpse as Dixon stared at him from his knees. The soldier was dead; he had to be dead. There was nothing to fear.

"You're beyond fear," BJ told himself. He repeated it, then got up, walking cautiously around the man. He kicked the corpse's side with his boot.

How disrespectful, he thought.

"Disrespectful," he said. And then he kicked again.

Truly dead. Dixon lowered himself on his haunches, balancing by using both rifle butts as a skier might do. Then he dropped the dead man's gun, let it bounce against the earth. He gripped the dead Iraqi's shirt. His fingers dug into the man's flesh, soft and pudgy, like a girl's.

Dixon gave a heave and pushed the man over.

Thick pockets sat at the front of the belt, the top of each secured by string looped around a long, narrow wooden knob. Two held banana-style clips of 7.62mm ammunition. A metal clasp and ring topped a third pocket. Dixon reached for the ring, and started to tug on it before realizing he was holding the trigger mechanism of a Russian hand grenade. He stared at his fingers for a moment, then gingerly pulled the small grenade—an old but deadly RGD5—out of the flap.

It was wet with blood. There was at least one more in

the ammo pocket. He teased it out, gently feeling along the tube at the top, past the fuse lever, to the smooth round body before gripping it. BJ pulled it out and placed both grenades next to each other on the ground. He reached into the belt again and felt something sharp and jagged, his fingers flinching back against the blood-saturated webbing material.

It was part of the man's pelvic bone, smashed out of place by one of the bullets that had killed him.

Slowly, Dixon pulled his hand away. He took another breath, then retrieved the gun clips. He slid the grenades into his chest pockets.

As he stood back, the corpse began to move.

He took another step back, trying to raise his gun. But the rifle suddenly felt heavier than three bags of cement.

The corpse jumped to its feet, arms extending over its head in victory, Death vanquished. It danced and flung itself in a swirl around the desert.

Dixon's breath caught. He closed his eyes and willed the cloud and its black noose away. He felt the gun hanging from his hand, felt the strain in his shoulders and his neck. He felt the pain in his leg and in his ribs, felt each bruise and scrape, felt the air slowly emptying from his lungs.

When he opened his eyes, the corpse lay back on the ground, head off-kilter, its mouth pasted in a sad frown.

Dixon curled the rifle under his arm and pushed on.

13

"There's no place like Home Drome. There's no place like Home Drome. Wow, look at that Dog. Oz!"

"Oh, you're a fuckin' riot, Shotgun," answered Doberman as they trundled into the Devil Squadron parking area in front of the hangars, an area affectionately dubbed "Oz" because of the wondrous things the maintenance wizards did there. As the two planes wheeled into their assigned spots, a large bear emerged from one of the hangars and began ambling in their direction—the Capo di Capo was gracing them with a personal welcome. Crewmen genuflected and fell over themselves to get out of his way.

Powering their mounts down, the Hog drivers descended to the tarmac. Sergeant Clyston waited a short distance away, his presence evident in the quick snap of the men scurrying to secure the planes.

"Hey, Capo, what's shakin'," said Shotgun, walking over.

"You better not have broken my airplane," growled the sergeant.

"Geez, who bit you in the ass?" said Shotgun. By common consensus, he was the only member of the squadron, officer or enlisted, who could get away with a remark like that to the Capo.

Clyston harumphed in response, then turned to Doberman.

"Captain Glenon, sir, I heard what you did with that MiG. Kick-ass flying, sir. I'm f-in' proud of you, and every member of this squadron is f-in' proud of you, even if they don't officially know what you did."

"You mean they don't know, or they don't know that they *don't* know," said Shotgun with a laugh.

"Yeah, thanks, Sergeant. I appreciate it," said Glenon, who wanted desperately to get out of his gear and grab something to eat.

That and take a leak.

Clyston took a measured step backward and did something that nearly knocked Doberman over: He lifted his hand up for a salute.

Glenon hesitated; truth was, he'd never seen Clyston salute before. In fact, he wasn't sure he'd ever seen *any* chief master sergeant in the Air Force salute before, certainly not to him.

But here was Clyston, grizzled bear of grizzled bears, seriously waiting for him to snap off a salute in return.

"Okay," said Doberman. He gave his best impression of a parade color guard—in truth, not a very good one—and returned the salute. "Thanks. Your guys, I mean, Rosen and Tinman and the rest out at Al Jouf, they were kick-ass too."

"Thank you, sir." Clyston remained at attention.

"I appreciate the sentiment, really. But, you know."

"Yeah. I know. You got a bullshit deal. But these guys appreciate what you did. They won't forget." Clyston glanced over Doberman's shoulder toward the crews examining the planes. He morphed back to his old self with a loud growl at one of his men. "Grimsley, you start on the *other* side of that first, for christsake. Geeee-zus-f-ker-eye-st."

Doberman started shagging along toward the life support shop, where he could change. He and O'Rourke would have to gather their thoughts for a round of reports on both the border incident and their time north at Fort Apache; he wasn't looking forward to intel debriefings, but they were a necessary part of the job. Inevitably, he'd forget some vital thing that somebody else would remember, and he'd have to answer a ton of questions about it, trying to stretch his memory when all he'd be interested in doing was playing cards or catching Zs. He started outlining what had happened with the tanks and the SA-7 as he walked; he had the play-by-play more or less summarized before realizing Clyston was tagging along with them.

"Something up, Sarge?" he asked.

"Couple of things," said Clyston. "New DO is a certified asshole, for starters."

"New DO?" said Shotgun. "I had ten bucks on Dog Man here getting the post."

Clyston's scowl deepened. "Between you, me, and the lamppost, sirs, I truly wish he was. I'm sorry if this is news to you, Captain."

"I don't want to be DO anyway," said Doberman.

"A Major Horace Gordon Preston," said Clyston, answering the obvious question. "You can tell he did time at the Pentagon. For my money, he belongs back there."

Coming from Clyston, the pronouncement was libel. And his next sentence explained why.

"F-in' zippersuit wants us to take down our Saddam sign."

"*Eat this, Saddam*? Oh, man, you can't do that," said Shotgun. "That's, like, our motto. It's what I'm talking about. You have to leave that up. You have to leave that up."

"I didn't say it was coming down," said Clyston slowly. "Only that Preston wants it down."

"What's the colonel think?" asked Shotgun.

Clyston shrugged.

"Skull wants it down?"

"I haven't talked to him about it," said Clyston. "Not my place."

"Well, I will," said Shotgun.

Clyston turned his head slowly to O'Rourke. "I'd appreciate that, Captain."

More than the sign was obviously at stake. The sergeant was by far the closest man, regardless of rank, to Colonel Knowlington on the base. Rumor had it they had served together when the Air Force was still using biplanes. If Clyston mentioned it to Knowlington himself, the odds were overwhelming that Knowlington would make sure the sign stayed.

So it must be that the sergeant saw Preston as a threat, and not to him.

"I'll speak to the colonel too," said Doberman. "And we'll watch out for him. He's a good commander. Shotgun and I were just telling some clods from the CinC's staff at Al Jouf that, as a matter of fact."

"Thank you, Captain." The sergeant's smile extended slowly. "There's a meeting scheduled for 1300 hours to introduce the new DO—pilots, senior NCOs, and probably an f-in' cheerleading squad if Preston has any input on it. In the meantime, you sirs might want to run into Major Wong."

"Wong's back?" asked Shotgun.

"And last I saw, headed for lunch," said Clyston. "You really, really want to talk to him, Captain," he added, turning to Doberman. "You'll be glad you did."

14

Skull stared at the top sheet of the lined pad on his desk. He'd sketched a backward "7" in the lower left-hand quadrant; atop it was a sideways, script "v." Two small squares sat like ink blots at the top stem.

Anyone glancing at it would have thought the hieroglyphics meaningless. In fact, it was the outline of his mission.

A maniac's mission, as Paddington had put it. And obviously the reason CinC wasn't willing to dedicate more than a few Hogs and an old C-130 to it.

Not true. The Hogs were backing up four F-111's, and the C-130 wasn't old. There were a dozen other planes involved, counting the CAP that would be orbiting nearby, the ABCCC command and control plane, the electronics-warfare craft, the SAM suppressors, and the rest of the support team.

But truly, it was a shot in the dark. And truly, finding Dixon was going to take more than a little luck.

If anyone could do it, Wong could. Skull knew that. But still—a long shot.

And the slingshot they planned to use to get them out— that wasn't even worth thinking about. The best hope was that helo flights would be cleared into the area by the time the mission took off—possible, but not likely.

Best to worry only about his part of the mission. Because he wasn't allowed to disrupt his other missions, Knowlington's planes would be over hostile territory for as much as six hours, from the drop to the pickup. They had to stay low to avoid being picked up by the sophisticated Iraqi defenses—and they had to remain unseen (and unheard) to avoid tipping off anyone about the ground team's presence. At the same time, they had to back up the F-111's and drop the pods containing the STAR gear. To do all this, he'd have only four planes—assuming Sergeant Clyston lived up to his promise that he could have four ready without disrupting the other missions.

Easy. For a maniac or a Hog driver.

If the mission succeeded—if they got Saddam—Skull and the others were going to be world-class heroes. Every last one of them could run for president.

But Saddam wasn't why he'd sketched the 7 and v on the pad, or why he'd pushed so hard to get the mission approved, or why he'd decided he was flying it himself. He wanted Dixon back. And if there was a small chance that he might be able to get him—an infinitesimally small, minute chance—he had to go for it.

No MIA bracelets in this war.

It was an arrogant, foolish thought. Guys got killed, guys got captured, guys got lost. Who the hell was he to wipe that out? What gave him the right to risk somebody else's neck on a wild goose-chase for a corpse?

Rank gave him the right. He made these kinds of judgments every day.

All the more reason to be sane now, to assess the odds carefully, calmly—like the CinC and his staff. Not a word they had said at the meeting had been out of line or wrong. The odds were long, long, long.

"We're here to volunteer."

Skull snapped around, startled by Doberman's voice at the door. He hadn't heard the door being opened, much less a knock.

"We're going," said Shotgun, entering the small room behind Glenon. "What's the game plan?"

"Where is it you're going?" Knowlington asked them.

"Don't bullshit us, Colonel," said Doberman. His face was tinged red; his voice snapped with the bark that had earned him his nickname. "We just talked to Wong. We're in."

"Wong?" Skull folded his arms into his chest. Both Doberman and Glenon had just gotten back from an incredibly taxing gig supporting Scud-hunting operations north of the border. By rights, they deserved at least a few days off.

If not months.

"You guys get any sleep last night?"

"We slept like babies," said Doberman. "When we taking off?"

"Close the door," Knowlington said. He sat back, examining the two men standing side by side in front of him. They couldn't be more different physically. Doberman was short even for a pilot, and probably weighed no more than 120. Shotgun loomed over six feet; his burly frame had to be at least twice as heavy as Doberman's.

They were different temperamentally as well: Doberman ready to go off like a bomb fuse set too high; Shotgun about as laid back as a human could be, at least until he was diving on his target.

Typical Hog drivers, though, each in his own way.

"You giving us the deal, or do we have to torture it out of you?" asked Shotgun finally.

"Our end's straightforward," said Skull. "Four planes total, two elements. Take off from here around dusk. Zig out from KKMC around one or two SAM sites, then northwest to a point about sixty miles south of Kajuk, the village you hit yesterday. Two planes go up toward Kajuk to cover a drop about three miles south of the village; two hold back as reserves. Most of that is at fifty feet to hide from some serious missiles Wong's worried they're movin' in."

"Twinkie material," said Shotgun. "Piece of cake."

"That's sixty miles at fifty feet, in the dark," said Knowlington.

"Devil Dogs," said Shotgun. "Creme filling on the inside."

"We wait for word from the controller, then we move up and check an LZ southwest of the village," continued the colonel, "make sure it's clean, then clear an MC-130 in. At the same time, F-111's take out two of the SAM sites. We drop retrieval pods, then circle south in case we're needed. We don't want to be too close or we draw attention to the ground people. On the other hand, we don't want to be too far away. Our linger time is what gets us in the picture. Nobody else can stay up there that long. Other element comes north, we tank. Keep going back and forth as long as we have to. Drop should happen right at 2100; pickup should be four hours later. That's two tanks apiece; could be less, depending on how we manage our fuel and what else happens. Could be more."

"Lotta flyin' time," said Shotgun, nodding. "I like it."

"What's happening on the ground?" Doberman asked.

"MH-130 drops three men—two Delta boys and Captain Wong. They wait for Saddam and they look for Dixon. Saddam's due at midnight."

"What if he's late?" said Shotgun.

"Wong says if he's late he's not coming," Skull told him. "From our perspective, that just gives us a little more time to find Dixon."

"That's a long time to fly up there," said Doberman. "A lot of tanking."

"Could be," Skull admitted.

"Shotgun and I can handle it."

"The only thing I want you guys handling is sleep," said Knowlington.

"Screw sleep."

"What I'm talking about," said Shotgun. "We don't need sleep."

"I don't know. You both look dog-tired."

"I'm going," said Glenon.

Shotgun put his hand on Glenon's shoulder. "It would make sense for us to fly the mission," he said. "We've been back and forth across this terrain a couple of times now."

That was the thing about Shotgun. One second he was carrying on about food and making junior-high jokes and pretending he was the world's biggest bozo. Then, all of a sudden, he got more serious than Johnny Quest.

"I know you guys haven't had much sleep lately," Skull said. "And I don't want that to be a factor."

"Shit, all we did at Al Jouf was sleep," said Shotgun.

"I'm flying," said Doberman.

"You guys both look like you're for shit," said Skull.

"Hey, you ain't winnin' no beauty contest yourself, Colonel," said Shotgun.

"Dixon's a friend of ours, Skull," said Doberman. "You have to let us go. We're your best guys and you know it. You need us."

The truth was, Knowlington knew they'd both volunteer. Because they were Hog drivers. And he knew that what Glenon had said was true—he did need them.

But he hadn't necessarily admitted it to himself yet, at least not officially.

"Let me think about all this," he told them.

"Shit, yeah," said Shotgun, punching the air.

"I haven't decided anything, except that I'm getting something to eat," said Knowlington. He got up out of his chair, then stopped, realizing he hadn't told them about the new DO. "Look, one other thing. We have a new pilot in the squadron. His name is Major Horace Gordon Preston. He's a good pilot and a good officer. He's going to serve as Director of Operations. If you don't need the rest, we'll have a hello meeting at thirteen hundred in Cineplex."

"We'll be there," said Doberman.

Glenon's face twinged red again, and Skull wondered if he knew Preston from somewhere. But that was neither here nor there.

"All right," said the colonel. "I'll tell you my decision

15

As approved, the mission bore only the slightest resemblance to the one Wong had originally proposed. Not that it was impossible, just that it was far less than optimal. And even optimal was a hard play against the odds.

Wong and two troopers would make a parachute drop two miles southwest of a bend in the highway leading to Al Kajuk. Unfortunately, the drop could not be conducted as an HAHO (high-altitude, high-opening) from a C-141B as most other Iraqi infiltration missions were; there wasn't a plane available, and besides, the SAMs would have an easy time picking out the planes—and possibly notice the chutes along the way. So instead an MC-130 would be pressed into service, flying a low-altitude course right up to the LZ, where it would pop up for the drop from a relatively low eight hundred feet. The pop-up would have to come just seconds after F-111's hit the SAM site; between their bombing and the jamming provided by a Spark Vark, the Hercules should have an ample window to proceed undetected. It would then fly south, using its extra load of fuel to orbit in a "dark" area devoid of enemy defenses until needed. While this added to the mission difficulty, it couldn't be avoided; there were only a small number of MC-130 Combat Talons equipped with the snagging gear in the Gulf—in the world—and even without the stranglehold on available resources, it might not have been possible to line up another plane.

In the meantime, Wong and the ground team would proceed on their mission, establishing a lookout post to observe the convoy. They would also prepare a diversion, which might be needed to slow or stop the vehicles. Mission complete, they would hike approximately two miles back to the drop point, where A-10's would have dropped the Fulton STAR retrieval pods. Officially, Dixon wasn't part of the plan.

While the Fulton retrieval system had been used on Spec Op missions in the past, it was admittedly far from routine. Wong had never tried it at night, and in fact had only attempted a Fulton STAR pickup once, during a training mission. The results of that attempt were not worth dwelling on.

Which was why he avoided answering the direct question posed by Sergeant Davis, one of the two Delta Force volunteers he was briefing on the mission.

"Hey, answer the question, Captain," said the other sergeant, whose last and seemingly only name was Salt. "How did that pickup go?"

Wong cleared his throat. The two Delta Force Green Berets had already seen duty north and had been involved in Panama. Davis was a demolition and com specialist; Salt was reputed to be the best sharpshooter in the Gulf.

"After being dragged fifty feet, the line was released," said Wong.

"Shit," said Davis.

"It happens. The second pickup went more smoothly. In any event, my experience isn't relevant. As long as the weather is clear, the pilot should have no trouble making the pickup."

"Unless he drags us."

"That is why I have located the pickup on a slight rise," noted Wong. "The direction of the plane will take us over low ground."

"I've done this twice," said Salt. "It ain't pretty."

"It needn't be pretty," Wong told him. "This is purely voluntary. If you wish to reconsider—"

"Screw that," said Salt.

"As you wish." Wong turned back to Davis. "Any other questions?"

"How many people are going to be with the bastard?" Salt asked.

"Assuming that you are referring to Saddam," said Wong, "that is unclear. There could be as many as a full company or more. I personally anticipate something along the lines of a platoon. But our concern is not with them. We have merely to spot his vehicle and illuminate it for the F-111 bombers."

"What happens if the Iraqis object?"

"We will have a flight of A-10A's at our disposal. They can provide additional firepower if necessary."

"Hogs. Okay," said Salt.

"They don't fly at night," said Davis.

"Shit, what's the difference?" Salt spat on the hangar's concrete floor. They were alone; Wong had taken the precaution of posting a guard at the entrance. The mission had need-to-know code-word clearance.

"The sergeant is ordinarily correct," Wong admitted. "But the A-10's will be equipped with missiles that have infrared targeting capability. In any event, our job will be a covert one. The enemy should never be aware of our presence."

"Shit happens," said Davis doubtfully.

"Shit, from what I've seen, Hogs'll blow up anything you tell them to," said Salt. "Don't worry about it."

"I'm not worrying. I'm just wondering why there aren't more of us going," said Davis. "If we had a full team, we could take the bastard out ourselves."

"Decisions on manpower allocation were not delegated to me," said Wong.

"Ah, we can still nail him," said Salt.

"That is the last contingency," said Wong. "If the F-111's fail to arrive, the A-10's will fill in. Our mission is to remain as clandestine as possible."

"Clandestine. I like that," said Salt.

Wong quickly outlined the rest of the package's responsibilities, noting that the operation would be coordinated by a specially equipped MC-130 ABCCC plane with the call sign "Wolf." Electronics jamming and fighter escort would also be available, but were being arranged in a manner that wouldn't tip off the Iraqis to the operation.

"Just tell us when we go," said Salt finally.

"We will board the Hercules Combat Talon at 1700," said Wong. "In the meantime, I have some operational details to review with the aircrews."

"We'll be ready," said Davis.

"There is one other facet of the operation that I cannot brief you on," Wong told them.

"Why not?" Davis asked.

"To do so may jeopardize other aspects of our mission. What I can say is this—at some point, I will have to separate myself from you while you carry out your job."

"That's it?" asked Davis.

Wong nodded.

"Where are you going to be?" asked Salt.

"In the vicinity," said Wong. "Beyond that, I cannot say."

"You gonna pull that need-to-know bullshit on us?" said Salt.

Wong had debated whether to tell them about Dixon or not; the option had in fact been left up to him. He decided not to. It wasn't because that would jeopardize Dixon if the team was captured. It was because he realized the men would be reluctant to leave Iraq without Dixon if they knew he was still alive. And it might be necessary to do so.

In fact, it might be necessary for them to leave *him*. For he had already decided he wasn't leaving without the young lieutenant. Whether Dixon was part of the "official" plan or not, he was the only reason Wong was going north.

But there was no need to tell his men that.

"I assure you, any decision regarding operational details that I make is only the result of careful consideration," said Wong. "For everyone's own good."

"My father used to say that right before he reared back and whacked us," said Salt.

"I won't whack you," said Wong. "That I guarantee."

16

The dirt road dipped and twisted after it slid off the highway, skirting the edge of the hill. Dixon walked along it, not caring that he might be seen—he kept hoping for a sound, for a truck to materialize behind him.

He had seen dilapidated farm buildings down the road yesterday. On one side of the road there had been a fence and a run-down building; opposite it, across the road, there had been a tiny house where he had stopped to find food. He thought they were a hundred yards in from the highway, and kept expecting them to appear, glancing first for the wall, then across the road for the house. He began walking faster, less and less sure of himself, a hundred yards in, two hundred, three hundred, a full mile. His whole sense of direction was thrown off, his sense of reality jumbled. Where was the damn wall? Had he imagined the house? Was he even where he thought he was?

He'd killed several men here. No way could he have imagined it.

When he finally saw the low pile of rubble marking the

start of a wall on the left side of the road, he felt a jolt of excitement, almost as if he had spotted the spire of his hometown church over the trees on the highway leading to his town. He'd hidden behind the wall yesterday.

The house sobered him up. Half of it was gone, the roof wrecked and the walls blackened where they weren't simply rubble.

It had been whole yesterday. He'd gone there for food, only to be chased by a small squad of Iraqis. They'd missed him at first when he hid across the street; then the woman had gotten caught in the cross fire. He'd killed the first group, but barely escaped a second, which hadn't bothered hunting him down—they'd simply blown up the house.

There had been a baby in the back room. Dixon had left him to escape, figuring the Iraqis wouldn't harm him. A moment after he'd jumped out the back of the building, it had exploded.

Dixon took a step toward the house, but stopped; he couldn't face it. And yet his curiosity was overwhelming— he climbed slowly up the opposite hill to the wall, trying to find a vantage point that might somehow let him see into the ruins. He stood on the wall, but lost his balance, dropping off behind it on the slope.

Tiny little kid, buried under the back end.

His fault. He could have saved the kid.

If he'd never existed, the kid wouldn't have been killed.

A small truck revved in the distance, turning off the highway. Dixon got to his feet.

The wall would protect him, or at least prolong the battle. He'd shoot, they'd stop, he'd pin them down. Sooner or later, they'd overwhelm him. He'd save the grenades until the very end.

Or he'd kill them all, and wait for the next truck. Or the next.

BJ took out his canteen, gulped the last of the water. His stomach felt like a worn stone; he'd been hungry so long it no longer hurt.

He tensed when he saw the truck. It was a pickup, not a

troop carrier, not what he'd expected. Two men were in the cab, two more in the back. They weren't civilians, though; they wore yellowish-brown khakis.

As he pulled his gun to aim at the driver, the pickup veered off the road into the dirt in front of the house. Dixon froze, thinking for a moment they had seen him, waiting for them to grab guns and fire.

But he could have been a ghost as far as the Iraqis were concerned. The two men in the back grabbed something, someone, from the bed of the truck. He struggled as they dragged him—he was short, two feet shorter than they were at least. They pulled him along the ground to the front of the burnt-out building.

It was a boy, a kid somewhere between seven and nine years old. The child crumbled to the ground. One of the men scooped him up, trying to make him stand against the wall.

Shit, they're going to shoot him.

As the idea flashed into his head, a shot rang out, then another, and another. The man to the right of the boy fell down.

Dixon didn't realize he had been the one who fired until the hollow click of the empty clip shook through his fingers and reverberated up through the bones in his arms. He grabbed for a new clip, fumbling as he cleared the rifle, fumbling as he ducked behind the wall.

He wanted to live now, long enough to stop them.

The soldier with the boy was crouched down, one hand on the ground, wounded, returning fire with his pistol. The two men in the truck were scrambling to get out.

Dixon burned the fresh clip. The two men from the truck fell to the ground, writhing and bouncing with his gunfire. By the time BJ turned his attention back to the man with the pistol, he'd disappeared.

The boy was curled up on the ground. Dixon couldn't tell if he was dead or alive.

He needed to get the other man.

Reloading, BJ began walking sideways behind the wall, half-stooping, eyes pasted on the front of the building. The hillside behind the house was dotted with scraggly bushes and vegetation, but there was nothing big enough to hide behind.

Dixon walked until he had the rear corner of the house in sight. He moved a few more yards to his left, then stopped again, watching for any sign of movement from the building. He put his hand on the stones carefully, gradually shifting his weight as if testing to see if it would hold. He rose, then raised his leg to step over the wall.

A bee shot out of the house. He dove forward as the Iraqi soldier fired a second round, dust kicking up as BJ rolled and tumbled toward the road. He winced as something hit the ground nearby, then pushed himself to his feet. Despite the surge of adrenaline, he ignored the impulse to fire blindly. The sound of a shot whizzing near his ear sent him diving back to the ground. Then he launched himself almost like a sprinter, plunging across the road toward the pickup. Bullets flew near him, but if he was hit he didn't feel it. When he was within five feet of the pickup he tripped; as BJ flew forward, glass from the mirror splattered over him, broken by the Iraqi's errant gunfire.

The man had to be inside the ruins, shooting from the front of the building close to the corner. But Dixon couldn't see the Iraqi, nor could he get a good shot at him without coming out from behind the truck. BJ pulled his legs up, trying to squeeze himself into the tiniest target possible. He swung the rifle up toward the building; a bullet ripped through the side of the truck a few inches from the barrel. Lowering the gun, BJ began edging along the ground toward the front of the cab. Another round sailed into the side of the vehicle, passing through the metal with a loud crackle.

The house was about ten yards away. Dixon leaned his head away from the truck, craning his neck as he tried to see the building. The edge of the road a few feet away popped with a fresh slug. Sooner or later the Iraqi would manage to get a bullet through the truck and hit him.

Dixon looked down the side of the truck for the gas

filler, thinking he might set the gas tank on fire and use it as a diversion. But it wasn't on his side of the pickup.

A shot sailed into the cab of the truck, spitting out near the dirt a few feet away.

He might be able to toss a grenade into the house.

If he missed, or even if he didn't, the explosion could kill the boy he was trying to save.

Dixon sprawled along the ground behind the truck, trying to see the kid. The slight slope up toward the house, which was probably helping shelter him, made it impossible to see where the child was.

Another shot ripped through the pickup, almost exactly where he'd been huddled.

Dixon took the grenade from his pocket, holding it in his hand. Jacketed in painted steel, it weighed about half a pound, with a diameter about as wide as a matchbook. The smooth skin and elongated shape made it very different than the pineapple grenades he'd seen in World War II movies.

And those movies were as close as he'd ever come to a real grenade.

The round pin hung off the side. Pulling it released a clamp at the top; the mechanism wasn't difficult to figure out, though Dixon wasn't sure how long the delay was.

In the movies, there had been scenes of grenades being thrown, landing, and then thrown back before they exploded. The actors solved that by setting the fuse, counting, and then throwing.

They had dummy grenades, though.

He leaned the AK-47 against his knee and rocked his body back and forth, grenade in his right hand, left forefinger looped into the pin. He pulled as he swung away from the truck, but the pin didn't budge; Dixon just barely kept himself from tossing the grenade without setting it.

A bullet ricocheted off the truck bed two feet away. He pulled desperately, but the ring still held. He yanked, trying to lever his weight against the catch. The rifle fell over in the dust; his right hand flew against the truck.

The pin was in his left hand.

Panicking, he wailed the grenade into the air, throwing it well beyond the house. He grabbed for the rifle, scooping up dirt and rocks as well as the stock, fumbling it into his hands as he levered himself to his feet. Dixon caught his balance and dove around the bumper of the truck, raising the rifle to fire blindly. A bullet passed so close to his head he felt the breeze.

As he pushed the trigger on the gun, the grenade exploded on the hill behind the house, sending dirt and serrated metal in a wide spray. Dixon squeezed off a three-burst round at the corner of the building, then began running forward full speed, expecting the Iraqi to nail him at any second. He smashed against the wall of the house, rolling from his right shoulder to his back to his left shoulder, pushing along to an opening that had held a window until yesterday. He pulled flush with the space, firing as he did, working it like he truly was a commando and not a misplaced pilot, assigned here by mistake and then stranded in the confusion of a mission gone way wrong.

His bullets burst in the dusty rubble, dragonflies snapping their wings. He stopped firing, seeing the Iraqi on the floor just below the window, dead.

Letting go of the trigger on his rifle somehow made Dixon lose his balance; he stumbled backward, caught himself, swirled around with the thought, the fear that one of the men he'd shot in the front yard wasn't really dead, was holding a gun on him. But the three bodies lay where they'd fallen, arms akimbo, heads jerked at bad angles in the ground. One man's eyes caught him as he sank slowly to one knee. The corpse watched him force a slow breath into his lungs, glared at him as he stood and began checking each body carefully, making sure his enemies were truly dead. After he did so, he returned to each man, searching their bodies quickly for anything that might be useful. He found only a knife, but in the truck bed were four rifles similar to his; along with two full boxes of clips. It was only when he tried to load one of the clips into his gun that he realized the guns were actually different models—AK-74's, which used smaller-caliber bullets. BJ left his and took two of theirs, stuffing banana clips into his pocket and belt. He fired off one of the guns, making sure it worked.

As he lowered the rifle, he heard a sound behind him. He spun quickly.

The Iraqi boy stood six or seven feet away, trembling.

"It's okay," Dixon told him. He shook his head. "It's okay. You're okay."

The boy's white pants were torn and badly stained. His T-shirt was a faded yellow, entirely intact and fairly clean, though he'd obviously been wearing it a long time. He wore a pair of sneakers at least two sizes too big; they seemed to be Nikes, though their markings were missing.

"You're all right?" Dixon lowered the rifle. "You okay, kid?"

The boy opened his mouth, but said nothing. He started to cry.

"It's all right," Dixon told him.

It surely wasn't all right, but what else could he say? What could he do?

"Why did they want to kill you?" Dixon asked. "What were they doing?"

The Iraqi boy took a step toward him, then another. Fear leaped inside Dixon's chest—what if the child was booby-trapped, or had a weapon, or saw the strange American who had appeared from nowhere not as his rescuer but as his enemy?

Before Dixon could do anything else, the boy threw himself into him, clamping his arms around his neck as he draped himself across BJ's chest. Tears streamed from the kid's body, soaking through Dixon's shirt, mixing with his dried sweat and coursing down the side of his chest and stomach.

"It's all right," the lieutenant told the boy, patting him awkwardly with the gun still in his hand. "It's all right. You're okay."

The boy began to wail, his voice starting as a low moan and quickly rising. Dixon started to push him away, but the child held on tightly, his body shaking with his cries. There was nothing Dixon could do but pat his back, hoping somehow that would calm him.

Grief ran from the kid like water from a busted pipe. Dixon felt his own eyes swelling; he remembered his mother dying, tried steeling himself against it, walling himself off, but finally there was no stopping the tears. He let the rifle fall and took hold of the kid as he sobbed. The first few drops felt like fingers tearing through the frosty ice at the top of a pond, but those that followed were like warm oil, soothing the corners of his face, soothing the aches of his body. BJ lost his sense of place; he lost his sense of himself, his hopelessness, his fear—most importantly, his determination to die there in a blaze of gunfire. A frightened self poured out with the tears. The part of him that trembled before battle, the part that froze at one point in every combat sortie, the part of him that was paralyzed by confrontation, the part of him that wanted to give up, the self that had closed his eyes the night his mother died instead of taking one last look—that William James Dixon poured out of his eyes and left his body with a shudder.

The man left behind wasn't beyond fear, but he understood it in a different way; he neither welcomed it nor ran from it. He simply accepted it as a fact.

The tears stopped. Dixon put his hands around the boy's sides and lifted him away from his chest, gently placing him on the ground. The kid too had stopped crying. He took a step back, looking at Dixon with an expression of shock, as if he had finally realized that Dixon was an enemy soldier. He cringed and threw his arms around his thin chest, holding his tattered shirt.

"I'm not going to hurt you," Dixon told him.

The kid shook his head. It wasn't until the boy pointed in the direction of the road that Dixon realized the kid was scared not of him, but of the sound of a vehicle approaching down the road from the direction of the village.

17

Skull tried to keep his face military neutral as Major Preston continued his speech. Any other guy new to an important post in a combat squadron would keep his remarks—if any—briefer than hell. But this was vintage Preston, the full-of-himself officer Knowlington remembered from their stint together at the Pentagon a little more than a year ago. People who knew him then said the major could outtalk a Congressman; Skull now had proof.

The worst thing was, Preston kept telling the assembled Hog drivers that, even though he was a pointy-nose fighter-jock pukehead, he was really one of them. Really.

Not in so many words, of course, but the drift was clear. And it went over like a Big Blue fuel bomb tumbling out the back of a Combat Talon I.

Being a pilot in the Air Force meant that you were one of a very select minority, the cream of chocolate milk. Being a fighter pilot—any fighter pilot—meant you were the cream of the cream.

And yet, there was a severe prejudice against Hog drivers

because of the planes they flew. Unlike the sleek F-15 Eagles and F-16 Vipers, A-10As couldn't come close to the sound barrier. They could pull maybe half the g's a pointy-nose could. Now granted, they were kick-ass at the job they were designed for—close-in ground support, tank-busting especially. And the first few days of the ground war, which saw them flying far behind the lines and doing things their designers never dreamed of, proved not just the mettle of the planes, but the skills and sheer balls of their pilots. Given all that, there was still a feeling out there that A-10's and their drivers were second-rate. Hog drivers definitely tended to react to it in various ways, none of which were particularly pretty.

They were reacting now, grinding their teeth as Preston told them once again they had nothing to be ashamed of.

"Uh, hey, no offense, Major," said Lieutenant Jack Gladstone finally, "but we ain't ashamed of nothing."

"Damn straight," murmured a couple of the other lieutenants. "We're not second-rate at nothing."

"I didn't mean you were," said Preston.

"Yeah, but you're making it sound like we are," said Gladstone.

"No. I didn't mean that." Fortunately for Preston, nearly all of the squadron's front-line pilots were out on missions. Even so, the audience was pretty riled. Doberman, studiously trying to ignore the proceedings in the back, was frothing. Wong was his usual nonplussed self next to him—he wasn't a pilot, so apparently he didn't care.

And Shotgun was stuffing his face with what looked like an apple pie, though God only knows where it came from.

Doberman's lips started moving. A bad sign.

Skull cleared his throat, getting up from the folding chair near the side of the squadron room. "We're all glad Major Preston is aboard," he said. "Now we have some work to get done. Hack, I think one of those newspaper people is waiting outside to talk to you about that MiG you shot down yesterday."

Preston hadn't mentioned the fact that he had nailed an MiG—probably he thought everyone knew already—and

Knowlington's seemingly offhand comment was enough to temporarily calm the rising tide of dissension. The new DO had enough sense to finally shut his mouth after a line about how much he was counting on everyone to help him out. He nodded to Knowlington, then joined the men filtering out of Cineplex.

"Class-A farthead," Doberman said as he approached Knowlington.

"Relax, Captain," said Skull.

"Come on, Dog, he ain't that bad. I was in a unit with him couple of years back," said Shotgun. "Good pilot. Very clean turns."

"Very clean turns? What the fuck is that supposed to mean? Very clean turns?"

"Doesn't spill coffee when he pumps the rudder," said Shotgun. "What I'm talking about."

"Captain Glenon informed me that he and Captain O'Rourke will be on the mission," said Wong, bringing toddler time to a close. "Who are the other two pilots?"

"Oh, they did, did they?" said Skull, frowning at them. "Yeah, they're coming. If they don't fall asleep."

"I might catch some Z's on the way back," said Shotgun. "I'm thinking of packing a pillow, just in case."

"The other pilots?" asked Wong.

"I'm flying this mission," Skull said. "I have Bozzone in mind to take the last slot. I told him to be ready to fly tonight, but I haven't given him the details."

"Billy's kind of low-time," said Doberman.

"True," said Skull. Lieutenant Bozzone was a good pilot, but had only been on one mission since the Gulf War started. He hadn't flown much before coming to the Gulf either. On the other hand, he had been training for night flights and was used to using the AGMs to read targets. Skull didn't doubt his abilities, but there was no arguing with the fact that he didn't have a lot of cockpit time.

"What about Duck?" Shotgun asked. "He's always up for an adventure."

"I need Captain Dietrich to lead a mission in the morning," said Skull. "He's taking four Hogs out to Al Jouf after a bombing run. If both of you guys are going, he can't."

"Billy's just a kid," said Doberman.

All of them were to Skull. But he didn't say that.

"I've been reviewing the latest satellite data and other intelligence," said Wong. "The missiles we spoke of have been positioned. I have a ninety-percent confidence that they are SA-11's. There are also several triple-A batteries, and positionings of low-altitude heat-seeking batteries. The information has been relayed to the F-111 commander. One group of the heat-seeking weapons will have to be targeted in the initial attack, and of course you must keep the others in mind during your operations near the village."

A few squadron members drifted toward them from the other end of the room, obviously interested in what was going on. While Skull hated keeping his people in the dark, the mission was code-word secret.

"Let's talk about this in my office," he told Wong, Doberman, and Shotgun, ushering them toward the hallway.

"Colonel, what newspaper reporter?" asked Preston, intercepting them outside.

"Hack." Skull shook his head, but decided not to bother explaining that he'd only said that to bail the idiot out. He continued down the hall.

"Uh, Colonel, could I have a word?" Preston asked.

Skull stopped. "Sure."

"In private?"

"Is it a private thing?"

"Well—"

Skull gestured to the others. "You've met Glenon and O'Rourke, right? This is Captain Wong."

Preston gave them all a quick nod. "Actually, I wanted to get myself on the roster to fly ASAP. Tomorrow, if possible."

"All the slots are filled," said Skull.

"There are four planes that aren't listed for missions," said Preston. "There are plenty of low-priority targets available. I'll find a wing mate and take one. Maybe Shotgun'll fly with me," added Preston, trying to make his voice sound chummy. "Gun and I go back to Germany. Used to plunk Volkswagens."

"Those planes are spoken for," Doberman said.

"What exactly is going on, Colonel?"

Skull scratched his forehead, rubbing the edges of his eyebrows with his thumb and middle finger, thinking. Preston had been flying combat since the beginning of the air war, and while it had been a while since he'd sat his fanny in a Hog, he had tons of experience. He'd be an obvious choice to take the mission—after days of orientation, or reorientation, flights.

No time for that.

"Colonel?" repeated Preston.

Why was he hesitating? Because he didn't like him?

Because Preston had tried to screw him when they both worked at the Pentagon a year or so ago?

Maybe Preston was a jerk, but he was a good pilot. He'd already nailed an MiG.

"You ever use Mavericks to fly at night?" Skull asked.

"You're not supposed to," said Hack. "Specifically advised against that. I've done plenty of night flying, though."

"In a Hog?" said Doberman.

"Of course. We used to drop logs and drill with CBUs and Mavs. Problem is the damn screens have such a small angle it's hard to get your bearings, so using them to do more than find your target can be disorienting. Right, Shotgun?"

O'Rourke smiled, but said nothing.

"What's this about, Colonel?" asked Preston.

Fly the number one and number two guys on the same mission? Along with the squadron's best pilots?

Why the hell not? You had to use your best weapons, no?

"Colonel?"

"All right. Come with us into my office, Major. Assuming you're up for flying tonight."

"Tonight?"

"If you're too tired or don't feel up to it—"

"Of course I'm up for it," said Hack.

"And you got to like long shots," added Shotgun. "And Devil Dogs."

Preston's chin twitched for a second, but only for a second.

"I like long shots," he said.

18

The easiest thing in the world was to say no.

The general looked at him expectantly. Jack Sherman was so heavy the desk he was sitting behind groaned as he shifted his elbows.

"It's a classified mission," repeated Sherman. He put his hands down and drummed his fingers, the beat vaguely reminiscent though difficult to place. "So you can work things out from that. I'm not authorized to say anything else, and to be honest, I don't know much more. You'll be briefed fully if you volunteer. I mean, obviously it's going to be hazardous."

Lars nodded. A voice inside was telling him to walk away—not just from the request to fill in for a sick copilot, but from the whole Gulf War. From everything.

General Sherman's round, light brown face broke into a smile. He obviously thought he was doing Lars a favor, pushing an assignment that would—

That would *what*? Get him promoted? Get him a medal?

He didn't need no damn medal. He needed to get home, go see his daughter Sushie again.

"Some of your experience will come in handy," added Sherman, still tapping. "That was one of the considerations in asking you."

Experience?

"It's nothing you haven't done before," said the general. "And it is in a C-130. An MC-130."

I'm not a coward, Lars thought. But I can't even land the damn plane a hundred miles behind the lines. And an MC-130 wasn't going to be running toilet paper across Saudi Arabia. The Herks were equipped for low-level penetration of hostile territory. They could perform a variety of missions, none of them exactly easy.

Lars had notched serious hours in three different training programs and a NATO exercise at the helm of a Combat Talon MC-130E some years before.

Years ago. Centuries ago.

"Herk pilots are at a real premium, especially good ones," said the general, who seemed to be slipping into salesman mode. Lars had first met Sherman when he was a major, but they'd never been particularly close. Sherman tended to play the hail-fellow-well-met thing a bit too far, though otherwise seemed like a decent officer.

"Guy gets sick, everybody's scrambling," added Sherman, his voice almost singing as his tapping grew more complicated. "Things are picking up, huh?"

Lars managed an affirmative grunt. The tune—a sixties TV show?

"Holdout for a signing bonus, huh?" suggested Sherman.

F Troop? Sushie watched that on Nick at Night.

No way.

"Get the Spec Ops boys to take you on permanently? Only a few of us over there; I'm sure they wouldn't mind."

Lars managed a smile. "Us" was a reference to the fact that they were both African-American.

If Sherman had been white, would it have been easier to blow him off?

Lars had never turned down an assignment before, not a real one. Not because he was scared.

He'd never been scared. This was just weird—the sort of thing he ought to see a shrink about.

That would go over big.

Lars could feel the sweat already pouring down the back of his neck.

Just say no.

"So, you up for it?" asked the general.

Against his better judgment—against everything—Lars felt his head bob up and down.

"Great. Plane's already being prepped. Your pilot is a nice fella, white guy, but okay. I've flown with him. DiRiggio. Lots of experience with SOC. Hook up with him, he'll give you the deal. Uh, watch his breath, though. Real garlic-eater. Knock you out."

Sherman smiled—it was tough to tell whether he was joking or not.

"Air Force captain name of Wong—no shit, Wong— he's in charge of the operation. He'll be on the plane. He's assigned to an A-10 squadron, but there's a lot more to him than it seems. Let me give you a heads-up," added the general. "Guy works for some admiral at the Pentagon and has no sense of humor."

"Great." The word stuck in Lars's throat.

"But hell, you'll probably do this with your eyes closed." Sherman slapped the desk in a crescendo and stood to walk Lars out. "Easy gig for you."

"Oh, yeah," Lars said, somehow getting his legs in gear.

19

Dixon pulled the boy along with him as he scrambled along the rear of the house. When he reached the corner, he dropped to his knees and put down one of the two Kalashnikov assault rifles, pulling the other under his arm as he leaned out to scan the road.

A battered Zil dodged some of the worst ruts as it lumbered up from the direction of the village. It slowed, then stopped a few yards from the pickup, whose front grille and bumper Dixon could just see from the back corner of the building.

The truck driver leaned out the window, staring toward the pickup. He yelled something, then turned his head toward the house.

Dixon ducked back. Probably, the driver saw the dead men, because he ground the Zil's gears and revved the engine.

Kill him quick!

Dixon jumped to his feet. By the time he reached the front of the ruined building, the Zil was a good fifty yards away and gaining speed. He squared to fire, but realized he was unlikely to stop the man, even if he managed to hit the bouncing truck; all he'd be doing was confirming any suspicion that he was still there.

BJ lowered the rifle and looked back at the house. The Iraqi boy stood by the edge of the building, holding the other AK-74.

Dixon motioned for the boy to come forward. The kid hesitated, and for a slice of a second Dixon worried that the boy was going to shoot him. But then the kid smiled and ran to him. When he reached Dixon, the child spun around, mimicking what Dixon had done as he shouldered the large rifle down the road.

Dixon put his hand on the barrel of the gun, gently lowering it.

"What's your name, kid?" he asked.

The boy looked at him, not understanding.

"Name?" Dixon patted his chest. "I'm BJ. BJ. Who are you? Huh?"

"Budge," said the boy finally, patting himself.

"Budge?" Dixon laughed. So did the kid. "Budge, huh? That's a good name. Budge."

The kid patted his chest. "Budge," he said, laughing.

"So, Budge, what the hell should I do with you, huh? Why were those goons trying to kill you? Who were they? What'd you do?"

Budge didn't understand.

BJ tried miming what had happened before, but the boy didn't really understand. He said something in what Dixon figured was Arabic, but his words were as incomprehensible to Dixon as Dixon's must be to him.

"What the hell are we going to do, Budge?" Dixon asked finally. "Are there other people around here who want to kill you?"

He was careful as he mimed that, not wanting to make the kid think that he was going to harm him. The boy thought it was a joke or a game, laughing.

"One way or another, there's plenty who want to kill

me," said Dixon. "If you're with me, they may shoot you too. Probably they would."

Budge shrugged, but obviously because he didn't understand.

"If I leave you here, will the goons come back and kill you?"

The boy blinked his green eyes, then said something, patting his stomach. Probably he was saying he was hungry.

"You know where there's food?" Dixon asked. He mimed the question, using the boy's stomach to start.

Budge shook his head. The obvious place to find food was in the village, but it wasn't as if they could simply show up at the local 7-Eleven and buy a couple of hoagies.

Or maybe they could. Dixon had some Iraqi money in his survival kit. He could give it to the kid, send him into whatever passed for a store in these parts. Or even a house.

What if somebody asked the kid where he got the money? Or simply followed him back?

Turning Dixon in would make Budge an immediate hero. He wouldn't even have to do it on purpose.

Why were the men trying to kill the kid?

Trust him? He was seven or eight most likely, certainly no older than ten. How smart was he? Smart enough to trick anyone who was suspicious of him?

Smart enough to trick Dixon?

Irrelevant. The question was, would he know to keep his mouth shut?

When Dixon was nine, he had a full load of chores on the family's tiny vegetable truck farm, a separate operation from the corn and soybeans. He manned the fruit and vegetable stand every day during the summer, handling the tourists and the local town folks who stopped by. It was more boring than hard; rarely did he have to help more than two people an hour.

What if someone had appeared in the middle of the tomato patch behind the stand, just walked up, and saved him from being robbed? What would Dixon have done? Tell his mom?

Sure, he'd be happy and grateful.

What if the guy had been in some kind of trouble himself? Would Dixon have been savvy enough to keep quiet, sneak him some food?

Maybe. If he realized the guy was in trouble. But you could be really dumb as a kid, innocent in all sorts of ways. This kid might be grateful that Dixon had saved him, but that didn't mean he wouldn't give him away.

Dixon could leave him. But that was like shooting him, wasn't it?

He'd already made that decision.

"What I think we're going to do here, Budge," Dixon said, squatting so he was eye-level with the boy, "what I think we're going to do is go into the village. We have to be very quiet. People there want to kill us. Do you understand?" He mimed the words, walking with his fingers, shielding his face with his hands, pretending to be fired at. The boy leaned forward and hugged him.

"That's going to have to do for now," said Dixon, starting toward the road.

20

Hack furled his fingers around the A-10A stick, waiting impatiently for the other pilots to complete their checks. The F-15's cockpit wasn't exactly massive, but the Hog's work space seemed smaller than the trunk of a Honda Civic. The instrument panel was a solid wall of old-fashioned dials and buttons; the only display was the small tube below the windshield at the right-hand corner slaved to the Maverick missiles. It was a miracle the plane even had a heads-up display.

Hack bounced his feet up and down on the rudder pedals, trying to shake out his boredom. The Warthog's GE turbofans were diminutive and almost silent—at least compared to the F-15, which had a guttural, throat-shaking roar even at rest.

He had to stop comparing the damn Warthogs to Eagles. He was a driver now, and a backseat one at that—Knowlington had him flying wing to Captain Glenon, the second plane in the second element.

Made sense, couldn't argue. Actually, Knowlington

seemed a hell of a lot more on the ball here than he had back in D.C. Had a peculiar way of running a squadron, but part of that might be because he had less than half the normal complement of personnel, except for the sections responsible for keeping the aircraft airworthy.

That Sergeant Clyston was a real piece of work. Hack was going to sit on his butt good to get him to do things the way they were supposed to be done. Stinking sergeants thought they ran the frigging service. Straighten him out no time.

Can his ass once he took over the squadron.

Maybe.

Two things surprised Hack. One was the fact that Knowlington didn't seem to be drinking—or at least was being considerably more discreet about it than he had been at the Pentagon.

The other was that Knowlington and his squadron were held in high enough esteem that they had been tagged to work with Delta up north in what had to be a high-priority, not to mention extremely difficult, mission.

Not that he'd thought Knowlington was a bad pilot. On the contrary, he'd heard the stories about what he'd done in Vietnam. It's just that he'd thought the colonel was an over-the-hill geezer with one foot and half his head out the door.

"Devil Leader to Devil Flight," said Knowlington over the squadron frequency. "All right, let's get this show on the road."

One by one, the others acknowledged. By the time Major Preston pressed his transmit button, he'd already nudged his Warthog off her brakes and begun to trundle up toward the starting gate to keep pace with the others. He ran through his checks one more time, scanning the instruments, glancing at the INS, quizzing his compass. His stomach began flipping over, and for a brief moment the veteran Air Force pilot felt like a teenager taking Dad's car to the grocery store the first time. Then instinct took over; he pulled the double throttle bars to their stops, spooling out the engines and rocketing down the runway.

After a fashion. Damn Warthog was slow, slow, slow.

And while it might not be fair to compare it to an F-15, there was no way not to as the plane heaved itself up into the air, chugging along more like a pickup truck with wings than a modern airplane. Hack's stomach tightened as he left the ground. He couldn't get the feel right, and started to jerk to the right, his left wing pitching up in answer to his awkward pull. But the A-10A was a forgiving sort; she caught a gust of wind and steadied her wings, rising behind her companions in a slow, steady march northward.

A fresh wave of jitters hit Preston as he searched the dusky sky for his wing mate. It took three long glances to find Doberman ahead on his left, exactly where he was supposed to be. He checked his INS; still overly nervous, he went through the sheet of way-markers on his kneeboard. He was precisely on course, flying the Hog as smoothly as if he'd racked up a hundred hours in the past month, but he could feel his heart pounding.

He'd been like this in the Eagle too. A lot of times it took until the border for him to calm down. The first snap vector or the first heads-up from the AWACS or the first radar contact of an enemy—once something *real* happened, he was fine. But until then he was just jangled nerves, no matter what he was driving.

Shit. Thinking like a Hog driver already.

Hack flipped through the sheets on his kneepad, studying the frequencies, the way-points, the notes on fuel, burn, and the rest. Finally he lifted the last page and exposed the three items he'd pasted to his board on his very first solo years ago—a Gary Larson cartoon, a quote from the Bible, and something his father always said.

He laughed at the cartoon, just as he had on every flight he'd ever made. He nodded at the quotation, which was from Ecclesiastes. Then he repeated his father's advice:

Do your best.

Do your best. That's all you ever needed.

Preston checked his throttle, shifted a bit on the ejector seat, nudged the Hog to slide a little further out off Doberman's wing.

Like the others, Preston carried four Maverick AGM-65Gs, one each loaded in the LAU-117 launchers that flanked the main wheels. The G-model Mavericks were serious weapons, featuring three-hundred-pound warheads, more than twice the size of the "standard" B model and extremely adept at pounding armor. But the real value of the missiles was the infrared imager in their golden noses; A-10A pilots in the Gulf had discovered that the IR gave the plane a primitive nighttime capability.

Primitive indeed. It would be looking at the ground through a straw. But the others had already used the missiles to fly night missions; if they could do it, Hack could too.

Besides the missiles, Shotgun and Doberman each had a pair of what looked like napalm containers slapped to the hard points on either side of their bellies. The pods held the Fulton-STAR retrieval systems the ground team would use to escape.

The other two Hogs were carrying illumination flares in rocket-launching canisters. Preston hadn't actually used the launchers for anything but rockets—and as a matter of fact, he wasn't even entirely sure he had done that. But the principle was fairly simple. The LUU-2 would spit out, opening its chute and igniting. The hot air would hold it up and it would descend, lighting the night like a set of klieg lights for five minutes or so. The "lou-twos" or logs would only be used if things got sticky and the Hogs needed to use their cannons.

Two other important weapons were attached to the planes. Every A-10 carried a pair of Sidewinder air-to-air missiles at the left edge of their wings for air defense. An ECM pod sat on the opposite hard point. The counter-measures in the ALQ-119 were older than Hack; the device was next to useless against the SAMs the F-111's were going to hit. In fact, even the F-15 Hack had just been flying would have been pushed to the limit dealing with it.

Do your best, he reminded himself, trying to push the negative thoughts away. He rechecked his position and twisted his head, scanning the sky for the millionth time even though they were far behind the lines.

All things considered, Preston had the easiest job of the mission. After a quick refuel at KKMC, the planes would fly together across the border, as if coming in for an attack. The dance would begin at a coordinate they called "Wendy's"— Shotgun had supplied the nicknames—about fifty miles due south of their actual target area. The planes would make a show of turning west toward a GCI or ground radar site that had been hit two days before; the maneuver was supposed to make anyone watching think they were going to attack it again. After about two minutes of flying time, they would reach "Krisp." Knowlington and Shotgun would hit the deck, diving to fifty feet and starting a zig-run north to scout the LZ for the Hercules. Doberman and Hack would continue toward the GCI for about a minute and a half before breaking off, turning back south to refuel. Assuming all went as planned, they'd relieve the first two planes in a staging area about fifteen miles south of the LZ, orbiting there until—if— needed. They'd be about a two-minute scramble from the hot zone. The A-10's would trade back and forth, waiting and re-fueling, until they were needed to cover the pickup. Then they'd go home.

Two pairs of F-111's were doing the heavy lifting—one taking out the SAM site and the other, several hours later, going after Saddam's car. The Hogs would back them up.

"Four, you're supposed to be further back in trail."

Glenon's ferocious yap jerked Hack physically; he slammed the stick of his Hog to the left, pitching the plane on its wing to fall back before realizing that he needn't have taken such drastic action. He swooped back level, cursing Glenon as well as himself—he hadn't been that close, for christsakes, just a little tighter on Devil Three than they had briefed. No reason to bark at him.

"Four," he said, acknowledging. He let the distance work out to a mile and a half, in the meantime pulling closer to the axis of the flight. You could waste a lot of fuel getting too close, because then you'd be making constant adjustments on the throttle.

In theory anyway. Damn Hog throttle was just an on-off switch.

"Devil Leader to Devil Flight. Ease up, boys," snapped Knowlington. "The night is young. We have our first way-point in zero-two. Nice, gentle turn."

The colonel's voice had the smooth, suave assurance of an all-night deejay spinning golden oldies in the wee hours. Hack eased his fingers, rolling his neck and trying to snap some of the tension out with the cracks of his ligaments against the vertebrae. The sky ahead darkened as he flew, blue hazing into a gray that slid into blackness. He took the turn, and then the next course correction, now on a direct line for Iraq. The planes had climbed all the way to eighteen thousand feet. It was high for a Hog—and the lowest altitude he'd ever been at crossing the border.

They'd be going a hell out of a lot lower before the night was through. Fifty feet in the dark.

Damn long time since he'd done that. Had he ever actually done that, even in an exercise? He wasn't sure.

Hack blew a wad of air through his nose and worked his eyes around the cockpit, determined to keep his shit together. Nail this, and everyone in the squadron was going to respect him, no questions asked.

He hadn't even thought of that when he'd volunteered. But it was true—a bonus he hadn't counted on.

Assuming he made it.

"Wendy's," said Knowlington.

The transmission startled Hack; it felt like it was too soon, though a glance at his instruments told him they were dead-on.

One by one, the planes acknowledged and took the turn. Shotgun's acknowledgment seemed garbled, and for a half second Hack felt a mixture of anticipation and actual fear, desire to step up into the tougher slot mixing with the fear that he might screw up the harder job.

But there was nothing wrong with Devil Two or its radio. Shotgun's voice hadn't been garbled so much as consumed by another sound.

Bruce Springsteen, it seemed. Singing "Born to Run."

Snap out of it, Hack told himself. You're wound so tight you're starting to hear things. Nobody listens to music on the way to a bomb run over enemy territory, not even a Hog driver.

21

Skull's yellow pad had it nice and neat, a quick cut to the northeast followed by a dogleg south, a dive, and then a 160-degree turn and a jog north to the money.

Real life was messier, with the RWR warning that an Iraqi radar that shouldn't be there was trying to acquire him before they reached Krisp. There had been a GCI or ground radar site due west, but if the RWR was to be believed, that wasn't what was targeting them now; the radar was in a different band.

If the warning was to be believed, in fact, they were being hunted by a Roland mobile SAM battery, probably the most deadly antiair weapon the Iraqis had outside of the SA-11's Wong had spotted further north.

"Radar," said Knowlington tersely. "Hang with me and stay on course."

As he let go of the mike button to end the transmission, the warning indicator went clear. Skull's eyes hunted the dark shadows below for a sign of the threat. They were more than a hundred miles inside Iraq, heading toward the heart of the country. They were beyond the worst of the desert; the ground was more hard-packed here, hard-scrabble scrub as opposed to sifting mounds of sand. But no matter what the earth was made of, it would have been hard to pick anything out of the dusky shadows from this altitude.

Their planned zig would take them through the direction the radar waves seemed to have come from; the way they'd chalked it up, they'd pass right through the missile's prime acquisition envelope as they dove to fifty feet.

The German-made missile system, which Iraq had a good number of, had a range of roughly four miles. Designed for low- and medium-altitude protection, it was extremely nasty once locked on a target.

"I have no radar," said Shotgun. "Been clean."

"One," acknowledged Skull.

It had been roughly thirty seconds since the warning. They were one and a half minutes away from Krisp.

The safest thing to do was change course. But that might change their time on target, which would mess everything up—this was a delicate dance between the F-111's, the Hogs, and the Herk. Throw the schedule off a minute and he risked having the Hercules spotted.

Better, though not safer, to dive sooner, steeper, get under the Roland as well as the SA-11. That meant a much longer drive at fifty feet.

Lose some speed, eat more fuel.

Knowlington quickly looked at his paper map, double-checking the elevations in their path to make sure there weren't any surprises.

Doable.

"Krisp in sixty seconds," Knowlington told the rest of his flight. "Devil Three, I'm figuring that Roland, if it's there, at about two o'clock, four miles from Krisp, maybe a little further. You want coordinates?"

"I can do the math," snapped Doberman.

"We're going to break on my signal. Shotgun, you and I are going to dive down to fifty feet and get under it.

Doberman, you avoid the site when you come north." He
left it to Doberman to decide how.

"Two. I'm ready when you are, Skip," said Shotgun.

"Three."

Skull took one last look at his gauges, making sure he
had plenty of fuel. His preflight calculations had been pes-
simistic; the Hog was sipping daintily.

Maybe he was being overly cautious. No way Black
Hole would have left a working Roland out here. Probably
just an ECM glitch.

No way to tell.

"Krisp," Skull said, tipping his wing as he rolled the
Hog into a steep dive.

22

"If I get the chance, I'm nailing him."

"Who says you're getting the chance?"

Salt glanced toward the front of the cargo hold, where Captain Wong was consulting with one of the Herk's crewmen. "If I get the chance, I'm nailing Saddam," he repeated to Davis.

Davis shrugged. "Planes'll get him. We'll be a mile away."

"I'm not saying they won't get him." Salt edged his toe against his weapons rucksack on the floor of the plane. He wouldn't completely suit up until ten minutes to drop time, set for 2002. And he'd wait until precisely then; it was a superstition thing, and no matter how much it bugged everyone else, he stuck to it. By contrast, all Davis had to do was slap on his helmet and he was good to go. "I'm saying if I get the chance, I'm nailing him."

"Sounds fair."

"What else you figure he's up to?"

"Who?"

"Captain Wong. That need-to-know bullshit."

"Couldn't even guess."

"You got enough explosives to blow the road?" Salt asked.

"I got enough to blow up Saddam's ever-lovin' bunker."

Salt laughed. Unlike most troopers—unlike most soldiers, period—Davis rarely used profanity. "Ever-lovin' " was about as bad as he cursed.

"I wish this crate would hurry up," said Salt. "I'd like to have the road mined already."

"Probably won't even get a chance to blow it."

"We will."

"I will," said Davis.

"Yeah, fuck, you will." Salt had known the black sergeant almost since basic training; they'd saved each other's butts a few times—in bars, not combat. The two operations they had been on together, one in Panama and one before the start of the air war scouting targets, had gone as easily as visits to a church fair.

"I hate these low jumps," said Davis.

Surprised, Salt jerked his head toward his friend. "You scared?"

"You bet I am."

"Ah. Fuck you."

"I am scared," said Davis.

"Yeah." Salt patted Davis's leg. "Me fuckin' too."

23

The ground intercept station betrayed no sign of life as Doberman leveled Devil Two off at five thousand feet. But the station wasn't the point—Doberman continued toward it, holding the plane at an altitude that made it not only visible on radar, but also fairly easy to hear from the ground. If the Iraqis were looking for Hogs up here, they had two very visible ones to track.

But there was no indication that he was being tracked. The AWACS had passed off Skull's Roland read as a malfunction. There was nothing between here and Kajuk that could see them, let alone harm them. And the GCI site—just now visible in the Maverick's IR viewer—looked like a kid's squashed Erector set.

Doberman knew from bitter experience that the moment you thought you were safe was the moment you were most likely to get whacked. The Iraqi missilemen had learned to keep their radars off-line until they were absolutely ready to fire; the handful of operators who had survived the early days of the war were good enough to flick the set on, fire within seconds, then shut down to lessen the odds of a Wild Weasel or Tornado sending them to la-la land. Just because his RWR was quiet, just because the AWACS said he was clean, didn't mean he was safe. On the contrary, it meant he had to sit at the edge of his seat, as wary as ever. The threat could come from any direction.

He missed having Shotgun on his butt. Frankly, Preston didn't impress him. For one thing, the guy hadn't flown an A-10 in years; Doberman didn't understand why Skull let him join a mission where he'd not only be flying far behind the lines but at night. Better to take Bozzone, even if he was a kid. Billy had the moves and the stuff; all he needed was a little experience and he'd be a kick-butt driver.

Plus, Preston didn't like the A-10. Anyone could see he thought he ought to be back flying Eagles. Why the hell had he been sent here? Punishment?

Had to be something serious. A guy didn't just fall into the A-10 community after flying Eagles. Hell, no. Especially a guy who'd nailed a MiG.

Doberman checked his INS. The units had a bad habit of drifting while you were flying, throwing everything off. Naturally, it only happened on a mission where precise timing and location were important.

Like tonight's.

"Devil Three, this is Four. Uh, we still turning?"

Doberman cursed before hitting the mike button. "Turning," he said, angry with himself for letting his thoughts drift, even though he was only about two seconds off the mark.

"Four," acknowledged Hack.

Not like him to be late. Preston had him all out of whack.

As he banked south, Glenon began pulling back on the stick, beginning a gradual climb that would take them to just about fifteen thousand feet as they crossed the border. The tanker should be in a track about two miles further south.

Flying through enemy territory at "high" altitude went against everything a Hog driver was taught. The plane didn't seem to like it either; she didn't buck exactly, but she did seem to be dragging her wings, taking her time on the long climb. She might also be wondering why she was heading south with unfired missiles.

Right about here, Doberman thought to himself, Shotgun would chime in with something funny. But Preston stayed quiet.

Which was, after all, how they'd briefed it—silent com, talk only when necessary.

Damn, he missed Gun.

As Doberman's radar picked up a pair of approaching F-15's, a voice on the long-distance radio frequency demanded that he and Hack identify themselves. As he went to acknowledge, Preston beat him to it.

"Hey, assholes, we're on your side," said Hack.

If Shotgun had said that—and it was the sort of thing he might have said—Doberman would have laughed. But somehow Preston's remark pissed him off.

"Devil Three to Piranha Seven," he told the interceptor pilot who had queried them. "We're A-10A's from the 535th Devil Squadron, heading for a refuel. You got a problem with that?"

The Eagles carried electronics gear to identify friendly aircraft; the FOF "tickled" equipment in the Hogs and painted them on the displays as good guys. That should have been done by now. The AWACS controller would also have given them information about the planes, since it was responsible for tracking flights in the sector.

So why were they being challenged?

"Yo, Blaze, it's Hack. What the fuck are you doing?" said Preston.

"Hack? Major Preston? No way. I'm looking at a pair of flying pickup trucks. Hack's a real pilot."

"Stop busting our chops, Piranha," snapped Doberman. "If this is a real fucking challenge, then get your goddamn ident gear fixed. Stand the fuck down."

"Hey, relax, Devil Flight," answered the fighter pilot. "Just trying to giggle your nugget wingman."

"You don't bust chops by targeting me with your radar," said Doberman.

"Negative. Negative. You weren't targeted. Jesus," said the Eagle jock. "Relax."

"We have not targeted you," said the other Eagle pilot. "Radars are not targeting you."

Doberman, still playing righteous, didn't even acknowledge. The planes rocked off to the east, back to whatever it was they were supposed to be doing.

"Devil Three, I have your six," said Preston over the squadron frequency. "Blaze is okay. He's just a ball-buster."

"How the fuck did he know you were here?" shot back Doberman.

"How would I know? Probably the AWACS sent him to make sure we were who we were supposed to be."

"This mission is secret."

"Well, they know we're here, for christsakes," answered Preston. "Besides—"

"Yeah. Tanker," snapped Doberman, ending the exchange.

He began correcting to fall in behind the KC-135, which had turned south. The director lights in the belly were just visible.

Man, he missed Shotgun.

24

Major Ronald "Wick" Durk had always believed he could sense a mission's karma right out of the gate. Not that he believed in any of the Eastern mysticism crap that went with the karma thing. But he could sense a winning streak when it was coming.

And one wasn't, not tonight.

The F-111 pilot had nearly been diverted about five minutes after taking off from Taif in western Saudi to hit allegedly "live" Scuds found by a Delta team in western Saudi. He'd nearly had to scream at the AWACS trying to order him off his assignment. Not that it was the controller's fault—for all he knew, Wick's two-plane element was going after the low-priority bridge as originally posted in the ATO. Clearing up the misunderstanding without revealing the nature of his mission had not been easy.

And now his wingman had severe engine trouble, bad enough to knock him out of the game.

Hell of a time. They were less than five minutes away from their IP, the initial point or starting line for their bomb-tossing.

He glanced at his weapons-system operator next to him before contacting the ABCCC plane coordinating the mission. Mo had his head pressed to the cowling around the radar unit, seemingly oblivious to everything except the screen a few inches from his eyes. Two Paveway II two-thousand-pound bombs were sitting on the wings waiting to be launched; a Pave Tack targeting set in the belly of the plane was even now hunting down their target. The pod head rotated as the turret flexed, the forward-looking infrared radar examining the terrain ahead.

"Wolf, this is Bad Boy Leader," said Wick, contacting the command plane. "I've just sent Two home. He's limping, but he thinks he'll make it."

"Wolf acknowledges. We heard that." The controller was an Air Force Spec Ops captain sitting in the back of a specially equipped C-130 flying just over the Saudi-Iraq border. He was part communicator, part coach, part mother hen for the complicated mission. "We'd like you to continue into target as planned."

That answered that question. Not that he expected anything different.

"Bad Boy acknowledges."

He flipped the radio to its interphone circuit, allowing him to speak to Mo. "Sixty seconds."

His bombardier grunted. Mo didn't like to talk when he was working.

"We have the SA-11's. They'll have to get someone else on the SA-9's."

"Ugh."

"You comfortable with a ramp toss?"

"Ugh."

"Green Bay ever going to win the Super Bowl?"

"Ugh."

"Your mother a whore?"

"Ugh."

Wick turned his full attention back to the plane, confident that they were going to get a good splash. Mo had everything under control.

25

When flying at fifty feet above ground level, the hairs on
your forearms and wrists became small pieces of ice, sticking into your skin. Your knees locked, the joints pinched
by a mass of cold iron. The fabric of your flight suit got
heavier and heavier, weighted by a fog of sweat and adrenaline. And still you flew faster, your left hand resting on
the throttle, as if its mere presence there might coax a few
more ounces of thrust from the turbofans nailed to your
spine. You held the plane's stick firmly in your right hand,
your consciousness centered in that grip. Your eyes ran
ahead, not so much seeing as absorbing the sky and
ground, bleeding into its shapes and shadows. You were
the plane and you were the pilot and you were the space
where you were flying. And you knew that at any second,
if you lost just a fraction of your concentration, if you
flicked your wrist the wrong way at the wrong moment,
you'd pile into the earth.

Something twitched; Skull nudged left, lifting the Hog
to stay with the contour of the land. Something else

twitched and he took his turn right, precisely on his mark, thirty seconds from the landing zone. The village lay further northeast, to his right as he flew; the highway where Saddam would be hit sat further to the east.

And the SA-11's were dead ahead. There was a battery of the advanced Soviet-made missiles right where Wong said it would be. Skull could actually see the shadows without using the Maverick's nine-inch targeting screen.

The Iraqi radars were inactive. As long as the Hogs stayed at fifty feet, however, they would be obscured in the ground clutter, even if it turned on. The angle of the radar waves and the reflections off the earth surface made it impossible for the targeting devices to see them.

Or rather, difficult; Wong had warned that there was a theoretical possibility that the Russian-made radars could be arranged in a way to guard against exactly this type of attack.

He pushed the seeker head around, scanning the scraggly ground beyond the SAM site. It wasn't Iowa loam, but the land below was close enough to the Euphrates for farming, or so he'd been told. In any event, it wasn't sandy desert; more like hard-packed dirt interrupted by rocks and occasional vegetation. The hill where Wong believed Dixon was holed up was on his right; Skull avoided the temptation to scan in that direction, concentrating on his job, which was to his left.

"Wolf to Devil Leader. One, we have a wrinkle."

"One. Go ahead, Wolf," he snapped.

"Bad Boy Two is scratched. Bad Boy One has prime target. Can you mop up?"

The controller was asking them to strike the SA-9 site immediately south of the SA-11 the Aardvark targeted. While not a threat going in, the short-range heat-seeking SAMs could target the Herk when it made the pickup a few hours from now. Hitting them would necessitate quick action—Skull was less than three miles from the target, closing at roughly four hundred knots. Minimum range was around three thousand feet, maybe twenty seconds from now.

Not a problem.

"One." He nudged his stick slightly, pushing the targeting cursor at the same time to slide the Mav's IR head over in the direction of the Iraqi missile launcher, which lay to the west of the SA-11 due west of Kajuk.

He started to tell Shotgun about the change in plans, but O'Rourke cut him off.

"Two, yeah, I got ya, Chief. I'm looking at the LZ."

Knowlington took one last read on the altimeter—sixty feet above ground—then turned his eyes to the blur of the Maverick screen, pushing the targeting cursor into the thick hull of the lightly armored vehicle where the missiles were mounted. The day's sun had left the truck's metal skin hot, making for a nice, fat blob in the monitor. He locked the target, then poked his nose up slightly, a bit overanxious about letting go of the missile so close to the ground.

And then he launched.

If he told Shotgun he had fired—and most likely he did, because he had intended to—he couldn't remember later. Nor could he have detailed exactly how he dialed the cursor for the next AGM as a second SA-9 launcher—unbriefed—appeared in the screen roughly seventy yards to the north. But he had a good memory of pressing the trigger, and an even better memory of what happened next—the air in front of him turned into a wall of red streaks.

Flak, said a voice that belonged neither to Shotgun nor to Skull. It came from behind an iron wall in a F-4 Phantom twenty years in the past, his old "bear" growling out a warning on a mission long since forgotten.

Now, as then, Skull ignored the warning, sticking to his game plan. He tacked to the left, right through the exploding shells, swinging around as he scanned the target site with his AGM-65G. He had nothing but blurs—then his eyes caught a leaping tongue of flame on the ground, the result of a large Paveway-series laser-guided missile launched from the F-111 striking the SA-11 launcher. Another Roman candle erupted a half second later—probably the van that provided targeting data. Then everything was red and white.

Skull whacked the Hog hard to left, then hit the transmit button.

26

The village was smaller than Dixon had imagined, laid out along one main road that had been cut into the saddle of three hills. The road jagged away from a sharp rock out-cropping at the entrance; by climbing the rock Dixon had been able to scout the town before going in. A mosque sat at the center, elevated on a narrow plain in front of one of the hills; the other buildings were small, mostly made of concrete or something similar, their sides shadows in the dim evening light. Industrial buildings, either warehouses or factories, were wedged into the slope to his right; he couldn't see much of them from the rocks. Worried about being seen, he moved slower than a turtle across the slop-ing scrubland behind the village. The boy seemed caught up in the game his rescuer was playing; he moved behind him like a shadow, ducking when Dixon ducked, rising when Dixon rose. He made no sign that he knew the vil-lage. They huddled together as the sun set, waiting for the long shadows to make it easier to move. But the night wasn't nearly as dark as Dixon wanted. Or perhaps he was just getting more paranoid. They moved ever more slowly, stopping any time there was a sound or odd shadow ahead. They drew a semicircle around the village without seeing anything remotely resembling a store. At three spots along the street, clusters of men stood around vehicles; otherwise there was no sign of life. They were too far away to see for certain whether the men were soldiers or not. The vehicles they stood around seemed to be civilian, but Dixon knew that meant nothing.

Gradually, he and the boy worked back around the hillside, inching closer to a group of houses that lay below the rock he'd climbed earlier. Finally, they came to a flat, open space less than twenty yards behind three small buildings. A faint light shone through one of the windows of the house on the left. Dixon decided to send Budge there to ask for some food.

He mimed it out for the kid, who nodded.

"You really understand, Budge?"

The boy nodded again. "Budge," he said.

Dixon patted his shoulder. He considered simply waiting a few more hours and then breaking in, stealing what they needed. But something inside him was uncomfortable with that—as if he truly were back in Iowa, as if this weren't a matter of life and death.

"Yeah, all right," he told the kid. "Go for it."

A rattle echoed off the hills, the sound of a rattlesnake about to strike. Dixon dove forward, grabbing the boy as a bomb hit somewhere to the northwest, not terribly far from the hill. A second explosion followed; then the sky behind them turned red, fiery hands waving across the horizon. Antiaircraft rumbled, tracers arcing into the sky overhead. The closest gun was a half mile away; the rest were scattered around in a vast semicircle that seemed to form a fist around them.

"This way," he told Budge, jumping back to his feet. "This way."

Dixon picked the boy up under his arm, hauling him along as he ran up the slope to the rock, hoping he might see what was going on from there. The ground shook like the floor of an old auditorium when a rap group played. Dixon ran as fast as he could manage, clutching the kid and the guns to him, stumbling as much as climbing.

The thunder of the flak guns stopped. A truck or some other vehicle started its engine in the distance, but otherwise everything was quiet. The sky beyond the village to the northwest was red; whatever the American bombers had hit was on fire.

When Dixon reached the rock he hoisted Budge up first, then clambered behind him. But the topography made it impossible to get a clear view; whatever had been hit lay beyond or on the side of the short hill opposite the road they'd walked down. Dixon faced it, trying to orient himself north-to-south; it seemed the target lay a mile or more north of the highway, commanding an open plain just before the hills.

Probably another Scud launching site.

If that was true, it was possible it had been pointed out by a Delta team. They'd be around somewhere, maybe waiting for pickup.

Go in that direction and see what was going on? He could skirt the house by walking around the slope, get down to the highway, and walk along it. He could go to the spot where the Black Hawk had appeared last night—it was an easy place for a pickup.

The Iraqis might have it guarded.

Scout it first.

If not there, where? Back to the Cornfield, the old rendezvous point where the Iraqis had ambushed his team days ago? The kid would never be able to walk that far without food.

Maybe it would be better to sneak back to the village, go ahead and get some food and water. The attack might divert attention for a while.

Or it might make the villagers doubly suspicious.

Dixon looked at the boy, trembling on the ground, curled around his leg. Dixon saw a shadow on his pants and realized the child had pissed himself.

"Hey, it's okay, buddy," he told him, pulling him up. "Happens to the best of us."

His father used to tell him that, didn't he? When he was three or four?

Dixon couldn't really remember much his father had told him. It didn't matter, one way or another.

"It's okay, Budge, come on." He stood the kid up. "Let's go see what all this fuss is about, okay? We'll move around to the other side of this hill and see what we can see. We'll get something to eat later. Moving's better than standing still. Remember that."

He repeated the advice, as if he expected Budge to take it to heart.

27

Shotgun's stomach twitched. It wasn't hunger—Skull had twisted his plane directly into a spewing fountain of yellow lava, seemingly oblivious of the ZSU-23 antiaircraft guns even though Shotgun had broadcast two warnings about them.

O'Rourke cursed, leaning against his restraints as the cascading sparks enveloped the lead plane. At the same time, he nudged the aiming cursor of his first Maverick toward the bank of ZSU-23's, the image jumping around and refusing to lock on target. It took so long that before he finally nailed the cursor the air around him had begun to bubble with the hot steam of exploding 23mm shells. As the Maverick dropped off her rail, Shotgun tapped his throttle for luck and yanked the Hog into a tight dip that would take him to the west and out of the Zeus's line of fire.

Had to give it to the Iraqis—they had lined the stinking flak guns up damn good. And they had a million of them here, more than last night, or so it seemed.

Tracers arced over his left wing as he pushed the Hog into its bank. He felt the plane rumble as he flipped the wings hard the other way, trying to dart north into a piece of open air. The violent maneuver tugged the hell out of ailerons, not to mention the wings and the rest of the plane, but the Hog didn't seem to mind, not even bothering to groan as her pilot shoved her over into a roll, gamely holding her rudder straight despite the violent g forces and exploding artillery fire. Finally clear, Shotgun leveled out, running due west as briefed, his eyes hunting for Knowlington.

His stomach twitched again. Devil One ought to be right in front of him, but it wasn't.

28

Captain Wong stood at the edge of the MC-130 ramp, waiting in front of the open doorway. He had his arms linked with the two Delta troopers who were jumping with him, not wanting to take even the slightest chance of mistiming the jump. The combat transport dipped suddenly, turning and rising so sharply that the sergeant on his right slipped toward the opening. Wong tightened his arm, pulling the man back.

"Not yet," he said, though it was unlikely the sergeant could hear him.

Red flashes began sifting through the sky behind the plane, followed by violent greenish-yellow sprays.

Good, thought Wong.

In the next second, the jump light flickered and Wong stepped forward into the rushing air. He spread his arms and in the same instant, the ripcord pulled. The chute of his low-altitude rig popped open as Wong pushed his arms back into his chest. They'd gone out below five hundred feet, even lower than planned—Wong barely got himself situated when his rucksack hit the dirt behind him. He got his legs ready, the ground coming up hard; as he hit the ground he rolled to his right, turning his body into a shock absorber. He sprang up, undoing the harness that had held his rucksack below him on the jump. As he furled his chute, he noted a group of convenient rocks; he was able to stow the darkly colored chute beneath one of them.

The two troopers came down within a few yards of him. They gathered their chutes silently, shouldering their gear and then joining Wong near the rocks to hide their chutes as he checked their location on his GPS.

They had landed ten feet off the mark. The inaccuracy irked Wong, but was within the acceptable margin of error for the mission.

"I'm jumping at 32,000 feet from now on," grouched Salt. "We couldn't have been a hundred fuckin' feet off the ground. Fuckin' pilot shoulda warned us."

"I believe we were lower than planned," agreed Wong. "But nonetheless we were on target. Your knee?"

"Ain't nothing," said the sergeant. "I ain't no fuckin' pussy."

"Wrap it as a precaution," said Wong. He reached into his belt and removed a piece of ace bandage he kept handy for precisely such contingencies. Salt frowned but took the bandage, diligently winding it around his knee. He continued cursing, apparently unable to go more than thirty seconds without using at least one expletive.

In the meantime, Davis unfolded his AN-PRC-119 and its keyboard to transmit a short, coded message indicating that they were on the ground in the proper location. Though bulky, the unit ensured that the transmission could not be intercepted and give their presence away.

Transmission sent, the sergeant repacked his equipment. As he shouldered his rucksack, the earth shook with a violent explosion, undoubtedly a fresh secondary from the attack that had been launched as the Hercules approached the drop point. A gush of red lit the sky to the northwest, throwing a pinkish shadow in the direction of the hills surrounding Kajuk, which lay to its right. Both Delta troopers turned toward it.

"Sergeants, no one admires a good explosion more than I, but our task lies this way," said Wong, pointing to the east. "And I would prefer to reach the highway before the trucks."

"What trucks?" asked Davis.

"You'll hear them presently," said Wong, starting off.

29

Lars felt the Herk hop upward as the rear door snapped shut. He snapped the transmit button, radioing Wolf that their passengers had disembarked, then held on as the pilot began a sharp bank west, at the same time pushing the nose to get back close to the terrain. Besides the heavy flak vest, he was wearing a full helmet and night-vision gear; their weight seemed to triple the effect of the g's the plane pulled as it whipped through its finely choreographed paces. They had popped up to five hundred feet to make the drop, lower than they had planned, when a blip of the radar detector forced a last-second deviation in the game plan. But the strike aircraft had done their job well, for the MC-130E's sophisticated equipment gave no indication that they were being tracked.

No radars were active as they descended, flying toward the earth's nap. They had more to fear from bullets than missiles—antiaircraft fire cascaded into the sky to the north and east as the Herk banked to turn southward.

Lars's hands began to shake as the pilot continued to descend.

"Turbulence," remarked the pilot.

Lars grunted. He tightened his hands on Herky Bird's control yoke, trying to will them stiff. Anyone with a rifle on the ground could hit them, even with his eyes closed.

Lars pushed his helmet to the side, trying to scratch an itch without removing it or the night goggles, which magnified the outside starlight enough so he could see. He felt his head growing woozy, took a breath. The hum of the plane and the dampened, surreal glow of the cockpit's instrument panel pummeled his senses, trying to convince him he was in a dream, not reality.

"We made the drop too low," said DiRiggio.

No one answered. They hadn't been off by that much, thought Lars, and besides, the commandos could handle it. He read their present altitude—falling through three hundred feet above ground level. The terrain-following radar showed a clear, unobstructed flight path—nothing to run into.

He looked toward the FLIR screen on the left near the pilot, then jerked his head to the left, looking through the pilot's side window as an immense fireball shot into the sky from the direction of the SAM battery that had been hit to darken the alley for their drop. The yellow-white flames turned inside out, blackness erupting from the inside as the fire burned through its fuel.

"Wow," he heard himself say.

"Got to be the missiles frying," said DiRiggio. "How's that temp?" he asked the flight engineer, who was perched like a wise man in a seat directly behind the two pilots. The seat was elevated, ostensibly to give him a better view, though a few wags thought for sure the men who had designed the flight deck were former sergeants intent on telling pilots who *really* ran the Air Force.

"Green," replied Kelly, the engineer. They'd seen some spikes in the temp on two earlier in the flight, and three's oil pressure had flickered just before the airdrop. "Gauge was flaky a second, I think. We're fine."

Lars managed a long, slow breath, lowering his eyes to the horizon indicator. His heart began to slow. He checked the altimeter clock again, still gathering himself, then pulled himself back up in his seat, helping the pilot with a crosswind correction as they hung tight on their course.

They were safe now, out of the radars' detection area. A few more minutes of flying time at low altitude and they'd be free to climb—they were entering a dark zone in the Iraqi radar coverage.

The worst was over, for now at least. Granted, they had nearly three hours to kill before the extraction—and that was going to be sheer hell—but for now things were fairly easy. All they had to do now was orbit in the dead zone and wait.

"Not like flying a slick, huh?" DiRiggio said to Lars, using Herk slang for a "normal" C-130. Compared to the heavily modified Combat Talons and other special operations craft, the transport models had smooth or slick skins.

"It's the flak vest I can't get used to," Lars said, coaxing what he hoped was a jocular note into his voice.

"Probably a good idea, though."

"Uh-huh."

Because the mission was classified, the crew had been told just the bare outlines, the absolute minimum they needed to do their jobs. Lars and DiRiggio knew that the Delta team was targeting a caravan of vehicles for F-111's. Lars figured that the target was a high-ranking Iraqi—possibly Saddam himself, given the location where they'd made the drop. Lars guessed that DiRiggio thought that too, and he wouldn't have been surprised if the rest of Herky Bird's crew had figured it out. But their code called for ignorance, and to a man they practiced it, concentrating on their jobs and pretending to know nothing beyond what was in front of them.

DiRiggio hit his mark and began angling into a slight turn eastward. They double-checked their indicators. They were still clean; the terrain before them empty desert. Lars listened for the transmission from Wolf that would tell them the landing team was down and in the right spot.

Their MC-130E carried the latest high-tech communications gear, but radio transmissions could still be problematic, hampered by everything from low altitude to atmospheric vagaries to interference from jamming craft. In theory none of those things were supposed to matter, but somehow communications remained as much an art as a science. Lars remembered an old Philco monster radio his great-grandpa had had in his Bristol, Connecticut, row house. It managed to pull in Yankee games from New York City, crystal-clear, even day games—once you hit the knob right. Took a certain flick, though.

"Jerry? Three? God. God!"

Lars snapped his head toward DiRiggio, unsure whether he was worried about engine three or something else. The major's face seemed to glow white in the dim cockpit, as if he were made of white marble instead of flesh. His eyes were round, large circles that stared at Lars, stared at him for a long moment, as if DiRiggio had woken from a dream and wondered how he'd gotten there. Then they rolled back in his head, the pilot's body flailing against the restraints, his arms snapping taut. The plane jerked to the right so hard the control yoke pulled out of Lars's hand.

"Somebody help me."

Lars wasn't sure whether the words came from DiRiggio or himself. He grabbed at the controls desperately, struggling to right the Hercules as its right wing pitched toward the ground barely fifty feet away.

30

Skull brought the Hog level at just under a hundred feet, not sure exactly where he was and half-suspecting that he was going to slam into a hill any second. He stepped through the last of the blurring tracers and found himself in the open air, though dangerously low. The plane quickly responded as he pulled back on the stick, plucking its nose upward toward the sky. If he'd been hit—and surely the odds had favored it—the Hog had shrugged it off. The plane responded crisply to his control inputs.

Not wanting to believe his luck, he hesitated before checking the row of warning lights on the dash.

Clean and green.

What had the rattle been? Shock waves from the exploding shells? Or was he flying with holes in his sides?

Knowlington craned his neck around, checking the exterior of the plane through the Perspex. It was too dark to see, but he had to look, just as he had to recheck his indicators once more, working through them slowly.

If anything, he had a bit more fuel than the preflight calculations had predicted.

He'd always been good. But he hadn't been this lucky since the old days—the really old days, back in the Thud.

"Devil Two to Devil One. I'm having trouble locating you, Boss," said Shotgun.

"One," said Skull, keying his mike to let Shotgun use the radio signal as a primitive direction-finding beacon. In the meantime, he got out his small flashlight and pulled the paper map off his flight board, shaking it out with his left hand as he got his bearings with the help of the plane's nav gear. He'd flown slightly to the northwest of where they had planned, but was more or less in the right place.

He saw Shotgun bearing straight at him from the east, less than a mile away.

"Gun, you're on me," he said, tucking his wing in an evasive and hopefully attention-getting roll. "Time for glasses," he added as he recovered.

"What I need is one of those NOD doohickeys," complained Shotgun. "Night vision. What I'm talking about."

"I'm surprised you haven't traded for one yet," said Knowlington. While he was still a bit put off by some of Shotgun's personal habits—not to mention the music he played—Skull had come to respect O'Rourke and his skills. O'Rourke goofed around a lot, except when the shit started to fly; then he was the sort of no-nonsense, can-do pilot Knowlington wanted watching his six.

"I almost had one off these Green Beret dudes at Al Jouf," replied Shotgun. "Went for a FAV instead."

"A FAV being what exactly?"

"Fast Attack Out-of-my-way Vee-hicle," said Shotgun. "The 'O' is silent. Your basic dune buggy."

"You strap it to your wing?"

"Geez, Colonel, why didn't I think of that?"

"That's why I get the big bucks," said Knowlington. He leaned the Hog into a wide bank, now precisely on the course they had laid out before the mission. They were approximately twelve miles from Kajuk, south of a highway that ran west to east over mostly empty scrubland. They were far enough away not to attract attention, but close enough to ride in to the rescue if things went sour. He dialed in Wolf and asked for an update.

The F-111 had done its job well, taking out one of the SAMs. There was still some doubt as to whether the missiles had been SA-11's or not; their radars had never been activated. A pair of Tornados had been tasked to sit on the remaining sites in case they flickered to life. While the sites would present a danger to the F-111 tasked with actually nailing Saddam, Wong had felt that taking out all of the SAMs would have caused the dictator to go elsewhere.

Which he might just do anyway, Skull realized. But you took your shots where you found them.

Skull advised Wolf that he and his wingman would orbit for another forty-five minutes, then go and tank as the other two A-10As came north.

"Wong ought to be finding Dixon right about now," said Shotgun after the exchange with the command ship was finished.

Skull shrugged to himself, not sure what to say. He hoped O'Rourke was right, but knew better than to be so wildly optimistic.

He should have pulled strings and insisted on the original plan, with a full-bore search for his man. He cursed himself for not being more forceful.

Honestly, though—what more could he have done?

If anyone could find Dixon, it was Wong. But damn it—they should have launched a full-blown SAR mission. The hell with Saddam—any American was worth twenty, a hundred dictators.

Not true, not even close. And he'd done the best he could as far as getting the mission authorized.

Skull checked his instruments as he continued southward, easing off on the throttle to conserve fuel. The Maverick IR head painted the terrain empty and lonely in his screen, a green-hued plain of desolation.

"Turning," he said, cuing Shotgun as he began a fresh bank.

There was no way to do this part of the mission comfortably. You flew and you waited, you flew and you waited. It was worse than the interminable ferry flight he'd made from the States to the Gulf, surrounded by darkness, waiting for something to happen, partly wishing it would and partly hoping it wouldn't. Skull tried not to let his mind wander, concentrating on his airplane as he came back north, nudging the Maverick viewer around in what he knew was a fruitless attempt at widening the area he could see.

At least there was no temptation to drink.

Maybe he was over that now. Maybe getting back into the adrenaline rush of combat was the shock therapy he'd needed.

The idea of bourbon in his mouth seemed mildly nauseating.

"Turning," he told Shotgun again, reaching the northern end of their racetrack pattern. The Hog seemed to anticipate him, pushing her wings down and gliding through the smooth bank as if she were showing off for the crowd at a Sunday afternoon air show. The plane looked ugly—hell, it didn't look like it even belonged in the sky. But sitting in her cockpit putting her through her paces, he found it hard to imagine a prettier aircraft. She went where her pilot wanted; she could walk through a standing wall of triple-A; she could carry a heavier bomb load than most World War II bombers. Every plane should be so ugly.

Skull checked his watch. They had a half hour to go.

Waiting sucked.

Wong had a pair of fancy binoculars that let him see heat sources, basically handheld IR. Still, finding the kid was going to be like finding a needle in a haystack. The prime search area was more than a mile from the point where the two Delta boys were going to watch the highway for Saddam or Strawman, as everyone on the mission now referred to him.

Boys. Kid. Dixon was twenty-three. Old enough to fly a Hog well enough to nail a helicopter on the first day of the air war, no mean feat.

But still a kid.

Skull had nailed three MiGs and hit the silk once by the

time he was twenty-three. He'd seen two of his close friends go down, never to come back.

Had his commanders thought of him the same way?

"Vulture Three, Vulture Three," said a distant voice in the faint crackle of Knowlington's radio.

At first he thought it was a transmission from a flight overriding their frequency. Then Skull realized it was a distress call on Guard, the emergency band.

"Vulture Three," said the voice again. Static crashed over it like an ocean wave.

Was he identifying himself or talking to another airplane?

"Any allied airplane, please respond," said the voice as the channel cleared. "Vulture Three, requesting assistance from any allied plane."

"Vulture Three, this is Devil Leader. What is your location?" answered Skull.

The response was garbled, but Knowlington heard co-ordinates approximately ten miles directly west of their position. His head turned that way, as if he might catch a glimpse of the stricken plane.

There were no other allied planes in the area. Detouring his orbit would add a little more than a minute to his response time back to the ground team.

"Shotgun, you catch that?"

"Catch what?"

"The transmission on Guard," said Knowlington.

"Negative."

"Not at all?"

"Nothing but static."

"Hang with me," he told his wingman. "We're going west. Come to 255 on my signal."

"On your back," said Shotgun.

Skull tried hailing Vulture Three again before telling Wolf what was up. The controller acknowledged, volunteering to alert the AWACS control plane in the area and hurry up the two Devil Flight Hogs that were tanking.

It was only after he snapped the mike off and found his new course that Skull realized Vulture Three was the call sign of one of the buddies he'd lost in Vietnam.

PART TWO

VULTURE
DEATH

1

Wong thumbed the contrast wheel at the top left of the AN/PAS-7 thermal viewer, dulling the glow of the approaching vehicle's engine. It was more than a mile away, just turning north from the dogleg that would finally bring it into view.

There were two people in the front seat of the sedan. From his vantage twenty yards from the highway, it was difficult to tell whether the men were soldiers, though that seemed obvious—the car was following a military transport, and besides, who else would be driving at night in Iraq? He could draw no other conclusions, however; a civilian vehicle might be part of Saddam's advance party or it might not.

"Truck a problem?" asked Salt, lying next to him.

"Negative," said Wong. "The Zil-130 six-by-six is empty except for its driver. The sedan has two passengers, neither of whom would appear to be our target."

Salt hastily set down the M82A1 Light Fifty sniper rifle. The long-barreled heavy rifle fired the same cartridges as the Browning fifty-caliber machine gun; equipped with armor-piercing shells, it could get through an armored car at roughly one thousand yards. Salt sighted toward a slight bend that brought the road roughly 350 yards away from their position.

"What kind of car?" Salt asked.

"I am not acquainted with the model."

"You don't know what kind of car it is?" asked Davis, hunkered on the other side.

"I am an expert on weapons, not automobiles," said Wong.

"You sure it ain't a Mercedes?"

"It is not a Mercedes, nor a station wagon," said Wong. "Please keep your voice down."

"It's a piece-of-shit Jap car," Salt told the other sergeant as it came in view of the starscope on his rifle. "I could nail it."

"The provenance of the sedan is irrelevant," said Wong. "They are not our target vehicles. Saddam would not be traveling alone, and in any event, he is not due until midnight."

"Nothin' says he can't be fuckin' early," said Salt.

The two vehicles continued up the highway toward Kajuk. Wong scanned behind them to make sure they were alone, then turned the infrared viewer northward, scanning past the intersection with the main highway, then up the road toward the nubby hill that guarded the turnoff to Kajuk. A T-72 tank sat in a shallow depression just to the west of the intersection; there were at least a half-dozen soldiers scattered there. Wong made out a small observation post on the nearby hill manned by two men. A second post, this with three or four soldiers, a Jeep-like vehicle, and an armored car or personnel carrier, sat in the middle of the road at the very western edge of the hill, commanding a curve in the highway.

The post on the hill presented an immediate problem. If the soldiers there were equipped with the proper night-vision equipment, mining the road would be difficult. Still, doing so was important—if the bombers were late or there was confusion about the target, cratering the roadway would increase the chances of killing Saddam.

Of the two northern points they had selected as candidates, one had no cover at all; it was in a gully directly exposed to the observation post. The backup candidate had a few rocks scattered around it and was further away; it seemed the safer choice.

Wong watched the truck and the sedan pass the spot. If the highway were blocked there, the rocks would make it difficult to pass but not impossible. Blow up the other spot, however, and the vehicles would have to backtrack a good distance before they'd be able to detour across the open desert. They would be easy targets even for Salt with his sniper weapon.

The truck and the sedan continued northward, passing parallel to the team's position and heading for the T-intersection with the main highway. The charred remains of a Scud launcher and some antiaircraft weapons littered a bulldozed area at the side of a small rise a quarter mile or so to the southeast of the intersection; Captains Glenon and O'Rourke, with some help from a group of F-16's, had blown them up the previous evening. The scarred skeletons of the support vehicles sat in the dim light, ghosts jeering from the sideline.

The oversized T-underpass at the intersection itself had been obliterated during the attack, but the Iraqis had bulldozed a detour at first light. It took the vehicles a few moments to negotiate it, bouncing along the ruts before regaining the highway and continuing toward the tank checkpoint.

Wong swung his view back to the hill. Dixon had been near the base at the far side, opposite the area where the observation post was. Wong readjusted the contrast on his viewer, panning the area. The AN/PAS-7 thermal viewer was an excellent device, remarkably rugged and, at least as night viewers went, relatively light. It looked something like an oversized camera, with a single porthole to squint through at the top of its large metal case. Its ability to read heat sources was particularly useful in picking out bodies from a distance. But it did not have the range Wong would have liked.

Two minutes of observation by a J-STARS with its attendant armada of sensor craft would have told him everything he needed to know. Five minutes with a properly equipped drone, a real-time feed from a thermal-viewing satellite . . .

Wong sighed. It was always a trial when your mission did not rate significantly high enough to command proper resources.

"Captain, it's almost time for our check-in," said Davis.

"Proceed."

The sergeant ducked back behind the small rise to activate the encrypted radio unit. Wong turned his attention to the west. He would flank the hill, approaching it in a semicircle. It wouldn't be necessary to walk more than a mile. There was some low cover, and the moon was not bright enough to cast a strong shadow.

"I can hit anything along that elbow," said Salt, referring to the safer stretch of road.

"You must establish your aiming point along the ravine, our primary site," Wong said, pointing further north. "I'll have Sergeant Davis plant the charges there."

The Delta trooper took his AN/PVS-7A night goggles and scanned the terrain. They worked by magnifying available light rather than heat.

"Damn easy to see from the post on the hill," Salt pointed out.

"True. But charges there will stop the convoy, especially if the detonation is keyed when the first vehicle passes. The rest will have to back up. You will have a much longer time to shoot. I believe also that you will command a wider area."

"Yeah, okay," said Salt, nodding. "Worth the risk." He continued scanning the area, assessing the defenses.

"They acknowledged. We're set," said Davis. He tapped his demolitions pack, a special hard-shell suitcase that contained a remote trigger and a set of small C-4 explosive packs. "We ready to plant these?"

"Take note of the observation post on the hill before proceeding," said Wong, pointing it out. Salt gave Davis his viewer. "An infrared viewer may spot you on the roadway. Move along that ravine side to limit your exposure, and slide your charges out along the road."

"More like a ditch than a ravine," said Salt. "I thought you said they wouldn't have night equipment."

"The possibility that they do is diminishingly low," said Wong. "But it cannot be ruled out. We are therefore better safe than sorry."

"*Davis* is better safe than sorry."

"Yeah." Davis handed back the viewer and took his demo pack. "Wish me luck."

Salt grabbed his friend's arm. "What about that spot there, Captain?" he said, pointing about a quarter of a mile further south than the bend he'd targeted before. "The drop-off on that north side is immense. That would make them come this way, if they could get through the rocks, and I'd have a good angle on them."

Wong studied the spot.

"Excellent choice," he told the sergeant. "But in that case we will have to move further south with the designator."

"Fuckin' easy," said Salt.

"Looks good to me," said Davis, examining the area with his NOD. "Take us fifteen minutes."

"Take your time," Wong told him.

"We can set up the sniper rifle behind that little slope up there," said Salt, pointing to a spot about a quarter of a mile from the road. He patted the metal stock of the gun. "Easy shot."

"Yes. I will meet you there," said Wong. He turned back to scan the area to the west.

"You're not coming with us?" asked Davis.

"No," Wong told him. "In the interval, I am going to scout the hill to our north."

"What?" said Salt.

"It has to do with the contingency of our mission that I referred to earlier."

"No fuckin' offense, Captain," said Salt, "but could you just talk fuckin' English."

"He's saying this is the need-to-know shit," said Davis.

"Precisely," said Wong.

"What the hell are we supposed to do if you don't come back?"

"You are to carry on with your mission. Be sure to identify the vehicle for the bomber before you fire. Exit precisely as planned if I'm not here."

"We're not fucking leaving you," said Salt.

"Hey, Captain. Seriously, what's the story here?" said Davis. "We're about two hundred miles deep in Iraq. You got to trust us."

"I do trust you," said Wong. "I trust you implicitly. That is irrelevant."

"Fuck," said Salt.

"Carry on with your mission. You should have approximately three hours before Straw or Stawman if you prefer arrives."

"If he arrives," said Davis.

"I believe he shall."

"We ain't fuckin' leaving you," said Salt.

Wong sighed. This was exactly the situation he had sought to avoid.

"I assure you, Sergeant, my assignment is ancillary to the main mission. And to put it bluntly, Sergeant, I am expendable. If all goes well, I will meet you back here in precisely one hundred and thirty minutes. If it does not, you will carry on without me. Please, follow the plan and my orders to you now."

"Goddamn Air Force assholes," muttered Salt.

Wong checked his MP-5, then looked back up into Davis's face. The sergeant seemed to be trying to find the words to say something.

Wong shook his head. Davis finally shrugged and scooped up the explosives kit. Wong made sure his extra clips were easily accessible, then turned to start the long loop around the Iraqi positions.

He'd taken only two steps when he heard a fresh set of

vehicles approaching from the distance. He froze, turning his head toward the sound, holding his breath as the faint rumble grew slowly but steadily. There were at least four or five vehicles approaching, maybe more. Even before he began trotting toward the others with his IR viewer in his hand, he knew one of them would be a station wagon painted with the red crescent.

2

Lars screamed as he pulled against the controls of the MC-130, pitting his muscles not just against DiRiggio's but against gravity. The big plane danced on her wing, slicing a diagonal in the sky, losing altitude even as he managed to keep her nose pointing upward. She was ready to roll—she wanted to roll—and as he struggled Lars considered just letting her, hoping against hope that there would somehow be enough room to get her back level. But even if he'd been twenty thousand feet higher, there was no guarantee he'd recover from such a violent invert, or even that the wings and control surfaces would survive intact. It was him and it was gravity; the plane was caught in the middle, skittering just above the cold sand.

Lars's arms and chest disintegrated, his legs melting to flaccid bands of flesh. He threw his right arm literally around the control column, and with his left punched DiRiggio. He hit him as hard as he could, once, twice, then felt the yoke slam back hard against his jaw. With his knees and elbows and chin he smothered the controls, urging the plane upright, willing it into something approaching stable flight. The ground loomed, an optically enhanced blur of oblivion. A stall warning sounded. A million thoughts occurred to him, a checklist of possible evasive action; he even considered popping the landing gear and wheeling in. But all he did was hold on, riding it out like a surfer caught in a monster tsunami.

The surfer would have swamped. The Herk somehow managed to level off inches from the gritty dirt. A moment later they began to climb.

"All right," he said over the interphone circuit, which connected to the others in the plane. "All right. All right."

He repeated the words several more times. Kelly, the flight engineer, reached forward from his station and held him on the shoulder.

"The engines, do I have the engines?" Lars asked.

He did—he had to, or the plane wouldn't be reacting as smoothly as it was.

"Captain, we're fine," said the sergeant.

"We're fine," repeated Lars.

"You're right on course," said the navigator. He spoke funny, as if half of his mouth had been Novocained—he'd been slammed violently as Lars struggled to control the plane. "Is the major okay?"

Lars forced a glance toward DiRiggio, who was slumped back in his seat.

"I don't know," he said. "I think—he may have had a heart attack."

"Definitely."

"I had to hit him. I had no choice."

"Couple of guys banged up in the back, but no serious injuries," said Kelly. "I think I busted my finger."

He continued talking, but the words bounced around Lars's helmet, not truly registering. A crewman gave a fuller report from the back, but Lars couldn't make out any of it. He just flew, staying in their preset track but pulling up to three thousand feet, judging that the risk of being detected was worth the leeway with the plane. What he really wanted to do was take it to fifteen angels, to twenty, to thirty—get the hell *up* there, climb and keep climbing.

Climb and go home.

The flight engineer and navigator pulled DiRiggio from his seat, lifting him over the center control console and past the flight engineer's seat. His head flopped down against Lars's arm as they pulled him out, skin ghost-white, eyes rolled back like a bizarre toy. The two men took him back off the flight deck to the rear crew area, where the two paramedics aboard quickly began working on him.

Or at least Lars assumed they did. He was alone, sitting in the middle of a precarious bubble, struggling to keep himself afloat. He couldn't breathe, he couldn't think—he ripped off the helmet and goggles, prying them away. His head rushed, as if he'd just surfaced from the bottom of a deep lake. He blinked at the massive wall of instruments in front of him, numbers and needles floating in space. He readjusted his seat restraints, felt his heart calming. Slowly, he began pushing the plane back toward the earth, flying in the track they had briefed.

"DiRiggio's on oxygen," said Kelly, returning to the flight deck ahead of the navigator. "We have to get him help. Fast. Real fast."

Lars kept his eyes fixed on the dark landscape in front of him.

"Captain?"

The flight engineer leaned over the console. Lars cocked his head so he could see him from the corner of his eye, but said nothing.

"We got to go back, don't you think?" said Kelly. The middle and ring fingers on the engineer's left hand were taped together.

"We really have to go back," said the navigator.

Lars concentrated on the plane, working into his bank south. The border was twenty miles south; it would take at least—at least—thirty minutes to reach a base with a hospital big enough to handle something like this. He wasn't even sure where that might be; maybe King Khalid.

He could cut almost a straight line there out of this leg of his pattern. There'd be one tricky point near the border, but otherwise it was an easy run. And he could get an escort—hell, he could get half the Air Force.

He wanted to do it. He wanted to get the hell out of here.

But should he? If he left now, the three-man Delta team he'd dropped would be stranded. There were no other STAR-equipped C-130's available; if there had been, he wouldn't be here.

They could scramble SAR assets. That was the backup plan. Send a helo.

Not really. Certainly not while the SA-11's and the other SAMs were still down there. The SAMs would make mincemeat of a helicopter. They'd factored that in already—that was why Herky Bird was here.

They could divert planes, take out the SAMs, put real force down there. Hell, they should have done it that way to begin with.

But they hadn't. And the truth was, this probably put less people at risk. Working at night, quietly, slipping in and out—that was the best way.

As if SAMs wouldn't mince him up. As if the Herk didn't just miss getting smashed to pieces by that flak— forget about the missiles.

Two night grabs—he had to do it twice. Five hundred feet in the pitch black, reel them in, go back, do it again. All at the edge of the acquisition envelope of one of the most powerful surface-to-air systems in the world.

No way. No way.

Lars had done it in an exercise, though. He had done it. He'd ducked under a Hawk radar without being detected, and evaded a Patriot battery as well—at least as difficult as the mission tasked here.

But that was long before he came to the Gulf, long before he knew fear.

"Captain?"

Lars stared into the darkness. It was his call to make.

Who did he owe—three men on the ground, or the pilot in the back of the plane?

Three men who had the odds against them anyway?

Or a fellow officer and Herk pilot, a nice guy with a family back in the States, a guy more or less like him?

Go home. Get the hell out of this. No one was going to blame him for running away now.

Lars reached down and pulled his radio gear back on.

"Major DiRiggio has had a heart attack," he told the crew, though of course they all knew by now. "We're going to complete our mission as best we can, and then we're going to go home. The men on the ground are counting on us."

He meant to say something else, something about DiRiggio wanting it that way—a lie maybe, but the kind of lie men often need to hear. But fear choked off the rest of the words.

No one said anything. Lars's hands shook so violently as he began to bank in his pattern that he feared he'd roll the plane.

3

Skull read the altimeter ladder in the HUD, making sure he was low enough to be heard from the ground, then glanced at his watch and the map, trying to figure out exactly where Vulture Three had been when he sent the call. There was of course no guarantee that the pilot had had his position correct, nor was it possible to know precisely where he had been when he pulled the eject handles. But search and rescue was basically about taking logical guesses. Skull began to turn the plane south, figuring it as the most likely direction.

Unless the pilot came back up on the air, however, no amount of guesses were likely to turn him up. The Maverick viewers could see only a tiny area at a time, and when they were designed no one was thinking of using them to spot bodies. And an Iraqi airfield lay due north, about five minutes away for a MiG with its pedal to the metal, increasing the tickle factor if not the degree of difficulty.

"Work out from me to increase what we're covering,"

Skull told Shotgun as they began their second sweep. "I think you can take it further south on your turn."

"Yeah," replied Shotgun.

"I'm going to turn now," said Knowlington.

"Two," replied his wing mate.

The Maverick screen remained a blurry, undefined mess. But at least that meant no one was down there to shoot at him—Skull was at three thousand feet, a juicy target flying at barely 250 knots or miles an hour.

"Devil One, this is Coyote," said the controller in the AWACS coordinating flights in the sector.

"Devil One."

"We have no Vulture Flight," said the AWACS.

"What exactly do you mean by that, Coyote?" snapped Skull.

"There is no Vulture Flight on the ATO at this time."

The crewman paused between each word, strongly implying that Skull had made a serious mistake. The plane's powerful airborne radar helped it keep track of everything happening north of the border; while it was possible that a plane had been hit without Coyote knowing about it, it was extremely unlikely. The fact that the call sign did not appear to be a valid one—the plane was not even listed for duty that night—would convince even the most openminded controller—and certainly his commander—that the transmission had been bogus.

Or some sort of auditory hallucination.

But Skull knew what he had heard.

"Acknowledged, Coyote," he said. He maintained his course heading north, studying the viewscreen.

"Devil One, this Coyote," snapped a new voice obviously belonging to controller's supervisor. "Please advise your current status."

Skull blew a long breath into his mask, then calmly noted his location and course.

Which wasn't the answer Coyote wanted.

"There is no Vulture Three," said the officer flatly. "We have no data indicating a downed plane at this time.

Colonel, we're concerned here that you're being sucked into a trap."

"I appreciate your concern. Maintaining search pattern." Skull could almost hear the exasperation in the static that filled the radio band.

"See, now that's why you get the big bucks," said Shotgun over the short-range radio. "I woulda told him to jerk off."

O'Rourke would have been perfectly within his rights to suggest they break off their search. Most if not all of the wingmen Skull had flown with, from Nam to Panama to Red Flag, would have at least asked if he was *positive* he'd heard the distress call.

But Shotgun was a wingman's wingman. And a Hog driver.

"Turning," said Knowlington, starting his sweep. He hit the radio and broadcast a call on the Guard frequency used by stricken aircraft, asking Vulture Three to acknowledge.

Static.

It was a hell of a coincidence, he had to admit. Twenty years before, he'd lost his own Vulture Three during what had been a routine mission to hit a supply depot in North Vietnam. Skull had taken a four-ship of Phantoms north for the strike. It was about midway through his second tour in Vietnam—he'd flown Thuds on his first—and if the truth be told, the mission had seemed almost boringly routine. They encountered no flak and no SAMs en route. Skull had a good look at the target through the cloud deck as he launched the attack, and a strong memory of his backseater telling him they were clean, meaning that the Vietnamese had not managed to mount a defense. The sky remained empty as Knowlington recovered and the planes regrouped, flying southeastward to the coast as they had planned.

It happened that a coastal air-defense battery was being hit by Navy A-4s at the same time; Knowlington saw a few black puffs of gunfire in the air, and four or five separate fires on the ground as he banked over the water and waited for his flight to catch him. It seemed like glimpsing the corner of a movie screen through an open door as he passed through a theater lobby, a quick vivid glimpse that disappeared as he put his head back to the task at hand. His wing mate caught up; they tacked south, waiting for the other two planes in the flight.

Vulture Four arrived shortly, having been separated from Three as he went after a secondary target. Three never showed.

The Vietnamese had launched several MiGs to respond to the Navy attack, and things got tangled quickly. With fuel reserves low to begin with, Skull hadn't been able to mount a proper search. The Navy did fly several flights in, but no trace of Vulture Three was ever found.

Skull forced his eyes down from the Maverick screen to the fuel gauges, running a quick check on his reserves. They had used considerably less fuel than planned, but he'd have to think about going south for the tanker soon.

He keyed back into the command and control aircraft running the Strawman mission for an update. Everything was quiet.

So had he imagined the distress call?

That sort of thing had never happened to him before. Not even when he was drinking.

Maybe it had and he'd just shut it out. Or didn't even realize it.

"Skull, I got something hot down there," said Shotgun. "Uh, looking about two, no, one and a half miles at, say, two o'clock off, uh, your nose."

"One," said Knowlington, dipping his wing as Shotgun continued with more detailed coordinates. He pushed the Hog lower, easing the throttle back so slow that he was practically walking.

If this was a ruse, he was a sitting duck.

A road cut across the desert; in the screen it looked like a twisted piece of litter, the narrow cutting from a newspaper fresh off the press.

"Vulture Three, this is Devil One. Vulture Three, please acknowledge," Skull said over the emergency band.

A bright shadow appeared at the top corner of the Maverick screen. Skull edged his stick to the right, the Hog stuttering a bit in the air—his indicated airspeed had dropped precipitously. He caught it smoothly, the plane gliding toward the growing glow in his monitor.

Long cylinder. Maybe a fuselage.

Maybe a heated decoy.

RWR clear.

Would be if they were planning to use shoulder-launched heat-seekers.

Flares ready.

Knowlington turned his eyes toward the windscreen, trying to sort through the darkness for something—anything.

If it's ambush, he thought, let's get it over with.

"Vulcan Tres, Vulcan Tres," crackled a voice over Guard. "Vulcan Three to approaching allied aircraft."

Vulcan, not Vulture. Shit.

"*Vulcan* Three, this is Devil Leader," said Skull, flicking his talk button. "Relax, friend. Give me a flare."

Static flooded into his headphones, and for a long moment Skull feared that maybe he *was* imagining the whole thing. But suddenly a sparkle of red pricked the sky two and a half miles southeast of his nose.

"There she blows!" sang Shotgun.

"Coyote, this is Devil One," said Skull. "I am in contact with *Vulcan* Three. Repeat, *Vulcan Tres*. French flier. I have a flare—" He looked over and noted the position on the INS, reading it off as he walked his Hog toward the downed airman. "Requesting verification procedures."

"Copy, Devil Flight. You are in contact with Vulcan Three. Stand by."

"Hell of an apology," said Shotgun.

"Devil One, I can hear you! I can hear you!" said the downed pilot. He was shouting, and added two or three sentences in indecipherable French.

"Relax, Vulcan," Skull told him. "Can you give me your status?"

"*Merci, merci. Je ne comprends pas.*"

"What?" asked Skull.

"De rien," answered Shotgun. *"Nous sommes* Hog drivers."

"Ah, *cochon. Le Hog.*"

"Le Hog," agreed Shotgun.

"Magnifique."

"What I'm *talkin'* about," agreed O'Rourke. *"Comment allez-vous?"*

"Je suis perdu."

"Nah, you're not lost. We got your butt," said Shotgun, adding words that seemed roughly the equivalent in French.

"You speak French, Shotgun?" said Knowlington after his wingman and the downed pilot exchanged several more sentences.

"Got to," said Shotgun. "You never know when you're going to wake up in Paris, hunting down a *café au lait.*"

"Devil Leader, we have an SAR asset en route, call sign Leander Seven. Request you contact him directly."

"Devil One copies. We have one downed pilot, tells us he's in reasonable shape. No enemy units at this time. My wingman speaks French and is talking to him. Feed him the questions."

"Coyote."

"Man, I love it when they're humble," said Shotgun.

"Just run through the authentication," said Skull, dialing into the search and rescue helicopter's frequency.

4

Doberman eased the Hog toward the director lights on the KC-135, sliding toward the refueling boom. The tanker had edged over the border and they were running well ahead of schedule. There was no need to rush, but he couldn't help it—he wanted to tank and get the hell back north.

Check that. He wanted to see BJ back on the tarmac at Home Drome, walking around like a newborn colt, a little embarrassed when Shotgun slapped him on the back. Gun would say something like, "Fuckin' A, kid," and Dixon would turn red. Kid was so pure he didn't even curse.

Fuckin' A.

That was what he wanted.

And to do that, he had to get his ass back north.

Taking out Saddam in his pretend Red Cross car wouldn't be bad either. The job was tasked to a pair of F-111 sharpshooters, Earth Pigs that wouldn't even be leaving their base for at least another hour.

Red Crescent. Whatever.

He wouldn't mind taking that shot himself.

The tanker twitched right. Doberman pushed on, nudging his rudder pedal gently to stay with it. The boomer in the tail of the Boeing was watching, ready to aim his long straw into the fueling port in the A-10's nose.

The lights on the big tanker told him he was there.

"Let's go, let's go," Doberman said to himself as the nozzle clunked in and the fuel began to flow.

5

Air Force Technical Sergeant Rebecca Rosen was a cliché: the tough-girl tomboy playing hard-ass to make it a man's world. She was the junkyard dog scrapping with all the other dogs just to prove how tough she was.

She *was* tough. She'd been raised in the worst part of Philadelphia in, as it happened, a junkyard. Or, as her uncle called it, "the crème dalla crème of the salvation industry."

"Dalla" was supposed to be "de la," but no one corrected her uncle, who though only five-eight could tear a car door off its hinges without breaking a sweat. Few people corrected his niece either; there was almost never a need to. Rosen had a real talent for fixing things, and the Air Force had given her not just the training but the discipline she needed to put her skills and intellect to work.

Like her uncle and the cousin she'd been raised with, Rosen had a reputation for cracking people who got out of line—her personnel records put it more delicately, if in greater detail. Barely five-two and about 110 pounds,

Rosen used every volatile ounce of her body to fight; she'd
learned to wrestle pinning junkyard mutts as a ten-year-
old, and had yet to find a tougher opponent.

It was also true that her clothes and skin smelled more
like JP-4 than Chanel No. 5. And while she wasn't ugly by
any stretch, it had to be said that she wasn't particularly
pretty either. In fatigues and with her cropped hair pulled
back, she could look almost severe.

On the other hand, there was more to Rosen than the
cliché, more than the tough kid who wrestled dogs and
could fix just about any part, electronic or mechanical, on
anything that moved. There was, for instance, a young
woman who had discovered poetry during a bullshit col-
lege program she'd signed up for to shake off some of the
boredom of downtime in the mid-eighties.

Sitting in a large auditorium with a hundred other stu-
dents, most of them several years younger, Becky Rosen
had heard poetry for the first time. Maybe not literally, but
certainly figuratively. On the first day of class the profes-
sor stood in front of the podium and wheezed through a
poem by Walt Whitman declaring America's greatness,
and then one by Emily Dickinson contemplating the nature
of death and duty. Rosen found herself fascinated, so fascinated that she ended up taking enough courses to get a
BA—and at the time of her assignment to the Gulf was in
fact only a few credits from a master's.

Not that she planned to use the degrees for anything.
They were an excuse to read, entertainment better than
movies—activities almost as engrossing as single-
handedly overhauling an entire A-10A herself. From the
day of that first class, she had spent at least ten minutes
every night reading.

But tonight, sitting in her quarters in Tent City at the
heart of the Home Drome, Technical Sergeant Rebecca
Rosen couldn't find anything to read, or at least nothing
that sparked. Not Whitman, not Hemingway, not Jones, not
the volume of Joyce she'd promised herself she'd slog
through. Not even Dickinson.

She tried to sleep, but couldn't. Every time she closed

her eyes she saw Lieutenant Dixon, lying dead on the ground near a cave that housed Iraqi chemical weapons.

William Dixon. BJ. KIA. RIP.

God, this is morbid, she thought to herself finally. She sat up and pulled out her small notebook from under the bed. She had been trying for the past few days to start a journal, vaguely thinking she might write a book about the Gulf when she got home—maybe get a million-dollar book contract and buy her own aircraft maintenance operation when she got home.

Or a junkyard. Hey, you went with what you knew.

She'd barely filled two pages so far with a few notes on the people she served with. She looked at her scrawl, barely readable even by her, then turned to a fresh page, starting to describe Tent City.

A well-ordered chaos of temporary quarters, theoretically intended for low-class enlisted types, but housing even hoity-toity officers due to a severe shortage of facilities and poor political prowess on the part of muckety-mucks many echelons above.

Or not.

Her pen fidgeted on the paper. She thought of Dixon, his baby face. They'd kissed once, almost by accident. She felt the kiss now, felt him pressing against her body, rubbing his hands against her breasts.

Which he had not done.

A damn, damn shame.

She tried writing again, thinking of a routine day, but segueing into a dream she'd had before bugging out of Fort Apache, the clandestine Delta command post in Iraq.

She was in her uncle's junkyard, back by the buses where her cousin Crank used to smoke dope. A turkey vulture swept down.

Red-headed turkey vulture. Never saw that in Philly, no way.

But that was the dream.

She thought about it, and then her pen began moving, the words arranging themselves on the blank paper:

Vulture Death
spread his wings
and laughed
boasting with his dark eye

I stood my ground

His head fired the sky
   but I stood
His wings pummeled the air
   but I stood
His claws ripped my neck
   but I stood until at last he tired and flew off.

But that was just a dream

Becky put down the pen and reread what she'd wrote. Death and more death.

Her fingers tore the page out. She crumpled it up and shoved it in her pocket, then pulled on her boots to go see what needed doing in Oz.

6

Dixon and Budge stopped for a rest amid a small collection of bushes just below the summit of the hill. Even in the dark, the scrubby vegetation wouldn't provide much cover, but it was better than nothing. They didn't seem to have been followed, and as far as BJ could tell the hill was unoccupied. It was lower than the hill opposite to the northwest, with occasional rock outcroppings and jagged terrain, difficult for the antiair vehicles to climb. Or at least Dixon assumed.

The boy had recovered from his panic, or maybe he was just too tired to do much of anything—he sat on the ground next to his rescuer, knees pulled up in front of his chest.

"Hey, Budge, what do you think?" Dixon whispered. "You think there are Scuds on the other side of that hill there?"

He pointed with his thumb. The boy tilted his head, but said nothing.

"I'm not sure what the bombers hit," Dixon continued. "I'm not exactly sure what kind of planes they were. I fly a Hog," he added. "An A-10. I'm really a pilot. I came north to help target Scuds. A-10's a great plane. They're made to fly real low and support ground troops." He began miming it with his hands, zooming in low and working the cannon with a stutter. He pretended to be in the cockpit, then threw his hands out like he was the plane, crouching and dancing. Budge smiled.

"We call it a Hog—short for Warthog. Kind of a joke too, because it looks ugly and it moves slower than a farm truck. I could have flown Eagles—I was selected to. But I had to, uh, see, I had some personal stuff going on." Dixon knew he was just babbling on, but the kid nodded, as if he understood and wanted him to continue. It felt good to talk; he'd been alone so long. "My mom died, she was dying. And my father's been laid up with strokes since I was about your age. You lost your parents too, huh?"

BJ hadn't thought about that before, but now he realized it must be true—perhaps the kid had seen them die.

"Parents dead?" he asked.

Budge nodded solemnly, then said something in Arabic. Dixon listened, trying to pick up the meaning in the tone of the words. They were flat, though, and the way the kid moved his hands, he could be miming a parade.

Until he jumped up and began mimicking what BJ had done, flying a Hog.

"Yeah, kid, we'll fly. We'll fly out of here. If we can find our way. I know there's got to be another Delta team around here. I just know it."

Budge kept flying. Dixon extended his arms, and for a moment the two of them flew together, bumping wings and laughing as if they were out on a playground a million miles from the war.

"Okay," Dixon said finally. "All right. We have to get serious, Budge."

The kid stopped and looked up at him. BJ slung the rifles over his shoulders and held the boy gently by the neck as they walked.

"What we're doing here is kind of like a game," Dixon said. "Kind of like hide-and-seek. Except the guys looking for us have guns, and they're not going to count to ten before shooting. But we're smarter than them, right? You and me. We'll kick their butts if they try to do anything."

Dixon let go, considering their next move. The plain to the west and southwest of the hill seemed open; they could sneak back to the cornfield, several miles away along the highway west. They could get water there, and it would be easy to hide during the daylight.

He remembered passing a building or two. They might be able to get food—better to try there than in the village, where there were other people and troops around.

But first, he wanted to look to the south, see what was there.

Hide out tomorrow. As soon as it was dark, look for one of the Delta or British SAS teams that were Scud-hunting. There ought to be at least one team a few miles further west. And beyond that there was a forward base, Fort Apache. They could go there, walk a few miles every night.

They'd get out of here somehow, Budge and him.

They began sidestepping toward the southern slope of the hill. Dixon slipped and Budge grabbed him, holding him up for half a second before tumbling over him. They rolled a few feet before coming to a stop.

It was so comical Dixon started to laugh, until he saw the flare of a cigarette ten yards away.

7

The station wagon was the third car in the procession, trailing two troop trucks. Immediately behind it was a German transport, followed by a pair of armored cars. A Mercedes sedan was next to last, sandwiched between two Zils with canvas backs. The caravan was about two miles from the spot they'd picked to put down the explosives. The rest of the vehicles followed at intervals of ten to twenty yards. With their lights out, they traveled no more than forty miles an hour—but that was more than enough; there was no way to get the explosives down to the spot they'd picked out. Wong sent Davis to alert Wolf, then stopped Salt as he bent to set up his sniper rifle.

"We'll have to stop them or slow them down so the bombers have a chance to target them," Wong told him. "Wolf will have to scramble the A-10's, and they will be at least five minutes away."

"I can get a shot."

"One may not be sufficient, even with the light fifty,"

said Wong. "Do you think you could hit the first vehicle with the grenade launcher when it draws parallel to us?"

"I'll have to get closer to make sure I hit."

"Do it then," said Wong. He reached down and grabbed the explosives set. "Wait until the last moment, but make sure that you strike it. Take your next shot at the Mercedes—the station wagon appears empty, and in any event will be struck by the A-10."

"Where the hell are you going with those explosives?" Salt yelled as he started away.

"I will attempt to divert the tank and give you more time to use your sniper rifle," Wong yelled. "Please, you have less than three minutes to get into position."

PART THREE

LAZARUS

1

Dixon pushed Budge down, and in the same motion swung the rifle on his right shoulder around to level it at the glowing cigarette ten yards away. The dot of red blurred into an oval meteor, flaring to the right. Dixon slid his trigger finger into the AK-74, his stomach pinching tight. His entire body jerked against his finger, pushing his life and hope into the quick burst it commanded, but there was no rumble at his side, no pull upward from the front of the barrel, no bullets flying across the darkness into his enemy.

In his haste and fear he had put his finger against the guard, not the trigger.

The cigarette disappeared. The smoker miraculously had not noticed them.

Dixon waited for the air to come back into his lungs. When it finally did, he unfolded his finger as deliberately as he could and placed it where it belonged. The boy lay curled on the ground next to him, his neck on the other rifle.

Dixon reached over and gently removed the gun. He put his finger to his lips, then held it up, wagging it to tell Budge he must be quiet and wait.

"I'll be back," Dixon whispered, patting Budge reassuringly. The child bobbed his head, seeming to understand.

Moving silently, the second rifle slung over his left shoulder, Dixon clambered across the slope toward the spot where the cigarette had flared. He bent his head forward, eyes peering into the dimness to try to sort the shadows into shapes.

A dozen steps and he entered a patch of light thrown by the moon; he inched back, eyes adjusting well enough to see the edge of a wall eight feet away around the slope. In the dimness the enemy position looked as if it were made of books, immense dictionaries or encyclopedias stacked on their side. BJ hugged the ground, eyes pinned on a narrow globe at the middle of the row of books—the head of a soldier who leaned against the sandbags, peering down the hillside through a pair of binoculars or a starscope.

A red dot flaring behind and to the left of the globe showed Dixon where the cigarette-smoker was. The dot moved further back, behind the bend, out of Dixon's sight and aim.

Were there others? Dixon narrowed his mouth, stifling his breath into long, quiet pauses so he could hear. If there were other Iraqis, they were silent, not even fidgeting.

The man with the binoculars said something to his companion. He stretched back and the other man got up, took the glasses.

Now was the time to fire. He could get them both with the same burst—get them both with the same bullet.

Trucks approached in the distance below, driving from the south in the general direction of the hill. The men began speaking excitedly, tapping each other. They leaned forward across the wall, trying to share the binoculars.

Best to sneak away, Dixon realized. He and the kid

could slip down the hill while their attention was drawn to the trucks.

He took a step back, kicking loose rocks.

One of the Iraqis jerked his head around. Dixon's finger snapped, this time against the trigger.

2

Doberman mashed his throttle, urging the turbofans to give him every ounce of thrust they could. The wind had shifted to kick the Hog in the face, holding her back at precisely the wrong moment. The pilot cursed and strained against his seat restraints, as if his weight might make a difference to the aircraft's momentum.

If stinking Preston hadn't screwed up his first attempt to hook into the flying tanker, they'd be there by now.

Stinking rusty major who thought he was hot shit just because he'd flown pointy-nose teenagers.

"Keep up with me, Four," Doberman snapped to his wingman.

"Four," grunted Preston. He sounded as if he'd gotten out of the plane and was pushing it uphill.

Actually, Doberman's indicated airspeed was 465 knots—close to an all-time Hog record for level flight with a combat load. But he was still a good two or three minutes away from getting into target range.

Once there, it could take considerably longer to find the convoy.

"I'll call the targets," Doberman said. "The station wagon's our priority. Screw any SAMs or Zsu-Zsus—leave them for the Tornados. Wolf has them right behind us."

"Four."

Stinking Wong. Why the hell couldn't he get the goddamn time right?

Doberman glanced at the Maverick targeting screen. He had the outline of a highway at the top right corner. It was the highway that led to Al Kajuk and intersected with the one Strawman was on. Swinging along it would make it easier to find his target.

But it would also take him through the lip of the remaining radar coverage of the SA-11's. Flying at medium altitude, he'd be an easy target.

Worth the risk.

"Follow my turn," he barked to Preston, hanging a hard right, eyes glued on the Mav screen to guide him.

"Four. We're moving off the briefed course, into—"

"Follow my turn."

"Four."

Wolf, the mission controller, called back, asking for an ETA.

"In target range in zero-two," said Doberman, afraid that wouldn't be good enough.

The highway cut a sharp line in the middle of the screen. He plotted the target zone in his head, decided he'd look for the T, then pivot; the station wagon would sit to his right, roughly in the center of the screen, if he could hold this course.

More speed, more speed.

Ninety seconds.

"Wolf acknowledges. We have live bait. Ground team attempting to tie them down."

The controller said something else, but Doberman lost it. Before he could ask him to repeat it, his RWR went crazy. The SAMs had woken up, and they were angry.

Somewhere to the south, the electronic-warfare operators aboard the two Tornados tasked to the mission licked
their lips and lit the wicks on their spanking-new BAe
ALARMS; the high-tech radar-killers burst from beneath
their bellies, streaking upward as their integrated circuits
calculated the surest way of quashing the offending defenses.

But the speeding missiles were of small comfort to
Doberman. The Iraqis had already launched their SA-11
missiles, and there was nothing he could do but fly toward
them.

3

Salt felt the grenade pop from the blunt nose of the launcher like a paint ball phiffffing into the air. He didn't bother firing another, knowing the projectile would nail the lead truck. He turned quickly, bending his head as he tried to sight the Mercedes through the M-16's starscope. He couldn't find the target at first, and by the time he dished a grenade in its direction, the first one had exploded, distracting him enough to screw up his aim. Davis yelled something behind him. He'd left the Satcom and grabbed the SAW, opening fire in the direction of the convoy. The earth turned into a barbecue pit, flames bursting all around them, rockets streaking upward, the tank beginning to fire, the armored car—actually an armored personnel carrier with a special cannon—thumping the ground. Men poured from the troop trucks. At least two heavy machine guns flailed.

Salt popped another grenade, but in all the confusion it was impossible to tell where it hit. He threw himself down over the sniper rifle, pulling his body back over the long gun as the ground reverberated. It was all a matter of being patient, as impossible as that seemed—you took your shot only when it was there, and to get it there you had to move deliberately. He squirmed around behind the sight, swinging the light fifty on its tripod. He moved the crosshairs across the vehicles, past the truck and the muzzle flash of the APC. He got the station wagon first, saw a driver but no one else, slipped his aim back toward the Mercedes.

Empty.

Davis screamed something. Salt ignored it, scanning the ground near the Mercedes. The car began to move; he picked his shoulder up slightly and put a round into the front tire. The round blew the tire and wheel apart, but the vehicle kept moving. He pushed his shoulder down, zeroing his aim on the thick, bullet-proof glass at the driver's window, waiting for the man to raise his head so Salt could see where he was going. The Mercedes bumped forward, aiming to get behind one of the trucks for cover. Just as Salt was about to swing toward the engine compartment, the man raised his head. Salt squeezed.

The car's thick glass was advertised as bullet-proof. What the manufacturer meant was that it was bullet-proof against ordinary bullets and guns. The weapon Salt fired was anything but ordinary, with its 12.7mm armor-piercing bullet hand-finished and loaded by the marksman himself. Still, the glass altered the bullet's shape and trajectory, knocking it off its mark.

Unfortunately for the driver, that meant it entered not his neck but his skull. The blast took off the top quarter of the Iraqi's head.

The gun's heavy recoil momentarily cost Salt his aim; by the time he sighted again, the car had jerked to a stop in the middle of the road. Davis yelled again, and Salt felt something wet and hot hit the side of his face, the ground trembling with the impact of a 125mm T-72 shell less than twenty yards away.

4

Skull watched the Pave Low helicopter rear upward from the mass of black shadows, jerking nearly straight up with the motion of a champion weight lifter clearing five hundred pounds. Its dark shadow hovered a second, then slashed forward across the black wilderness, heading for the fresh flare launched by the Frenchman. He looked to be about two miles from them, perhaps less.

Skull replotted the fuel reserves, while Shotgun asked the downed Frenchman something about cafes. It was cutting it close, but there was just enough to run back to Kajuk, fire the Mavericks, and then tank.

As long as they met the tanker at the northern extreme of its track. And they got a tailwind.

Hell, if they got a tailwind there'd be two gallons to spare. Maybe three.

Let's get on with it, he urged the helicopter silently.

Knowlington pushed the Hog onto her wing, sliding through the orbit around the Frenchman. Wolf gave an update on Kajuk in staccato: Doberman and Preston were attacking, the RAF Tornados were launching their radar-killing missiles at a SAM site.

"Boss, he's hearing something," said Shotgun, breaking in. "And it ain't *le hélicoptère*."

Knowlington had started to ask for a direction when the air in front of him burst into flame.

"Leander Seven, hold off, hold off!" he barked, whacking his stick hard to the right as he pulled the Hog out of the worst of the antiaircraft fire. The plane began shaking like a pickup dragging four shot-out tires over a dried-out streambed. Skull rolled into a chest-squeezing turn that took him nearly ninety degrees from his original path, looping out under the stream of gunfire.

One consolation—if he'd been hit, the maneuver would have torn the plane in two.

"Fuckin' Zsu-Zsu in the shadow of that road, uh, half mile, three quarters north of the Frog," said Shotgun. "Shit. Something else."

"Yeah. I'm on the son of a bitch," said Knowlington, trying to get it into his targeting screen. The four-barreled mobile antiaircraft unit was one of three vehicles hiding in a shallow area of shadows near a roadway. As he struggled to lock the flak-dealer in his targeting screen, its red spit turned to narrow points; the gun was turning in his direction.

Knowing he'd be unable to climb quickly enough to avoid the spray, Knowlington pushed his nose down and twisted his wings, shaking off the g forces as he sticked and ruddered into a nearly ninety-degree turn, clear of flak about two hundred feet from the ground and dead on target at one mile.

Michael Knowlington had had less than twenty hours in an A-10A cockpit when he was assigned to command Devil Squadron. At the time, it was only going to exist on paper, a bureaucrat's accounting for planes en route to the boneyard. But the war—and Schwartzkopf—had intervened, plucking not just the allegedly obsolete Hogs but their supposedly washed-up commander off the discard pile.

His first few flights had been tentative. He'd had to unlearn a dozen habits better suited to the high-powered aircraft he'd grown old with. In a way, Skull's past glories held him back; the differences between the Hog and the other planes made him think too much about what he was doing, made flying a hair-twitch more intellectual than it needed to be when shit was raining hot and heavy. But the stream of unguided antiaircraft fire that had caught him off guard had changed that. He didn't think now, he flew. As he snapped clear of the flak, he nailed the Maverick's targeting cue onto the Zeus and let go of the missile. The AGM-65 slid through the air to the left as it was dropped, momentarily riding out the Hog's momentum. But as her engine ignited, she cleared her head, setting her chin on the ZSU-23 flak gun. She struck exactly 3.2 seconds later, ending the hail of bullets.

"Trucks moving on the road. I got people," said Shotgun.

"Yeah," said Knowlington, pushing the Hog to the east as his AGM crashed into the tin armor below the flak dealer's four-barreled turret. "You sure that Frenchie's real?"

"Authentication checked out," said Shotgun. "And the guy knows his restaurants. I'm talking serious snails. Targeting one of the trucks."

"I got your butt," said Skull, pulling the Hog around south of his wingman's.

"Just don't kiss it," said Shotgun. A Maverick dropped from his wing, its solid-fuel motor igniting with a red sparkle.

Had these guys been here all along? Even if the authentication procedure checked out, there was no guarantee someone wasn't holding a knife to the Frenchie's throat.

"Splash one Zil," said Shotgun as the ground flared with his missile strike. "Bonus shot—one slightly used pickup. I hope high explosives damage is a warranty repair."

The AWACS cut in, informing them that a pair of F-15's had been diverted to help.

"What the hell are they going to do?" blustered Shotgun. "They get nosebleeds under twenty thousand feet."

"Gun, I'm going to take it low and slow over our Frenchman. Tell him to get his butt out in the open. I want to see him alone."

"He's got people shooting at him, Boss."

"Just tell him."

Knowlington dropped the Hog down in a buzzard's swoop into the shadows. He felt his way through the grayness, slipping the Hog to sixty feet. He leaned Devil One gently on her keel, improving his view out the side of the cockpit window. But it was just too dark to see a man cowering on the ground. He pushed around, fiddling with the IR head on the Maverick, hoping the glow of the Frenchman's body would show up somewhere.

Nothing. The viewer was just too narrow or perhaps not sensitive enough to see the pilot.

Served him right. When he was at the Pentagon, Skull had helped kill a proposal to outfit A-10's with night-fighting equipment.

"Says you flew right over him."

"Yeah, I heard," Skull told Shotgun. The trucks O'Rourke had hit were still burning; they would be big blotches on the IR if he could ever get the damn thing oriented right.

Which didn't make sense, because, hell, now he had them right in his face and the screen was still blank. No matter how he pointed the FLIR head on the Mav, he had nothing.

Seeker head wasn't working right.

Oh.

Skull banked the Hog through another turn. Leander asked what the hell was going on.

"We're hosing these guys," answered Shotgun. "Be with you in two shakes."

Knowlington gave the shadows one more look with his Mark-One eyeballs. All he could see were shadows dancing on shadows and an eerie reddish glow cast by the fires Shotgun had started when he hit the trucks.

Only thing to do was fire off one of his LUU-2 illumination flares.

It was a very dangerous move. The flare might help the Iraqis see the Frenchman. It could also make the Hog an easy target as he ducked low to make sure the pilot was for real and alone. But Skull couldn't clear the helicopter into an ambush.

"Leander Seven, I'm going to drop a log," Skull said over the rescue frequency. "Hold back. Shotgun, get between the Iraqis and the helo, just in case there's more we missed. I'll take some turns, knock down anybody left by the trucks, and look for our guy."

"Two," snapped Shotgun. "Give me three seconds."

Knowlington needed more than that to get into position. He saw a few pinpricks of red on the ground, but couldn't tell if the Iraqis were firing at him or the downed airman. He goosed off the flare, accelerated, then slammed back to take a look. The stark effervescent light cast by the lou-two as it slowly descended on its parachute swing turned the world into a scene from a Grade-B sci-fi movie, earth devastated after a nuclear accident.

Still couldn't see.

Screw it.

Skull tucked his wing, swooping toward the flare and charging in the direction of the Frenchman. He plunged so low he got beneath the slowly descending LUU-2; the light silhouetted the dark hull of the plane and made it an obvious target, but Knowlington didn't worry about that—he was too busy flying. He skimmed along the ground and found three Iraqi soldiers blinking assault rifles toward him.

Skull blinked back, teasing his GAU-30. The soldiers disappeared in the swirl of erupting dirt, uranium, and explosives. He nosed upward, continuing his path toward the trucks Shotgun had hit. Shadows scattered—he fired at them, realizing they were Iraqi soldiers. He fired high and there wasn't time to bring his aim down as he winged over the position, wheeling back around at the edge of the bright circle of light.

As he churned back around, he spotted a stick figure about fifty yards from the spot where he'd obliterated the first group of Iraqis. He began crawling as Skull approached, moving toward the south.

Had to be the Frenchman.

"I'm on that other truck," announced Shotgun.

It took Skull a few seconds to spot the vehicle a quarter mile ahead on his left, a six-wheeler that looked more like a boat than a truck. A moment after he saw it, Shotgun's missile turned its hull into molten steel and foam.

Skull turned back toward the first group of trucks, looking for the soldiers he'd seen. They were gone, obviously hiding from the Hog and its monster cannon.

"Leander Seven, the heavy stuff is cleared away," Skull told the SAR helicopter. "Few ground troops by the burning vehicles. We'll walk you in if you feel up to it."

The Pave Low pilot replied with a string of curses indicating he was more than up to it. The big Sikorsky popped up, racing forward into the bright arc of the still-burning flare. As Skull banked behind her, one of the crewmen lit up the mini-gun at the door, spraying the area near the destroyed trucks. Meanwhile, the Eagles that had been tasked to help out announced that they had arrived with a swoop down to a thousand feet. Their massive engines shook the ground like lightning bolts from the Norse god Thor.

Which just happened to be their call sign.

The French pilot shouted something over his radio. Skull caught a glimpse of him running to the helicopter.

"Said we're magnificently ugly," explained Shotgun as the Pave Low abruptly lifted up and began heading south. "Those French know beauty, let me tell you."

"Thor Flight, appreciate it if you can run Leander home," Skull told the F-15's. "We have a prior engagement."

"Thor Leader copies. Thank you, Devil Flight; thumbs up to you."

Skull had already snapped his Hog onto the course for Kajuk. Shotgun acknowledged that he too was on the proper heading.

"Say, Boss, not that I'm complaining, but we're out past bingo, aren't we?" Shotgun added, referring to their fuel situation. Bingo was the not-altogether-theoretical turn-around point, the spot where you had to fly home or risk running out of gas.

"Might be," said Skull, making sure he had the throttle at maximum.

5

Wong felt the first shell of the T-72 explode in the distance. The tremble knocked him into the dirt; by the time he managed to get back up and grab the suitcase with the explosives, another round had landed. This one landed parallel to him but well to the east, a good hundred or more yards away from where he'd left Salt and Davis. But the tank had to be neutralized, or sooner or later his men would be killed.

Perhaps sooner—a third salvo landed behind him, close enough to lift him off the ground and deposit him chest-first six or seven feet away. The explosives case landed square on his back, knocking the air out of his lungs. As he struggled to breathe, Wong rolled over and tore open the case. He hastily wired three of the C-4 charges for firing; reaching for another, he heard the whiz of a fresh shell heaving through the air. He froze, waiting for the explosion he sensed would be less than twenty yards away, more than likely fatal. But the shell landed with a dull plop, burying itself in the ground without exploding; still cringing, Wong grabbed the remote detonator, leaving the set charges on top of the open case. He ran as fast as he could toward the tank, the wireless detonator cupped against his body; as the T-72 launched another shell, he detonated the explosives.

His idea was to use the explosives to create a diversion and at the same time cloud the tank's laser range finder; he hoped to get close enough to the tank to draw its attention as the smoke cleared, giving Davis and Salt more time to pin down the convoy for the scrambling A-10's. Had Wong calculated the gambit according to his usual coefficient of probabilities, he would have been presented with an alarmingly small coefficient—but sometimes even he preferred not to do the math.

Of course, had he done the math, he would have taken a few more steps before igniting the explosives. The C-4 was not particularly suited to the task at hand, but it was nonetheless true to its inherent explosive nature—it made a nice, big boom as it was ignited, filling the air with grit, dirt, and pulverized rock. The force of the explosion knocked Wong flat, slamming his face against the hard surface. His cheekbone cracked—technically, the zygomatic cranial bone on his right side suffered a clean fracture—but Wong hardly felt it: the shock of the blast had already knocked him unconscious.

6

Doberman could see the dark shadow as it rode up toward him in the distance, a knife poking into the sky. His own ECMs were useless against the missile, and he had no way of knowing if the fuzz being thrown by the electronic-warfare craft to the south was working. He tossed some chaffe and pressed on, trying to keep his eyes on the targeting screen, where he had only blurs.

He needed to see the goddamn highway. He needed to see it before the SAM nailed him.

It was going to come right through the windscreen any second.

Nothing but blur in the screen.

The SA-11 would have been launched at long distance, would be blind and unguided because surely the radar-seeking missiles had nailed the ground radar and the ECM support craft had fried its onboard guidance system.

No, it was there ahead, a shining silver blur coming for him. He was an easy target, straight and level at ten thousand feet, struggling to see the goddamn car.

He was just about at the damn intersection. Should be right there.

Doberman took his eyes off the targeting screen for a second. Pinpricks of red and green light dotted the ground ahead of his wings. A wall of antiaircraft fire rose from around the village. The radar warning receiver was still going ape-shit. Someone—Preston—yelled a missile warning.

He was about to get nailed. He could feel it.

Served his damn butt right for wearing that stinking BS good-luck medal.

Doberman rolled his wings into a knifing dive, pushing the Hog as close to straight down as possible and swooping for the spot where the parade ought to be. The RWR freaked and Preston screamed and the Iraqi missile homed in.

Doberman put his helmet nearly on the Mav screen. The shadow of a truck materialized.

Finally.

He nudged the Hog's nose sideways, pushing her along the highway as she plunged. He saw a truck, saw another truck, saw a car, saw a big Mercedes, saw a troop truck, saw a nice, long, long station wagon.

Just your typical madman dictator out for a midnight stroll through suburbia.

"Bing-bang-boing," Doberman said aloud, his thumb dancing over the trigger in his old shooting ritual.

"Bing-bang-boing."

The Maverick kicked out from the launcher, barely separating from the plane. The two-stage Thiokol TX-633 solid-fuel rocket motor ignited, jerking the eight-foot-long missile out ahead of its mother ship. A half second later, another thunked into the air behind her, the cruciform delta wings at the rear whipping around ferociously as the guidance system put the missile on course.

7

The gun jumped in Dixon's hand, propelled upward by the momentum of the gases that sent a dozen bullets into the two Iraqis in front of him. By the time he jerked it down, the soldiers had crumbled to the ground. Dixon kept squeezing, shaking the gun up and down before realizing he'd burned the clip. He threw the rifle to the side and pulled up the other Kalashnikov, flinching as something seemed to move just beyond the sandbagged position he'd fired into. But there was nothing, or at least nothing that shot at him. He crouched down, leaning away from the hillside, still unsure if he was safe.

Budge was holding on to the back of his shirt, an anchor pulling him down toward the ground. Dixon reached his left hand around calmly, reassuring the kid as he scanned the hillside, still expecting someone or something to attack. He stayed crouched like that for an eternity, his senses perfectly focused, his whole world narrowed to a sphere no larger than five feet around.

Then he realized the air behind him had begun to hum.

Dixon slid around quickly, knocking the boy to the ground accidentally. There was an enormous flash in the distance beyond the hill, a sudden geyser of red steam, a pipe bursting under tremendous pressure.

And over the explosion, the faint hum of a Hog swooping upward after firing, hungry for another target.

Gunfire below. Vehicles on fire, explosions. A firefight. On the ground.

There had to be a Delta team down there, or British SAS troopers, commandos, allies—friends of *some* kind. People who could get them the hell out of here.

Dixon reached over to the huddled, trembling shape of the kid, lifting him under his arm like a loaf of bread. He left the empty AK-74 and began sliding down the hill on his butt.

"We're getting out of here, kid," he said as they slid. "We're going home."

8

Salt put a slug through the door of the sedan as it started to open. In the next moment a massive flash behind him threw him to the ground amid a whirling storm of dirt. He rolled over and spat out a mouthful of cordite, blood, and pulverized rock, then began to retch, puke pouring like water from his mouth. Somehow he got to his feet, grabbing his combination M-16/grenade launcher and running toward the highway. Davis had taken a position behind some rocks a few yards ahead, pumping rounds from the SAW into the armored car.

"He was in the Mercedes. Come on, come on," Salt yelled, tapping Davis as he ran but not stopping. He managed to load the M203 as he ran; having the grenade in the gun somehow calmed him, helped him run even faster.

A shell from the tank hit near the spot he had run from. Bullets whipped around him, crisscrossing the night with green, yellow, and red streaks. He seemed to be in a movie, outside his own body—not untouchable, not immune to being hit or killed, but removed from it, as if he could die and watch it all happen, analyze it, and even shake his head over what a fool he'd been. Because he was being a fool—he ran directly toward a fierce stream of tracers, kept running as an APC launched a shell over his head, kept running as he saw two figures thirty or forty yards away cross from the highway and duck behind a small rise in the terrain. The Mercedes was twenty yards away on his right, one of the troop trucks ten yards off to his left. He realized as he ran that the Iraqis had lost track of him in the confusion, though surely that could change in a moment.

The SAW ripped behind him; AK-47's answered to his right. Salt leveled his grenade launcher and kicked a 40mm grenade into the yellow sparkle. He took another step and threw himself to the ground. A half second before the grenade exploded, he heard a sharp, howling whistle from above, a wolf calling to its mate—or a Maverick, an instant before hitting its target.

9

Lars blew another long breath from his mouth, shaking his head, swallowing back the salvia flooding his mouth. He checked his altitude and bearing for the fifth time in the past sixty seconds—on course at one hundred feet, chugging steadily through the long arc carefully planned to keep the MH-130 from active radars. He had his protective helmet and night-vision gear back on and he'd moved to the pilot's seat—if he didn't feel more comfortable there, at least it was more familiar.

One of the British RAF Tornados tasked with suppressing the SAM sites announced that it had launched its missiles. Lars glanced nervously toward the window on the right side of the cockpit, as if he might see the strike, then turned his attention to the throttle console, tapping each lever in turn though not changing the settings. He wanted to seem calm to the others. He had to—not because he thought they might rebel if they realized he was nervous, but because it was his job to reassure them so they could work without worrying. You couldn't do your job if you were worrying about your commander; he knew that from his own experience.

It was probably irrelevant, because already they must hate him. Major DiRiggio, the real pilot, their real boss, was lying a few feet behind him on the other side of the bulkhead, barely breathing, possibly beyond survival. Lars had made the right decision—surely DiRiggio would have said himself that the mission came first. But the fact that Lars's hands were shaking and he was gulping for air didn't help matters.

"Herky Bird, this is Wolf. Advise your status."

Lars started to answer, then realized the flight engineer was handling the communications. They spoke over each other for a second, then again as Lars apologized. He glanced up at the switch panel above him, examining the settings as if there were a possibility that something had been changed without him noting it. He worked as slowly as he could, deliberately, hoping to project an aura of assurance. If he couldn't fool the others, perhaps he could fool himself.

Meanwhile, the mission controller brought them up to date. Strawman was being attacked; the Tornados were suppressing the SAMs. They were to proceed as briefed, though obviously well ahead of schedule.

They hadn't had a chance to tell Wolf about DiRiggio's heart attack, but now the controller in the ABCCC asked to speak to him. The navigator laid out the situation.

"Can you complete your mission?" asked the controller.

Lars felt his lungs cough for air.

"We will complete our mission," he said between gulps.

He had talked over the engineer again. This time, however, their words chorused together, exactly the same.

10

Major Preston watched the black-green hull of Devil Three plunge downward, blurring into the raging hellfires. The dark night sky seemed to fold over itself as the Russian-made triple-A hunted through the sky for the intruders. One of the SAM operators had managed to launch two missiles; both were in the air somewhere ahead. Preston felt naked. His A-10's ALQ-119 electronic counter-measures pod was older than the airplane and incapable of confusing an SA-8, let alone the SA-11's.

But Doberman flew right into the teeth of the defenses, despite Hack's warnings. All Hack could do was follow as his leader pitched downward almost directly over the target area, single-mindedly hunting for Saddam. He had a hell of an attitude but he had balls, no question about it.

Doberman snapped something over the radio. Preston's brain worked in slow motion, processing the words.

He'd launched the Mavericks.

Hack's turn. Someone blurted something over the radio; he only half heard it, trying to find a target in his screen.

The Tornado commander had just assured the Hogs that they had launched their ALARMS at the other SAMs, the ones that hadn't turned on their radar. Unlike American HARMs, the homing missiles could loiter above until the SAMs came back on-line.

Somehow, the idea of missiles orbiting overhead didn't comfort him. Hack slid his eyes over to the small screen at the upper right quadrant of his dash. He had the highway in the middle of the screen, no vehicles. The screen blurred, the IR head temporarily overwhelmed by the flash of Doberman's Maverick striking the station wagon.

There's a way to compensate for that, Hack thought. What the hell is it?

Close your eyes?

A second flash. Doberman had taken out the APC as well.

Cocky little son of a bitch was one hell of a pilot.

Past tense. He spotted the Hog pitching left in front of a looming shadow—one of the SA-11's.

Poor son of a bitch.

Poor nasty son of a bitch.

Something exploded in the sky a mile ahead to the east, obliterating the darkness Doberman had just flown into. Hack gaped at the curling red circles that mushroomed into yellow and black spheres. The fireball crinkled at its edges, as if it were made of paper. Then it flashed white and disappeared, its only trace the shadow it had burned on his retina.

Jesus, he thought. I've never seen someone die before.

Poor nasty son of a bitch.

He started to turn his attention back to his targeting screen when Doberman's voice came over the radio.

"Preston, you're up. Go for the tank by the hill."

What?

"Three, are you okay?" Hack said.

"What the fuck are you talking about, asshole? Take your shot. You're almost on the goddamn highway."

"I just saw your plane blow up."

"You just saw the missile miss me and explode. Take

your fucking shot. Then wheel if you can manage it and
cover me. And watch it—there's one more warhead in the
air."

Before Hack could respond, there was a second explosion in the sky, this one much higher and at least four miles
further away.

"Take your fucking shot!" screamed Doberman.

Hack, angry, incredulous, and relieved, tore his attention back to the TVM. He pushed his right leg gently
against the rudder pedal, nudging the plane ever so slightly
through an eddy of turbulence. Somehow he overcor-
rected, his elbow suddenly cramping as he moved the
stick; he came back too hard and felt the beginning of a serious yaw, the plane pitching back and forth as it tried to
follow the pilot's overanxious control inputs. He stopped
moving the stick, told himself that it was going to have to
be okay if he blew the attack—he'd be embarrassed but
there'd be a next go-around, assuming the Tornados hadn't
missed any SAMs and none of the arcing yellow and green
flares of antiair perforated his wings.

Maybe he'd underestimated the Hog drivers, not just
Doberman but every last one of them, willing to fly way
the hell up here and hang their butts out where everybody
in the world could hit them.

No longer confused by the jerks on her control stick, the
Hog straightened herself out, pushing her tail up and sticking her chin down, smelling a ripe and ready piece of Iraqi
meat on the ground ahead. Hack glanced at the HUD
screen, noted the altimeter ladder falling through six thousand feet, then put his eyes back on the Maverick monitor.
A big brick with a lollipop stuck on the top of it appeared
in the left-hand corner; the brick reared back and flared
into a glow so bright he thought the monitor would catch
fire. The targeting cue jumped as Hack moved it toward
the blur, sucking itself in.

But it didn't lock, instead jittering away as Hack
nudged his stick in the tank's direction. Had he been flying
an F-15, his touch would have been perfect; the plane
would have bucked her nose ever so slightly in the proper

direction. But Hack wasn't flying an F-15, and as he felt a whisper of resistance from the controls, he pushed harder. Confused but obedient, the A-10A jerked her nose upward to follow his command; Hack felt his stomach get weak again with the first hint of another yaw.

Do your best, he reminded himself, and this time he resisted the temptation to overcorrect. The plane's momentum carried it off the path he'd plotted, but he worked the cursor down as the tank reappeared in the upper quadrant of the screen. The cue slipped one way and then the other; Hack cursed and then realized with a shock he was down to two thousand feet.

As he went to jerk himself skyward, he saw the cursor plant itself square on the center of the lollipop.

11

The black turned deep blue and a wedge of yellow appeared above, morphing into a triangle of pure, perfect whiteness, a gleam that grew and consumed everything else. Wong felt the edges of the triangle sear his face, bursting with the heat of a phosphorus grenade. It burned straight through his skull, his ears tingling with the sensation not of heat, but cold, freezing cold. The triangle then turned from white to black, the sides of his skull folded into it. His body followed in a rush, vacuumed inside out, skin to organs, molecule by molecule. He was at the end of a long, geometric tunnel cut from an infinite prism, glittering with a blue-blackness that seemed the inverse of light, as if it were capturing all colors to enhance its own nature. As he stood and stared, the crystal flared, then began to vibrate, pulsing with its blackness.

"Interesting," Wong said aloud. "The metaphysical implications of this experience challenge many of my essential beliefs regarding the nature of existence. But I have a considerable amount of work to do. Perhaps we can continue this at another time."

And in that moment he was flung down on his back, his head bouncing off the hard rocks. He opened his eyes to an enormous headache and the flash of missiles and shells exploding all around him, bullets flying everywhere in the air.

He could see it all, but he heard nothing. The explosion had rendered him deaf.

In some ways that was a blessing, because he was in the middle of an enormous racket. Wong's explosive charges had indeed thrown the tank's aim off, but the T-72 crew was still firing. Wong had turned to look back in the direction of Davis and Salt when his eye caught a wavering shadow above the highway; red and yellow burst below it, followed by the quick flash of a gas tank exploding. A second flash, a second fireball, this one not quite as high. The long barrel of a howitzer or light tank gun somersaulted into the sky.

Obviously, the Hogs had arrived. And if, as was their wont, the A-10's were blowing up the biggest things they could find, the T-72 would be next.

Wong turned and began running about ten seconds before the AGM-65 hit the top of the tank, crushing it with the wallop of a hammer hitting the side of a soda can. He slid into the crater created by the C-4, narrowly avoiding a spray of heavy machine gun fire.

As he swung himself around on his haunches, Wong realized he had lost his MP-5 somewhere along the way. He had carried two pistols—a .44 magnum Desert Eagle and a SIG-Sauer P226. Both were admirable weapons with slightly different applications, not to mention limited utility in the present situation. The Desert Eagle carried only seven rounds, though admittedly these were monster magnum slugs capable of stopping anything smaller than a rhinoceros. The heavy gun's demanding kick made it more suitable to close encounters of the one-on-one kind, and Wong therefore chose the SIG, whose utter dependability and fifteen 9mm rounds were enhanced by a nature that could only be described as "sweet," even by someone like Wong who was not given to such imprecise and abstract descriptions. Pistol in hand, he got up and began running in the direction of the Delta team. Alternately ducking, diving, running, and spinning, Wong took several minutes to spot Sergeant Davis hunkered behind his SAW. As the M249 Minimi spat a fresh mouthful of 7.62mm toward the highway, Wong yelled to the sergeant, sliding in behind him as the light machine gun clicked through the last of the rounds in its plastic feeder.

Davis shouted something in response, but Wong still couldn't hear.

"I'm deaf," he yelled, or thought he yelled—he couldn't even hear himself.

Davis nodded vigorously, then reloaded the gun.

There were two knots of Iraqis firing at them. One was toward the north end of the highway, beyond the truck Salt had taken out with his grenade. They were firing willy-nilly, beyond the effective range of their weapons.

The other knot was directly ahead, with better aim and more guns.

Wong realized that there must be more soldiers, but they were either dazed by the attack or prudently waiting until they had clear and obvious shots.

"Where's Sergeant Salt?" he asked Davis.

Davis spoke and made a kind of looping gesture with his hand; Wong took it to mean that Salt had decided to try flanking around the Iraqis' position.

"The A-10's didn't know to hit the Mercedes," said Wong. "They would have gone for the station wagon. Is the Mercedes still intact?"

Davis didn't know.

"We have to get Strawman," Wong said. "Come."

Wong jumped up, running to his right in a diagonal toward the curving highway, intending to flank the stalled convoy. A DShKM "Dushka" heavy machine gun roared to their left, spitting its monster 12.7mm shells into the night, fortunately behind them. A shadow loomed dead ahead.

Wong extended his arm and pumped two slugs from the SIG in its direction, then threw himself down into a roll to duck any return fire. He rolled back to his stomach and got up into a crouch. The Dushka raked the night again, this time considerably closer to Wong and Davis, who had thrown himself to the ground a few feet away. The Russian-made heavy machine gun was being fired from the lip of the road about forty yards away on the left; it had an unobstructed field of fire and sooner or later one of its sprays was going to nail them. Wong reached to his web belt for his M26 fragmentation grenade; his fingers had just touched it when he saw Davis rearing back and pitching one of his own.

Forty yards was a good toss under fire, but the sergeant had a right fielder's arm. Fused to detonate on impact, the M26 sprayed its fragments through the air, killing the two men who had been operating the machine gun. Meanwhile, someone with an AK-47 fired a burst at them from the edge of the road. Wong sighted across the top of his pistol, but all he could see was darkness. He took a handful of dirt, tossing it to the left; as the soldier began firing in the direction of the noise Wong fired a single shot.

The Iraqi screamed, his anguish cascading over the battlefield. Wong crawled to his right a few yards, then picked himself up and began running toward the highway.

The Mercedes sat to his left off the road. There was a troop truck just beyond it. Wong still had the grenade in his hand and considered tossing it at the truck; he didn't, though, not knowing where Salt was.

A second vehicle sat about ten yards down the highway to his right. Its motor wheezed; Wong threw himself down as a shadow ran behind it.

Davis skidded in behind him, huffing; he'd lost his SAW along the way, and like Wong was armed only with his pistol.

"Someone behind the truck," said Wong. "Moving left to right."

The Delta trooper said something, but Wong still couldn't hear.

"Could be Salt," he guessed, and Davis nodded his head.

An AKSU Russian submachine gun declared that they were wrong, a statement underlined by a half-dozen 5.45mm bullets that ripped through Sergeant Davis's arm and leg. And just in case there was any doubt, bullets from a much larger Dushka roiled the dirt nearby, the impact of its bullets so strong that Wong could feel the earth vibrating beneath him as he pressed into the soil.

12

"Got it! Shit! Shit!" yelped Preston over the radio, sounding like a nine-year-old who'd just nailed a tin duck at a church bazaar.

Doberman, flying in a wheeling pattern that had him roughly opposite his wingman's path, glanced at the ground and saw the T-72 guarding the turnoff to Kajuk explode in a red-white geyser of frying steel. Preston was coming straight on for the hill behind it.

"Up, get up! Get the fuck up! You're too damn low! The hill! The hill! Jesus, get up!" yelled Doberman.

He cut his turn to try to keep Hack in view, but lost the dark-hulled airplane in the shadows near the hill. Doberman pitched his Hog downward, cursing the idiot and repeating his warning to pull away from the hill. Preston might be a jerk, but no one should pay the ultimate price for target fascination.

Pay attention to the plane, not the boom. Hog Rule Number Three.

And never run into hills.

Hack hadn't acknowledged, but Doberman didn't see a flash either, and now he was running right for a fresh stream of antiair coming from a battery west of the village. Doberman cut south, tossing some flares and chaff in case any of the SAM sites were still working. He temporarily lost his sense of where he was, swinging at too wide an angle to get back on his original target area. His low altitude—he'd ducked to five hundred feet to avoid the SA-11—made sorting things somewhat harder. He also had to watch out for the hills.

Doberman pushed back westward, climbing slightly and scanning for his wingman and trying not to pay too much attention to the AAA bursting behind him. Wolf cut in with something to the effect that Skull and Shotgun were on their way; Doberman didn't have a chance to acknowledge, finally getting a bead on where he was and cutting back with the idea of launching another Maverick and then putting the cannon to work. As he turned, his RWR bleeped a warning, then went off; in the next instant a gray streak of lightning flashed toward the earth three or four miles to the northeast. It was one of the RAF ALARM missiles nailing the last of the Iraqi SAM installations. The missile had needed only the slightest flick of the on-off switch to memorize its enemy's location; before the Iraqis could juice up again the British warhead landed, sending hot shards of metal into the nearby SAM as well as the destroying the radar van. A narrow thread of yellow flame rippled on the ground, then erupted brilliant red as the poised SS-11's caught fire.

A pair of yellow and black flame puffs rode skyward, framed by the light of the explosion; two more followed in quick succession. Doberman guessed they were a flock of heat-seeking SA-9's, launched in desperation. The short-range missiles were not a threat, since they had been launched at long range and lacked all-aspect targeting; they simply had too far to go to get a sniff of his engines.

The quartet of missiles rising now out of Al Kajuk, just ahead of his left wing and nearly parallel to him—those were a different story.

Doberman yanked and banked, goosing flares and trying to whip his turbofans away from the heat-seekers' noses. One of the SAMs, moving at Mach 1.5, shot out behind him then veered upward, utterly confused; it exploded in midair more than a mile from the Hog's hull. Another sucked in one of his flares and detonated instantly, bouncing a shock wave but no shrapnel against Doberman's tail.

But two others, launched in a fresh volley after he began his evasive maneuvers, stayed with him. Each sucked a different engine, lions working a tired zebra from both flanks. Doberman could feel them panting behind him; he goosed more flares and tucked right, tucked left, tucked right, very low now—so low, in fact, that he was at least ten feet below the summit of the hill that was growing in his front glass.

The missiles kept coming, gaining on him as he gave the stick a hard push left. An elongated football shoot by his canopy, so close Glenon could see the thrust surging from its rear end. He nearly took the control column out of the floor trying to turn toward it as it passed, away from the other missile. The air in front of him shuddered as the missile detonated; the Hog skipped sideways with the turbulent shock, more a brick than an airplane, succumbing to several of Newton's Laws at once.

The second missile exploded on his left, close enough to singe part of the tail fin. Doberman struggled to gain control of the plane, both hands on the stick, his head swimming. With his forward speed plummeting toward stall level, the right wing flipped out from under him; in the back of his mind he thought he'd flamed an engine. He worked to correct, but the wing was insistent; he spun through an invert so close to the ground that the wing tip seemed to scrape dirt. But despite the spin and the ground, he somehow managed to actually pull stable and begin to climb. He hadn't lost the GEs, or if he had it was only temporary, because they were cranking their turbofans now. Head scrambled, legs weak, he somehow managed climb over the highest hill, clearing the scrubby summit by perhaps six inches. The Hog lifted her nose with a snort as she flew into clear air; Doberman's heart pounded so hard he could hear Tinman's medal clanging on his chest.

Good luck or not, that sucker was now part of his flight gear. Doberman caught his breath, checked his instruments, and banked south to return to the battlefield. His fuel was a little low; it was possible he'd gotten nicked by shrapnel and had leaked a bit before the Hog's self-sealing bladders choked shut. Even if that was the case, the situation wasn't critical.

"Devil Three, this is Four. Glenon, where the hell are you?"

Preston sounded like a flight leader scolding a nugget for getting outside the formation.

"Where the hell are you?" Doberman responded.

"I'm two miles south of the highway," said Hack.

"Which fucking highway? There's two."

Preston didn't answer. Obviously he'd meant the east-west highway.

"I'm coming over Kajuk from the northeast," Doberman told him. "Orbit where you are. I'll come to you."

"Four."

The battlefield lay in a vector that perfectly split the intersection of Doberman's left wing and fuselage at forty-five degrees. The village sat in the crock of a hill. A line of triple-A installations made a staggered "C" to the east of the village in the direction of Kuwait; only two were still firing, their spew of red and black streaming harmlessly into the air some miles away. Doberman turned his attention to the TVM; he quickly found the tank Preston had hit half hidden by the shadow of the hill as he approached. Beyond it, several vehicles in the convoy were still burning. Nothing was moving, and there didn't seem to be any armor left intact.

Doberman tried contacting the ground team, but got no response; Wolf didn't immediately answer his hails either.

"Preston, you talk to Wong and his boys while I was fooling with those SAMs?"

"Negative. Uh, friends call me Hack."

"Three." Doberman realized he was being an asshole,

but Preston rubbed him the wrong way. "I'm banking west, trying to raise them. I have two more Mavs; I want to hold on to them until I know their situation. The convoy is definitely stopped."

When two more hails failed to reach Wong and his men, Doberman went back to Wolf. The ABCCC hadn't heard from the ground team either. The Herk that was supposed to make the pickup had suffered a casualty aboard—apparently a heart attack—but was proceeding anyway.

There was some good news. The Iraqis were desperately trying to radio about a dozen units; the controller took that as a hopeful sign.

Doberman didn't. It meant there'd be no chance for the ground team to linger. The whole operation had moved so quickly he doubted there had been time to find Dixon.

Son of a bitch. As far as he was concerned, that was the whole reason for the mission.

Son of a bitch.

And now they had other things to worry about—the AWACS monitoring the area spotted two Iraqi fighters taking off from an air base about seventy miles away. At the same time, two SA-2 SAM sites thought to have been eliminated suddenly came back to life.

The SAMs would only be a problem going home, and then only if the Tornados or somebody else didn't splash them. The Iraqi jets were another story. Tentatively ID'd as MiG-29's, they could get within missile range in roughly three minutes. Without a head start, the Hogs would never get away.

The AWACS controller prudently directed Doberman and Preston to snap onto an escape vector away from the Iraqi planes—and out of the battle.

"Negative," answered Doberman. "We're staying on station."

The controller's response—undoubtedly not pretty—was conveniently overrun by another transmission. Doberman tried the ground team again without getting an answer. He turned his full attention to the Maverick screen as he swung back south, as if he might somehow be able to see Wong through the tiny aperture.

"Devil Three, this is Four," said Preston. "Bandits are positively identified and heading this way."

"My radio's working fine," Doberman told him. It took a superhuman effort not to add something to the effect that Preston was welcome to run away if he was scared.

"I have your six," said the major.

Shotgun would have said something funny, but at least Preston didn't try and pull rank. And, in fact, he had given the proper Hog response—screw the enemy, I'm staying here until my job is done.

Which didn't make him all right, just slightly less of a jerk.

"Okay, Hack," Doberman said. "Your old buddies in the Eagles'll take care of the MiGs."

"We'll nail them if they don't."

Okay—that was something Shotgun could have said.

Doberman eyed the village with the Mav's infrared eye; he caught a grayish blur at the left edge of his screen that came into focus as a large vehicle, possibly an APC, though it didn't have the wedgy shape Dog associated with the Iraqi vehicles. No matter—there was something else behind it, a truck big enough to be a troop transport. And another. Doberman nudged his stick to try to get the lead vehicle back into his targeting scope; he slid his whole body to urge the plane around. He coaxed the pipper on target, locked, and fired as he muttered his ritual "Bing-bang-boing."

"I got trucks moving out of the village," he told Preston. "I targeted a personnel carrier, or what looked like a personnel carrier."

The Maverick smashed the vehicle as Doberman paused for a breath. As the explosion flared, the ZSU-23's to the east began firing, this time nearly straight up. Doberman banked west immediately; Preston said something, but it was garbled.

A thick spray of tracers arced for his nose as he turned, frothing in his path.

13

Salt pressed his chin against the dirt. The world had become a sharp buzz, the air above him on fire. He wasn't wounded, he was sure of that, but he was equally sure that if he moved, if he twitched, he'd get fried. Things were burning, things were exploding, but he couldn't see anything except for a hazy gray mist, the shroud they threw over you before dumping your body into the earth. He waited for it to clear, but instead of lifting, it drifted downward, its electric tingle moving closer and closer. Salt pressed himself further and further into the earth, dirt filling his nose and throat and lungs as he breathed. The sky flashed white with heat so intense he could feel every hair on his body singe. Only then did the mist start to evaporate.

He lifted his head, saw nothing in front of him. The wreckage of the Mercedes, a twisted collection of burned metal, fabric, and plastic, sat to his left. The door was open.

Salt pushed forward like a sprinter lining up for a race.

He took the M-16 and awkwardly sprang forward, unbalanced, low to the ground, legs propelling him forward in something like a stuttering dive rather than a trot or run. He pushed himself sideways, stumbling for three or four yards before collapsing in a roll. Something moved to his right. He got back to his feet and went in that direction, six yards this time, falling down a shallow hill, sliding like a kid belly-whopping without a sled down a snowy incline.

Two Iraqis huddled ten feet away. Either they were surprised by him or thought he was on their side, because neither moved as Salt rose to his knees and aimed his gun at them. Or perhaps the rest of the world was moving in slow motion. The Iraqi on the right moved his hand, down toward his belt; it got about halfway before Salt put three 5.56mm slugs in the man's heart. The Iraqi reeled to the side, stood straight, then collapsed straight forward like a plank pushed from the top, all the time moving at what seemed to Salt one-quarter speed.

The other man stood and raised his hands out to surrender. He took a step forward, and in the dim light of the battlefield Salt saw the grubby bearded face of Saddam Hussein.

You bastard, he thought, aiming his gun at the dictator's belly.

14

The Iraqi heavy machine gun sputtered its bullets in the dirt about ten feet from Wong. He could tell that the gunner couldn't actually see him, but the bullets were still close enough to make him cautious. Sergeant Davis lay on the ground a few feet away, writhing in obvious pain. Wong still couldn't hear anything.

There was no way to aim at the Dushka without exposing himself to return fire, a nasty proposition. The man with the AKSU Russian submachine gun had him pinned in a cross fire. Sooner or later, Wong feared, the Iraqis would use their superior numbers to advance under the cover of the fire. So he had had two choices—retreat and flank, or charge forward. In either case, he would be a target; it seemed better to go forward.

The odds of getting shot depended on the ability of the Iraqi gunners, of course. Still, a rough estimate might put them in the three-to-one range, the three lying in the favor of the enemy. Wong took a breath, remembering a koan from an old Zen master that translated roughly as, "The bullet you see is not the bullet you hear is not the bullet you feel, unless it is." Failing to make sense of the mystery, he jumped up and rushed for the truck where the man with the light machine gun was hidden.

Either his sheer audacity or pure luck protected him as he ran the twenty or so feet. Bullets from both guns whizzed past. The flash of an explosion nearby almost blinded him, then silhouetted his nearest enemy at the front of the cab.

Wong squeezed three shots from the SIG, then flung himself down, rolling beneath the chassis just in front of the rear wheel. The Iraqi soldier had stopped firing, though Wong wasn't sure he'd hit him. He crawled under the truck, fired the SIG again in the man's direction, then pushed out and began running. He'd lost track of exactly where he was, and when a figure appeared to his right he stopped, thinking it was Sergeant Salt. The man, perhaps five yards from him, was running toward the road carrying a rifle. Wong stared intensely and realized the gun was a Kalashnikov. He steadied his aim, fired twice, missing both times. The man stopped and turned to fire at him; Wong aimed again and hit him in the chest. The rifle flew to the side, but it took two more slugs for the Iraqi to go down.

Wong thought of grabbing the man's gun, and took a step toward him as a muzzle flash ahead caught his attention. He threw himself down into the dirt, then realized the flash had been about fifteen yards away, down a small incline. He pushed back up, his knee jerking sideways out from under him as he started running again. He winced away the pain and reached the hill in time to see Sergeant Salt standing on the left, holding his M-16 on an Iraqi who held his hands upright.

A bearded, potbellied Iraqi who could only be the Strawman.

Salt raised his gun to fire.

"Sergeant!" shouted Wong. "Sergeant!"

Salt gave no sign that he had heard Wong.

"Sergeant, do not fire!" said Wong. "That is a direct order."

Salt's gun remained level but did not fire. Wong's knee balked as he worked down the hill.

"I cannot hear you if you're talking," Wong said. "I appear to be deaf."

The Iraqi's face was stained with sweat or tears.

"I'm going to kill the bastard," said Salt, his voice muffled but suddenly audible. "I'm going to kill this son of a bitch for starting this goddamn fucking war. He deserves to die."

Salt raised his rifle to fire.

"You may be right," Wong told him. "But we're not the judges and you cannot shoot him."

"Our mission was to fucking kill him."

"Indeed," said Wong. "But he has surrendered."

"I don't give a fuck."

"Sergeant, you must realize that I am giving you a lawful order. The welfare of the prisoner is now of prime concern."

The Iraqi's hands were trembling, but he did not move.

"You gonna fuckin' kill me if I shoot him?"

"You will not shoot him," said Wong. His pistol was now aimed at Salt.

"Dyin'd be worth it to nail the son of a bitch," said Salt.

"I should not think so," Wong said. "And such a calculation is besides the point. My order is lawful and must be obeyed. I would note also that this is not Saddam. It is an impostor, a lure."

"What?"

"Saddam Hussein is taller and older. This man is in his twenties. Frankly, he is a poor substitute, though obviously he would confuse a crowd when viewed from a car."

Salt didn't change his aim. "I really ought to kill the bastard then. All this for fuckin' nothing."

Wong gently placed his left hand on Salt's weapon and lowered it. The Iraqi collapsed on the ground.

"You did a good job capturing him," Wong told him. "He will be invaluable."

"More valuable than me?"

Salt's question was more to the point than he knew. The

rigs that they were to use to leave allowed only two men each to be taken; there were or would be only two rigs. So if Wong found Dixon, someone would have to be left behind.

A decision he would have to make when all the contingencies had played themselves out. The plan had been to make the pickup within an hour of the attack—would Wolf hold to that?

"The prisoner is of more value than any of us." Wong walked over and pushed the man flat onto the ground. He quickly patted him down, retrieving a small revolver and a knife attached to his leg. The man also had a vial taped to his leg—probably for suicide, as well as some pills in a pocket bottle.

"Quaaludes, I believe," said Wong, tossing the bottle and pulling the man up by the back of his fatigue shirt. "He does appear somewhat calm."

"I thought you said you couldn't hear," said Salt.

"I couldn't. Your curses apparently jarred my senses back into working order. I am obliged."

Salt began laughing. "Fuckin' comedian."

Wong told the ersatz Saddam in his poorly accented Arabic that he would allow the sergeant to execute him if he gave the slightest hint of trouble. The man nodded, then began telling him that he was only a poor farmer from the north.

"We will conduct a proper interview at another point," said Wong, first in English, then in Arabic. The man babbled on, even after Wong pushed him up the hill.

"Where's Davis?" Salt asked.

"On the other side of the highway, in that direction," said Wong. While his hearing had returned, he had a peculiar ringing in his ears that made it seem as if he had his head in a fishbowl. "He's been wounded."

"Why are we going this way then?"

"Because he is pinned down by a heavy machine gun approximately thirty yards from here," Wong explained. "And unless we disable it we will not be able to rescue the sergeant. Will you take point or shall I?"

"Fuck you," snapped Salt, moving out ahead of him.

15

Hack winced as Doberman turned directly into the tracers he'd been trying to warn him about. He'd already pickled a Maverick at the Zeus; cursing, he dished another one out at the same target, the AGM falling off the rail just as his first hit.

He realized as the rocket motor flashed that he'd made a nugget mistake, the kind of thing a greenhorn scared-shitless lieutenant might do, not a veteran combat flier who was supposed be DO of a squadron. For he'd just lost his night-vision gear, as primitive as it was.

He was also out of position, swinging in the wrong direction as Doberman bucked and weaved. Hack swooped lower and back in Doberman's direction. The only surviving guns now were well to the west and north.

Something flickered across the thin quarter of the moon; Preston nudged left and found the dark hull of a Hog sailing just ahead, apparently none the worse for wear.

"There's a troop transport trying to get around the APC," Glenon told him. "Take it out."

"Can't. I'm out of AGMs."

Doberman said nothing, but the static that followed was more than enough to convey his displeasure.

"I used them on the gun that almost brought you down," Hack said finally.

There was dead air for a second.

"Bank and follow me back to the pickup zone. I have fuel leaks in two of my tanks but I've isolated them. I want to make sure I get the STAR pods down, assuming it's clear."

Hack followed along dutifully, sliding out on Doberman's flank. The prime pickup area lay two miles to the southwest of the village at the top of what looked like a succession of long steps leading back in the direction of Saudi Arabia.

Devil Three orbited once, then skipped low. While dropping a flare would have made it easier to see, it might also draw the attention of nearby troops. Hack couldn't see the oversized gift packs slide off the Hog, nor could he see the chutes, though he had his helmet against the glass, trying to.

"All right, check your fuel," said Doberman. "And stay in formation. We're going back and doing a box, like we briefed."

"I thought you were hit."

"I've taken care of it," Doberman said. "I got movement on the highway four miles west of here. Follow me."

16

Doberman nudged the Hog's nose into a thirty-five-degree dive, straight on the lead truck—or at least he figured it would be straight on the target, since he was transposing from the TVM, triangulating with the dark shadows before him. He wanted to keep his last Maverick in reserve and didn't want to risk a flare, figuring it might help the Iraqis find the ground team.

Besides, the GAU tracers would light up the night.

A shadow moved into the middle of his HUD. Doberman centered his targeting cue, waiting while the shadow grew fat. Something kept him from pulling the trigger—the man who normally calculated everything, who did the math on every shot backward and forward before pressing the trigger, hesitated because it just didn't *feel* right yet.

Damn. Shotgun was rubbing off on him.

The shadow didn't move. He was looking at a house or something.

No, it was the truck, but it had stopped. Two others were pulling around it to the right, live targets.

He shifted in his seat, as if merely moving his fanny would move the Hog onto the new targets. Somehow it did—Doberman squeezed the trigger and the black night flashed with the fire of death, the bullets slashing through the thinly protected side hatch of an armored car, up into the turret just to the right of the gun before flailing through the engine. Doberman rode the hot stream into the second vehicle, obliterating it with a long burst. He still had enough of an angle and altitude to get his gun onto a third vehicle approaching down the highway, but he was moving too fast and had come too low to do more than spit a few shells in its general direction before flailing off to the south to regroup.

"Three, I don't have a target."

"Yeah, just hang with me, Hack. That's all I want," Doberman told him, swinging a wide circle. "You just keep cool."

"Four."

He checked his fuel. Sealing off the flaky tank had worked. The game plan had called for them to fly all the way back to KKMC; even if he hadn't lost a bit he'd be close to bingo by now. He could change that easily enough, though; just run south and hit the tanker.

What about Preston, though? He'd had trouble before and he'd be tired now.

Whack a few more ground vehicles, or walk Preston home?

What Doberman really wanted to do was scoop up Dixon. It wasn't his job—Wong and the others were doing that—but he'd do anything to get the kid back, including landing and tossing him on the back of the plane. The kid was like Doberman's little brother—exactly like him, which was why he was in trouble in the first place, as a matter of fact.

He hailed Wolf, but they hadn't heard from the ground team either. He told the controller that the pods had been put down and mapped out the trucks they'd just hit. Wolf told him a pair of F-16's were coming north to assist. In the meantime, a flight of F-111's out of Turkey had been rerouted to hit the stranded convoy one more time.

From Turkey?

Doberman acknowledged, setting his nose back toward the convoy area, still unsure how long they were going to stay there. Hack radioed that he had just passed bingo. His voice was flat and matter-of-fact, the way a Hog driver's ought to be.

He could just send Hack home alone.

Might get lost.

Had to take him back. And give the devil his due, Hack had taken out the Zeus and he had ignored the MiG warning.

Which, come to think of it, had evaporated.

"Devil Three, this is One. Doberman, what's your situation?"

Skull's voice, unexpected and a bit tinny, nonetheless had a tone that permitted nothing but a full set of the facts, including a layout of the positions as well as their fuel and ammo stores.

"Go south," Skull told him. "You and Preston head back. We'll stay here until the Vipers arrive."

Doberman had heard Knowlington tell Wolf about the downed Frenchman. There was no way he and Shotgun had more fuel than they did. Even without doing the math, he doubted Devils One and Two could linger more than two minutes before heading desperately for the tanker.

But there was also no way to disobey Skull's directive.

"Glenon," said Skull.

"We're setting course now," he told him.

17

Dixon shepherded Budge down the hill, trying to move as quickly as he could without running into the Iraqis. It took forever and longer, every step slowed by caution and speeded by anticipation. The battle unfolded on the plain before them as they descended, flaring and dying and then flaring again. Several times they hunkered down and watched for falling debris as missiles erupted overhead. Installations to the north and east reverberated, hit by bombs or long-range surface-to-air missiles.

There were definitely Hogs involved. Their target seemed to be trucks or buildings about a half mile down the highway, perhaps further; there was gunfire there, and Dixon guessed that must mean the commandos were in that area. There was also a tank and an Iraqi outpost that had been struck on the left foot of the hill. He and Budge found a path and began running, nearly to the bottom now. Dixon picked up the boy and carried him about a hundred yards until he saw a truck sitting at the bottom of the slope, thirty feet ahead.

BJ nudged Budge to the right, aiming to get around the vehicle. Something flashed as they moved on the sloping soil of the hillside—a lightning bug flickering in the dark.

No, a man on the back of the truck, squeezing off a single, almost silent rifle shot. The truck was a Land Rover, sitting pug-nosed in the dark a few feet from the roadway.

Dixon pointed his rifle at the man. As he took aim, he realized another Iraqi vehicle sat less than five yards to the left of the Land Rover, obscured from Dixon's view by a bluff at the edge of the hill. It was thick and long, with a gun at the top—a tank or more likely a BMP, a tracked armored personnel carrier exported by the Russians.

The man in the Land Rover fired another round. He seemed to be trolling for a response, unsure what was out there, if anything. He moved too deliberately to be panicked, yet seemed to be shooting randomly.

It wouldn't take much of a shot to hit him. But the BMP was probably loaded with men. The bluff would prevent it from training its turret up the slope, but Dixon and Budge would be quickly outnumbered.

Infinitely safer to keep sneaking to the right, flank the position, and then cross the road. At that point, he could swing toward the firefight, maybe help out by coming up behind the enemy.

Assuming, of course, the Iraqis were shooting at something more than ghosts.

"Okay, Budge," he told the kid. "This way."

"Budge," agreed the boy. He got up and walked with BJ across the slope, then slid down toward the road with him. A trench ran along the highway; Dixon stopped Budge for a moment and pointed to it.

"Go, Budge," he said, pushing him forward.

"Budge!" yelled the kid.

They'd gone only a few yards when the boy yelped. As Dixon moved to clamp his mouth shut, he realized there was an Iraqi with a gun a few yards away.

Tugged from behind by Budge, he tumbled back into the ditch as the Iraqi began to fire.

18

Salt saw the Dushka and its crew about ten yards to his
left, set up behind the wrecked chassis of a truck. Mounted
on a thick tripod, the DShKM was a thing of austere
beauty, from its double-circle muzzle brake to the wooden
pegs of its rear handles. Capable of spitting just over nine
rounds of 7.62mm ammo a second, the gun was as rugged
and dependable as any machine gun ever used, and at least
as deadly.

Salt had a shot on only one of the three men behind the
gun. If the others managed to swing the weapon around at
him, he'd be dead meat—he had no cover himself.

Carefully, he began moving to his right, trying to flank
the position from the rear, hoping to get to a position where
he could hit the entire crew with one burst. The wreckage
of the truck helped camouflage him, but it also made it impossible to see the gunners. The Dushka's metallic thud
sent him diving to his right; it took a moment for him to
realize the Iraqis had fired not at him, but at whatever was
in front of them—Davis, most likely.

As a general rule, Salt didn't like officers, especially those giving him orders. He'd been willing to put up with Wong because his bona fides were there—the guy had, after all, done a HALO jump a few nights ago with some buddies of Salt's. But the bullshit about Saddam pissed him off.

Not that Wong didn't have a point. It was the way he'd expressed it that pissed him off.

That and the fucking SIG he'd pointed at Salt's neck. Salt had half a mind to just drop back and let Wong deal with the machine gun—more than likely they'd fry him, and he could whomp Saddam in revenge.

Not to overvalue revenge. He began crawling on his belly, paralleling the wrecked truck. He paused parallel to the rear of the truck; he could spring up and be behind them with two steps.

Three guys, three slugs. Didn't need cover.

Unless they were behind something themselves.

Sneak close to the truck, take a peek before he attacked.

The machine gun stopped firing with a jerk and a metallic snap. They'd run through the clip.

Salt's brain was still processing the sound as his instincts took over, propelling him to his feet with a leap. He took a step, brought the rifle to his side, took another step, and fired point-blank, the first burst catching the actual gunner, the second catching the man to his right, the third the man on the left.

Except that it didn't. He'd run through the clip, leaving the third man unharmed.

Salt cursed his stupidity, cursed his shit luck, cursed the world. He ejected the cartridge and reached for another. But as his fingers fumbled, the Iraqi drew a pistol, and before Salt could reload there was a tremendous boom in his ears, the sound of a massive bullet hitting home.

Hitting the Iraqi, not him. Captain Wong had run up behind Salt and now stood over him, a Desert Eagle smoking in his hand.

"Shit," said Salt. "Shit."

Wong said nothing, turning quickly and running to grab

the Saddam impersonator from the ground a few feet away; it wasn't clear if Wong had left him there or if the man had been trying to escape by crawling away. Wong dragged him over to the machine-gun position. He scanned the ground, then knelt next to it. By the time Salt got there Wong had disabled the weapon.

"They were out of ammunition," the captain told him. "Sergeant Davis is this way."

"Hey, uh, Captain—thanks. You saved my butt."

Wong gave him a quizzical look, as if he didn't understand or his hearing had once more gone on the fritz. But maybe that was just his way of saying, "You're welcome"—the Air Force captain was an odd duck.

"Sergeant Davis is this way," said Wong, pushing the prisoner ahead.

They found Davis huddled over his leg, half-conscious. He'd been hit by three bullets, one of which had shattered his bone. Wong quickly bandaged the leg and gave Davis a hit from the morphine syringe. The D boy had been fortunate—the wounds had come from a submachine gun, not the Dushka. The big machine gun would have taken his limb right off.

"At least he got the bastard," said Salt, who could see the body on the ground behind the nearby truck.

"Actually, *I* eliminated the soldier wielding the submachine gun," said Wong.

"You know, Captain, you talk kind of funny."

Again, Wong gave him a goggle-eyed stare. "I wasn't aware of that."

Salt started to laugh.

"I will never understand why everyone in the Gulf has such a bizarre sense of humor," Wong told him. Then the captain turned to the Iraqi and said something that apparently meant he was to carry Davis, for he went over to the sergeant and tried lifting him.

To Salt's surprise, the Iraqi was actually able to get him over his shoulder.

They ran back across to the road to the spot where Davis had left the com gear. Wong immediately went to work on it, fingers flailing over the controls like a mad typist finishing up the last bit of paperwork before a long weekend. Salt scanned northward. The tank had been taken out by one of the planes. There were two vehicles to the east right at the foot of the hill, guarding the highway. They were maybe a half mile from them. Salt couldn't remember now whether they were there when all of this had started—it seemed like aeons ago.

"Strawman was an impostor," Wong told Wolf when he succeeding in contacting the ABCCC craft. "We are proceeding to rendezvous site."

The controller apparently said something the captain didn't like; he frowned and said only, "Understood," before ending the transmission.

"Take the Satcom and go to the pickup site," Wong told Salt. "The STAR pod will have been dropped by now."

"You think Davis will make it?"

"If he's placed in the harness," Wong said.

"That's not what I meant."

"My medical knowledge is limited," said the captain. "Obviously he cannot survive here and must be evacuated."

"Where are you going?"

"I am going to complete my assignment," Wong told him. "If I am not there for the pickup, leave without me."

"What? When?"

"The plane is on its way. You will recognize the spot from the photos we reviewed after takeoff; set up near the highest elevation and present yourself southwards. Quickly; you have no more than twenty minutes. Apparently the Iraqis are scrambling every force at their disposal into this area."

"Shit. What about him?" Salt gestured to the Iraqi.

"He won't give you trouble. Place him in the second set of harnesses. The Hercules will make two passes."

"You trust me not to kill him?"

"Of course, Sergeant. You have your orders."

"Yeah." Salt frowned, then looked over at the Iraqi, who was bending forward under Davis's weight. The man seemed to have lost the glaze in his eyes; maybe Wong had sobered him up. "You understand what I say, fuckhead?"

"He doesn't speak English," Wong said. "Simply point."

Wong picked up Davis's SAW and several cases of ammunition.

"Hey, Captain. Thanks," Salt told him.

This time, Wong nodded and actually seemed to smile.

"All right you, move out," Salt told the Iraqi, gesturing. "Go."

Davis groaned as they started. Salt figured that was a good sign, and ignored the fresh explosions and gunfire in the distance.

19

In 1943, a U.S. Army paratrooper stood under a set of extremely high poles as a Stinson light observation aircraft trundled overhead. The Stinson dipped slightly, then held steady; a hook off its fuselage caught the wire at the top of the poll and the paratrooper shot nearly straight up into the air. Attached to a modified parachute harness, the paratrooper was pulled along behind the plane at roughly 125 miles an hour before being cranked inside the craft. It wasn't particularly pretty, but when the paratrooper finally clawed his way in, he became the first American successfully scooped from the earth by an airplane.

Not counting the sheep that had been strangled in the earlier experiments.

After the war, Robert Fulton improved the ground-hook system considerably, stepping up from sheep to pigs for his trials. On August 12, 1958, Marine Staff Sergeant Levi Woods attached himself to a thin harness tethered to a helium balloon and waited as a Navy P2V Neptune approached on wavering wings. The plane snagged a line held by the balloon and the sergeant was airborne. The tug that propelled him upward supposedly felt lighter than the pull of a parachute opening, though it should be noted that on being winched into the P2V, the pigs tended to attack the crew.

Streamlining behind the patrol craft, Woods extended his arms and legs, literally flying as he was pulled toward the plane. When he reached the hold, he had successfully demonstrated the Fulton surface-to-air recovery (STAR) system, and proven once and for all that Marines are crazier than most normal human beings.

The Air Force adopted the STAR system for Spec Ops during Vietnam. Air Force personnel being somewhat less crazy than Marines, the system was not actually used in combat during the war. But it continued to be a favorite of Spec Op troops, or more accurately their commanders, who frowned on risking small and slow helicopters in hostile situations when much larger craft like lumbering transports could be sent instead.

By the time Saddam decided to push into Kuwait, improvements in the C-130 meant that a covert team could be picked up by an aircraft nearly impossible to track. Compared to earlier versions as well as other transports and helicopters, the MC-130 variants were sneaky fast, avoided snoopy radars, and could make quick and effective forays into enemy territory without needing a sixty-plane escort. In theory, the STAR system gave the U.S. an almost invincible covert retrieval capability.

That was the theory. To Captain Lars Warren, stroking the control column to avoid yet another Iraqi SAM site, the reality was very different. As long as he stayed where he was—fifty feet above the increasingly bumpy and varied terrain—his Herk couldn't be seen by radar. It could be heard, however, and the night wasn't nearly so dark that it couldn't be seen—as a row of tracers erupting to his left vigorously demonstrated.

"We're okay," said the navigator, presumably meaning that the gun was being fired simply by sight, and not very well.

Lars didn't answer. He held his flight path steady, passing the tracers without getting hit.

Or at least, without knowing that he was hit.

"The A-10's have engaged the target vehicle," Kelly told him. "Destroyed. Everything's moving ahead, just with the timetable pushed up. Two Hogs coming west to cover us. F-16's en route as well."

Lars grunted. He didn't want a play-by-play. He didn't want to hear anything except for the loud drone of the Herk's four-bladed engines.

"Thirty-five minutes to show time," said the navigator.

"Okay."

"GPS looks good."

"Okay."

They were headed toward the Euphrates, not far from the heart of the country. They'd take one more turn, get on a direct course to the target area. They'd pop up about sixty seconds before hitting the target area and take a hard turn southwest. The balloon ought to be right in front of him, sitting pretty at five hundred feet.

Right.

They'd hook the line with the prong at their nose. A guideline ran from the wing tips to the forward fuselage to protect the line from the propellers. After the rope was snared, the crew would winch in the first two members of the team. He'd then come around and repeat the process for the last man. It would take between six and ten minutes to get them in.

Right.

There were a million Iraqis below, every single one of them armed to the teeth. There were a million antiaircraft weapons of every description—23mm, 56mm, shoulder-fired heat seekers, high-altitude SA-2's, Rolands, SA-6's, SA-9's, machine guns, pistols—even a stinking slingshot could nail them this low, this slow, this straight.

At least one flight of MiGs had taken off earlier and was still inexplicably unaccounted for. The AWACS and the interceptors scrambled to meet them lost them near their air base. Did that mean they had landed—or were they simply flying low like Lars was?

Lars heard himself give the crew a briefing on the situation. They were on course and in the green.

"Cool," he said. "Everything's cool."

Where the hell did that BS come from?

He checked his course again, careful to keep an eye on the terrain-following radar. The flight engineer went through the systems readouts. The navigator counted down to the turn. They hit the way-marker and he banked, fought off some unexpected turbulence, felt his hands turning to jelly, told himself he was sticking with it, heard the pilot gasping for air.

He was the pilot now. He was the one who couldn't breathe.

"Thirty minutes," said the navigator.

"Thirty," said Lars. "Everything's cool."

20

Shotgun began closing the distance between himself and Skull as they came up on the initial target area south of Kajuk. The ground team had finally checked in with the controller; Devils One and Two were going to take a pass and knock down any units that might try to follow Wong and the boys back to their pickup spot.

The way Shotgun saw it, the mission had been among the most boring he'd ever flown. Sure, they'd hit a heavily armed SAM site and saved a French guy, but he personally hadn't done much more than wreck two trucks. Hell, he could have gotten that at home.

Often had, come to think about it.

But that was the way your luck went. Sometimes you got the short straw and diddled around with pickup trucks and a ZSU that couldn't hit a BUFF flying at a thousand feet with four engines out. Other days you got to nail down a Scud, fry a dozen T-72's, and duck a battery of SA-6's, all before you finished drinking your coffee.

Would be nice to nail the Mercedes, he thought, focusing in on the sedan with his IR viewer. The doors were open, it was off the side of the road, and it was obviously not a threat, but there was nothing like poking holes in overpriced German sheet ‾metal to puff up your chest. Frenchie woulda liked it too.

"Gun, I got some vehicles on that highway at the base of the hill. You see 'em?"

"Not yet," he told Skull, pulling the viewer back out to what passed for wide-screen.

"Some sort of gun on one of them. I'm not sure if it's a tank or what, but it seems to be the only thing big left down there. Armored car or BMP maybe."

"Could be," agreed Shotgun, still trying to find them.

"I'm going to sweep around and run south toward those vehicles Doberman hit before they left. If you can't find anything else, take out the gun."

"It's what I'm talkin' about," said Shotgun.

"Watch your fuel."

"Always."

"Vipers claim they'll be here in zero-five."

"Tell 'em to take their time."

Shotgun checked his position against the INS and his paper map. He knew which hill Skull meant—it ought to be just left of center at the bottom of his windscreen, which should put the road right across the center of the Maverick's targeting video. But damned if all he had there were a few rocks.

Problem was, he was too high—eight thousand feet. Hog didn't like to fly this stinking high. Eight *hundred,* now that was an altitude to fly at.

Shotgun did the ol' tuck and roll, plummeting toward the earth as the plane squealed with delight.

And hot damn, there were the vehicles Skull had told him about, definitely a BMP and something smaller, transport or an oversized pickup. Hot spots on both suddenly flared, guns blazing away on the ground.

Shotgun wanted to reserve one missile so he'd be able to see the ground without resorting to a flare if things got hot again. On the other hand, it looked to be impossible to hit both with one shot; they were separated by five yards.

Hit the side of the BMP and go for the bounce.

He dialed in the Maverick and fired. Something on the ground blinked as the AGM's motor lit. Gunfire sparkled all around.

Iraqis couldn't be firing at themselves.

Shit. His guys must have wandered up there where they didn't belong. They were going to be damn close to the BMP went it went boom.

All he could do was watch.

gun fire took them down; the BMP began firing again, its two weapons clattering like oversized typewriters as they raked the ground in front of them. A dozen shadows moved from behind the personnel carrier toward the road.

No, into the ditch. They were sidling in his direction.

Dixon let off two quick bursts from his AK-74, then pulled the boy with him as he threw himself forward across the highway. He tried to hug the ground but keep moving at the same time; above all he kept his fingers tight on the boy's tattered shirt. He saw two rocks ahead, barely higher than cement blocks. He swung Budge around as he dove for them, keeping him sheltered as the bullets whipped around him.

If the rocks deflected anything, it was by pure chance. The light *whhisssh* of rifle fire gave way to the throaty thump of the cannon, the shells moving inextricably closer.

BJ choked on the smoke and dust, praying for a miracle, praying to hear a familiar sound from above—the throaty *whoosh* of an A-10A closing on its target. He prayed, and then in his confused desperation swore he heard it; he pulled Budge beneath him, expecting, knowing that he had finally lost his mind and was ready to die.

In the next second a short, shrill whistle announced the impending arrival of three hundred pounds of explosive on the top of the Iraqi BMP. A ferocious wind slapped Dixon deeper into the ground as a piece of flaming steel from the personnel carrier ignited the gas tank on the nearby Land Rover, turning the vehicle into a three-quarter-ton Molotov cocktail. The four or five Iraqis who hadn't been killed when the Maverick hit were fried as the truck's shell vaporized. Their ammo cooked off in a burst of Fourth of July finales.

And then there was a hush, the flames eating themselves into oblivion. Dixon felt the oxygen run out of his own body, as if sucked into the fire. He fought to get it back, gagging in the dust as his lungs began working again.

Something kicked underneath him. Dixon pushed himself sideways, fearing he had crushed Budge. He looked at the small body writhing on the ground, lost his breath again—then realized the kid was laughing, maybe out of fear or frustration, but no, he seemed to find the whole thing a gag or joke staged just for him. The boy giggled and cackled. Dixon too started laughing, as if they were in the middle of a giant amusement park, as if they were at Disney World and Goofy had just done a pratfall for their benefit.

"We'll go there when we get out of this, kid," Dixon told the boy, and the kid nodded vigorously, as if he'd read his mind about Disney World and going to America. "Come on—let's get the hell out of here."

Dixon hooked his arm around the boy's back and side, clutching him as he began running toward the light machine gun that had cut down the two Iraqis a few moments before. Having wished the Hog there, he now wished his countrymen to materialize before him; he ran forward, convinced it would happen, convinced the first miracle wouldn't have happened without this one being preordained too.

"We're American! We're American!" he shouted as he ran. "American! American!"

"Ammorican, Ammorican!" yelled the boy. "Budge! Budge!"

Dixon, half-running, half-dragging, started to laugh again. He was a kid himself, running through a bizarre fun house, trotting through an endless dream, his head spinning wildly. Days of hunger and almost no sleep, of thirst, stress—of everything that war was, of every bizarre thing that war was—spun like a tornado in his chest, holding him up, propelling him.

"I'm an American!" he yelled, and he heard something pop on his left, and he heard a voice, vaguely familiar, yelling from a few yards away on his left, "Get down! Get down! I see you! Get down!" And the thing popping on his left flared into the dragon mouth of a machine gun mounted on the rear of a truck, its breath flaming the ground in front of him and the air overhead, its tongue leering from between teeth dripping with blood. The dragon roared and lurched, snapping at him, trying to bite the tornado he had become. And all Dixon could do was run and laugh, run and laugh, shouting again and again, "We're American! Don't shoot! We're American, me and the kid. Don't shoot."

22

"Get down! Get down! I see you! Get down!" screamed Wong as the canvas at the back of the Iraqi truck flew off. He'd seen Dixon running forward from the road just after the A-10 struck the BMP, but had been unable to warn him away from the Iraqi truck a few yards away. As he had feared, the Iraqis had mounted a heavy machine gun on the back of the vehicle, and had shown amazing patience in not revealing it until they had a target. Wong leveled Sergeant Davis's SAW at the truck and blew through a good portion of the ammo box, raking the side of the vehicle but failing to stop the machine gun, which was protected by a low wall of sandbags or something similar. He did, however, succeed in drawing the gunner's attention—Wong ducked as a barrage of bullets whipped in his direction, pinning him to the ground.

Under other circumstances, he might have felt some satisfaction that he had been right about Dixon, and that he had beaten the odds and found the lieutenant. But a fresh

spray of bullets made it clear that the gunner on the truck
was well supplied with a long belt of ammunition, and as
the line of exploding earth danced inches from his face, he
realized his had been a Pyrrhic victory.

23

Shotgun had never felt so bad about smacking an enemy vehicle in his life. He actually stuffed six red licorice pieces into his mouth instead of his usual three as he pulled the Hog around to inspect the damage.

Nailed the sucker good. Land Rover looked smashed too.

He turned back to the small, fuzzy Maverick screen, viewing the wreckage. Glowing hot stuff, not moving. Little like a fishbowl with all the water run out.

Or maybe not.

Shotgun pushed the Hog southward as he scanned with the Maverick's IR head, trying to search the area where he figured the D boys would be—or at least where he hoped they had escaped to. He still had his STAR pods; they'd only be dropped if the ground team had trouble with Doberman's. They added weight and resistance to the plane, but he didn't notice it much as he banked and came around above the main highway, the Mav's head trained on the area he'd just hit. His eyes had begun to fuzz from fatigue—a good thing, he realized, since it blurred the numbers on the fuel gauges.

Something sparkled in the lower corner of his glass.

Machine gun.

Shooting at somebody on the ground.

Big machine gun, so it had to be Iraqi.

Damn, if that wasn't the best news he'd had all day. If they were still shooting at somebody, his guys were still alive. He hadn't nailed them accidentally.

Without really thinking about it, Shotgun slammed his Hog into a nose-first dive, tossing four or five g's in a full-body slam toward the earth. Air brakes screamed, flaps groaned, and the thick flare of a heavy machine gun, probably a Dushka, made a perfect X in the middle of his targeting screen.

And wouldn't you know it? Bruce Springsteen was on the CD player, just dishing up "Born in the USA."

O'Rourke lit his cannon as the Boss wailed. The GAU grabbed the bass, rhythm, and drum lines with its own particular take on slash-and-burn rock 'n' roll. The enemy machine gun disappeared beneath an onslaught of 30mm shells, vanishing along with its truck in a frothing white powder that turned red and black as the vehicle's gas tank blew.

Unfortunately, the tank had been less than half full; the explosion barely lit up the night, throwing only a lackluster fireball across Shotgun's path as he veered off. The fire wasn't even strong enough to sear his wings.

"I keep telling you idiots, keep your gas tanks full," Shotgun admonished the Iraqis as he recovered from the steep dive. "Woulda had a ten on the Boom Scale if you'd just held up your end of the bargain. Losing the war's one thing, but at least score some style points while you're at it."

24

As the machine gun swung its dragonlike fangs back toward Dixon, a hawk flashed above it. The Iraqi gun disappeared upward in a furious windstorm. Flames shot everywhere; dirt, dust, shrapnel, bits of plastic and rubber swirled through the air. A ball of fire shot off at an angle. Thunder roared with a massive, ear-shattering pop. Then silence returned, the night hushed by the faint whisper of two turbofans churning in the distance.

Dixon jumped to his feet.

"That was a Hog, kid," shouted Dixon, pulling the boy to his feet. "We're saved. We're saved. Shit—we were about an inch from getting creamed. Holy Jesus. Holy, holy Jesus."

"Lieutenant Dixon?"

Dixon looked up and saw a soldier running toward him carrying a light machine gun.

"I'm Dixon," he said. "Thank God you rescued me."

"We're not rescued yet. I'm Captain Wong."

"Lieutenant William James Dixon, 535th Tactical Fighter Squadron. Wong? You?"

"Yes. A pleasure to meet you in person." Wong had joined the squadron after Dixon was assigned to Riyadh, but had spoken to him briefly over the phone several times. Then as now, he spoke in a bored monotone, as if he were on a train platform waiting for the 6:03 to arrive. "We have a rendezvous to make," said Wong. "It's two miles away and scheduled to take place in five minutes."

"I guess we better get going."

Wong took a step, then stopped. "What's this boy?"

"Budge. I saved him."

Wong gave him a quizzical look, then bent to examine the child. He said something in Arabic. Words flooded from the kid's mouth.

"Your name is Budge," Wong told Dixon, translating a bit of what the boy had said. "BJ, I assume. Budge. He misunderstood. He thinks you're an angel sent from God. He doesn't understand who we are."

"What's *his* name then?"

"Nabi."

The boy nodded.

"Some Iraqi soldiers were going to kill him," Dixon told Wong.

"His parents were taken away. I believe he saw his father shot. My Arabic is not optimum," said Wong. "Most likely, the father was executed, along with the rest of his family. I believe we'll find he was a Shiite Muslim and/or part of the resistance, though there are other possibilities."

"Doesn't matter now," said Dixon.

"He can't come with us, Lieutenant. We have to run two miles; I suspect our transport is already approaching. They won't wait."

"He is coming," said Dixon.

Wong shook his head again. "We can't take him back."

"Are we going to make the rendezvous or not?" Dixon asked.

Wong frowned but said nothing. Turning, he began trotting to the southwest. Dixon started to follow, tugging the child to come.

They'd gone perhaps ten yards when the kid fell. He'd slipped well behind; it was obvious he couldn't keep up.

"Come on," said Dixon, running back to him. He picked Nabi up and took a few steps, but couldn't carry both the AK-74 and the kid, not and run at the same time.

He threw down the rifle, pushed Nabi across the top of his shoulder, and set off behind Wong.

"It's okay," he told the boy between his labored breaths. "We're going home. God must want us to, because there's no way we would have gotten this far without Him. Yeah," he said, running. "You don't mind if I still call you Budge, okay? It kind of sounds cool. That okay?"

The boy murmured something.

"Thanks," Dixon said. "Shit, Jesus—to make it back after all this. We're going home. Home."

And though his legs were liquid and his lungs wheezing, though he had a dozen bruises and maybe broken ribs and a bum arm and a banged-up head, he knew they were going to make it.

25

His Maverick's IR head remained out of commission, but Skull had no problem seeing the splashed trucks; one of them was burning rather spectacularly. Two other vehicles were stopped nearby, also damaged or destroyed. A pair of vehicles were coming down the highway from the west, maybe a mile and a half away. From what he understood of the layout on the ground, they weren't an immediate danger to his guys, but that didn't mean he was going to let them continue merrily along. He warned Shotgun even though he was back by the main battlefield, then pitched to climb and let off his last LUU flare. They popped at roughly nine hundred feet, lighting the sky like a bank of high-powered stadium lights as Knowlington continued upward before spinning around to attack. A little anxious, he started firing from three thousand feet, the shells falling in a bent arc toward the earth to catch the first vehicle, a six-wheeled truck, right across the grille. Two dozen uranium-enriched slugs made short work of its engine compartment, stalling it in a heap of steam. Skull kept coming, riding his rudder to put his nose across the path of the second vehicle. He let loose with more cannon, but could tell he missed; he jabbed the pedals and nudged his stick, but just couldn't hold the plane in the right position, altitude and speed burning off and the light of the flare distracting him. He pulled back and got a chop warning, the plane hinting that he had pushed things a bit too far and was in danger of losing all forward momentum. Knowlington ignored it, rearing the plane up by her nose and dipping around, goosing the throttle. The Hog divvied the air currents with her wing, skipping tightly back toward the target with an appreciative giggle, her nose centered on the truck. Knowlington clicked out a three-second burst, more than one hundred rounds of combat mix flaring from the business end of the Gat. He saw another shadow to his right and pushed toward it, aware that he was getting precariously low but still calculating that he could get off a burst. His aim was short; he zeroed again and nailed his trigger, but missed wide and now had to pull off.

As Skull banked, he saw a new group of shadows fleeing south from the vehicles Doberman had smashed earlier. But as he began to push the Hog in their direction, the flare inexplicably burnt itself out. He fired anyway, hoping he might at least scare the bastards. It was a waste, and he berated himself as he began to climb away, the Warthog gradually picking up speed.

"Devil Two, what's your situation?" he asked Shotgun.

"Geez, Skip, I was just about to ask you," answered his wingman. "Got a Devil Dog under way, and Bruce is poundin' in the earphones."

"You're a piece of work, Gun. What about the BPM?"

"Gone. Ditto a truck, and a flatbed or something they were using for a machine gun nest. Took the machine gun out too. Shame. Probably a Dushka. You ever shoot one of those, Boss?"

"Splash it or shoot it?"

"Shoot it."

"Negative. You see the ground team?"

"Negative. But I'm pretty sure I saw some fire being returned against that machine gun," added Shotgun.

Knowlington checked back with Wolf. The ground team had checked in, saying they were proceeding to Silo, the prime pickup point. Doberman had dropped his two pods there earlier.

The controller didn't mention Dixon. It'd been a long shot, too long—no right to hope for it, Skull told himself.

Wolf said the Herk seemed to be taking longer than expected to reach the pickup zone, but everything was shaping up nicely.

Except that the F-16's that were supposed to relieve them had been delayed.

"Can you remain on station?" the controller asked.

"We're going to have to," replied Knowlington. "Have our tanker move further north so we don't have too far to fly."

"What's your fuel situation?" asked Wolf, suddenly concerned. He paused to let Skull respond, but he didn't. "Maybe you should go south now," said the controller, probably doing the math himself.

"Negative, negative," said Skull. "Bring the tanker north and tell him to stand by."

"I don't know if we can do that."

"Then scramble the SAR assets to pick us up. We're not leaving these guys hanging."

26

Salt's GPS told him he'd reached the spot, but he couldn't see the pod containing the STAR kit. He was starting to get a little concerned—the Herk was due ten minutes ago, and he wasn't sure it would hang around. Walking home was not an option.

A light flared in the distance. One of the Hogs had lit a massive flare four or five miles to the west.

As Salt turned his gaze from it back toward the Iraqi holding Davis, he saw a dead body lying in the shadow ahead, a blanket over his head.

Poor dead bastard, he thought. Wind ripped his blanket off.

He took a step forward, instinctually moving to restore the corpse's decency, even if it could only have been an Iraqi. Then he saw it wasn't a body at all, but the pod he'd been searching for. The second lay a few yards away.

"There. Stop!" he told the Iraqi, gesturing with his rifle. "Put Davis down."

The man stopped, but didn't understand enough to put

the wounded sergeant down. Without time to explain or bother, Salt dropped the com pack and ran to the long metal canister. He pried it open, fingers desperate. The fall had jolted the cover, making it more difficult for him to separate the latched casing. Finally, he got it open just as he heard a plane in the distance.

One of the Hogs? Or the MC-130?

Salt fumbled with the gear, dragging the poles upright, setting them in the ground right there instead of running up to the high point of the area. He screwed in the connector for the helium inflator, cursing his bum luck, cursing everything. Where the fucking hell was Wong?

"I am right here, Sergeant," announced Captain Wong, running down the short hill that led to the rendezvous point. "There is no need to get overly flustered—the approaching plane is an A-10, not the MC-130."

Salt spun around as the captain ran directly to the pod, placing his gun on the ground. He removed two suits, which looked like padded olive-green ski gear. The hoods had fur fringe around them.

"Dress quickly, and prepare Sergeant Davis," said Wong. "I will prepare the prisoner."

"Fuck the prisoner," said Salt.

"He is more valuable than you or I," said Wong, going to the second canister. "He will go on the harness set with Lieutenant Dixon," he added, gesturing up the hill. "I trust he will be here shortly. He does not run quite as fast as I."

"Dixon?"

"My other assignment. Have you radioed to initiate the pickup?"

"I just got here."

"I'll make the transmission once the gear is set," said Wong. "The Hercules is supposed to proceed to Silo even if we do not broadcast."

"How are you getting back, Captain?" asked Salt.

"The future is not our present concern," said Wong. "Quickly now. The Hercules should arrive at any moment, and I believe I hear a vehicle in the distance."

27

If the Hercules had been equipped with an ejection seat, Lars would have pulled the handles by now. The blare of the RWR warnings, the flak, and the explosions drilled into his skull from all directions, carbon-tipped bits eating through the bone into his flesh.

Yet not one of the threats, real as they were, had been anywhere near the Hercules as it flew. MiGs, SAMs, a flight of F-15E Strike Eagles inbound to Baghdad crossing his path—everything had been miles and miles from his plane. He knew from Wolf that all hell was breaking loose near his target zone, but couldn't see it, flying too low and too slow; nonetheless, every flicker of pink, of red, of green panicked him. Somehow he managed to hold the control column steady as he flew on; somehow the big plane kept herself precisely on the path for the rendezvous point. They were making bad time—they were roughly twenty-five minutes behind schedule and getting worse— but there was nothing he could do about that, and it was decidedly better than being off course.

They were now inside ten miles of their pickup spot, not yet in contact with the ground team. Wolf had confirmed that the commandos were alive at least, and proceeding toward Silo, the code name for the prime pickup point. But the team had not checked back.

"I think we ought to go right in," said the navigator. "Hit our mark in case they're there but can't use the radio. This low, we're going to have trouble hearing them."

Going straight in was the briefed procedure, and Lars knew what the navigator said might be true. Still, Wolf ought to be able to get them on the air, or contact them through the A-10's flying cover. Lars opened his mouth to tell Kelly to contact the ABCCC again, but nothing came out. He worked his tongue around his lips and teeth, swallowed, trying to force some saliva toward his dry throat.

"Try another hail," he managed.

"Wolf would have told us if they'd come up. You're on course," added Kelly, leaning over his shoulder. The flight engineer was looking at the radar unit, or maybe just pretending to. "Everything's cool," added the sergeant, patting his shoulder.

"Yeah," said Lars, seeing his left hand shake but powerless to stop it. "Cool."

The assistant jumpmaster and the winch operator and the tail-position operator reported that they were ready. Someone else in the back said something; then there was another voice Lars couldn't make out. After they snagged the line they'd have to clamp it, then release it, then winch it, then hook it, then release it, then grab the men.

No, he had the order wrong. Hook, clamp, release, pull. No . . .

Just fly the plane. That was tough enough.

The Herk's GPS NAVISTAR computer projected a crosshair over the target zone as they approached, just as if they were making a covert drop in hostile territory. Lars felt his body hitching, weighed down by the helmet and heavy flak jacket. As he hit his turn and brought the Herk up off the deck, he caught a glimpse of the moon; it was nowhere near full but it would be bathing them in light, making them an easy target.

A flare lit in the distance off their right wing.

We're going to fry, he thought. Fry.

"Wolf hasn't heard from them. A-10's say we're clear and Wolf concurs. Go for it," said Kelly.

"Going for it."

"Going to take a first pass to get the lay of the land?" asked the navigator.

Lars realized he was too high and too fast as he came out of the turn that was supposed to get him right in front of the balloon.

"It's been a while since I've done this," he said, though he wasn't sure whether he expected sympathy or outrage.

He backed off power, got a little more crosswind than he expected, but compensated. He was doing too much; he couldn't handle all of this. He needed to be at five hundred feet; he was at seven hundred, sliding down slowly.

"Forty seconds. Confidence high," said the navigator. They were on course and somehow at the right altitude.

"Thirty-second slowdown." Lars cut his airspeed again, holding his altitude at a perfect five hundred feet above the ground. The flight engineer said something, but he missed it.

There was no flak in the air, nothing. Just like a picnic.

"Five-second slowdown," he said, but he stopped himself as he went to cut more power. The big plane was already down to 140 knots indicated, and its speed was still creeping downward.

Too slow and he'd stall. Then he'd really lose it.

Keep it steady. That was the key.

No way he could do this. No way.

"Do we have them on radio? What's the story?" he blurted out.

"Pencil flare ahead," Kelly shouted, practically jumping from his perch behind the pilot to point out the window.

The flare arched upward, slightly off to the right.

That wasn't the protocol, wasn't the way it was supposed to happen.

Was it?

"Shit, they're off—I'm replotting," said the navigator, trying to update the computer. "Damn it—was it them or what?"

Lars didn't need the computer, didn't need the terrain radar or even the FLIR. He nudged the big plane as gently as he could manage, edging slightly off keel, speed dropping low. The Herk's airframe had been modified to increase its stability at low speeds and altitudes, but it was still a struggle, still a battle just to keep it in the air, get it to where he needed to get it.

Had the small flare come from their guys or Iraqis luring them to their deaths?

"Shit, there! There, dead ahead!" shouted the flight engineer.

Lars pushed his head toward the windshield, but instead of looking ahead for the Mylar blimp that would show him where the line was, he closed his eyes.

28

A little less than a year before the Gulf War began, BJ Dixon's mother had died. She had suffered a massive coronary and gone into a coma. Then she briefly revived, only to plunge into a fugue state, teetering on death. Besides the severe heart condition, she was found to have several aneurysms of the brain. After a second, milder heart attack, her doctor said her time left was measured in hours, not days, but she somehow hung on for weeks.

The night before she passed away, he sat in a chair next to her bedside, praying. He had never been particularly religious, and the words were mostly haphazard snippets of things he remembered from childhood, interspersed with simple pleas for his mother's life. He had begun praying simply because his mother asked him to, but as he went on, he started to believe more and more in the words, and then in their power. Finally, he somehow came to think that his mother—who had been healthy and even strong all her life, who wasn't yet fifty—would live. When he finished his last prayer, he was convinced God would save her.

His mother died a short time later.

He didn't blame God exactly, nor did he lose faith—he hadn't had a vast reservoir of faith to lose. But the religious inclinations that he might have had drifted away. By the end of the funeral service, the biblical passages that his mother had picked out—intended actually for his father, who had been bedridden for nearly twenty years—were no more than vaguely ironic words with references to faith and an afterlife. Dixon was like millions of other men and women, neither believing nor disbelieving.

The war had done nothing to change his attitude. His panic during his first air mission, his triumphant shoot-down of an enemy helicopter, his free fall into Iraqi territory, his decision to sacrifice himself so another man would live, his wandering through the desert—none of these things had made him more or less of a believer.

But as he ran with the boy over his shoulder behind Wong, BJ Dixon felt strongly that God had saved him. It was the only explanation that made sense. His miraculous recovery might be explained by wild luck and chance—not to mention the heroic efforts of Wong and the other men who had landed here. But the Iraqi heavy machine gun had been aimed directly at him from less than twenty yards away. Wong had distracted it, the Hog had finished it, but only God himself could have sheltered Dixon and little Nabi from the fusillade. Dixon felt gratitude and exhilaration—he literally felt grace.

By the time Dixon reached Wong and the rest of the ground team, Wong was spinning out a cable mechanism near what looked like a pair of football goalposts. Two men in parkas were sitting between the poles, one slumping against the other.

"What's all this?" Dixon asked as Wong finished.

Wong reached over to the ground and tossed what seemed to be a green sleeping bag at him. "Into this suit."

"What is this?"

"The suit is part of the harness system. We're using a STAR retrieval system to board an MC-130. Please, Captain, prepare yourself. It will keep you somewhat warm and may help if you bounce along the ground."

Another man, short, somewhat fat, stood in another suit nearby; he watched Wong but did not say anything.

An airplane dipped nearly overhead. It had to be a Hercules—nothing else in the Gulf had such a throaty, turbine roar.

"He's too high and we are in the wrong position," said Wong. He held up a pencil-flare dispenser and fired, frowning as the small rocket disappeared. He stared northward as the drone grew louder, then shook his head. "I'll have to tell him to make another pass."

He ran to the Satcom rucksack.

"Shit," said one of the men between the goalposts.

In the next second the Hercules passed directly overhead, so low Dixon thought it would land in the dirt a few feet away. He jumped on top of the boy, who'd already thrown himself down. Above the roar Dixon heard the sound of a guitar string breaking; there was a scream and a *whoosh*. The plane was gone—and so were the two men, literally plucked from the ground by the system.

Wong hunkered over the Satcom, shouting; his words were drowned out by the airplane. Finally he jumped up and ran the few steps back to Dixon.

"Quickly," said Wong, gesturing at the suit. "We have six minutes while they recover the men and turn."

"We're getting snapped up?" Dixon asked, standing.

"Quickly. The suit has the harness sewed into it."

"Where's a suit for the boy? And where's yours?"

"The boy is not going. We cannot kidnap an Iraqi child," said Wong. He went to a large metal container and took out more poles. With a hiss, he inflated a blimplike balloon and began reeling it upward.

"I'm not kidnapping him. I saved him," said Dixon, holding the boy to his side. "Where's your suit?"

"There's no time to argue, Lieutenant. I will order you into the suit if you wish."

"Captain, no way I'm leaving him."

Dixon threw the suit down on the ground, anger welling

inside of him. As it landed, the man who had been sitting on the ground in the other suit leaped up, pushing Wong aside and slamming into Dixon.

Dixon flailed back, unsure exactly what was going on. Worn down by everything that had happened over the past forty-eight hours, tired and hungry, BJ pushed and punched, but it was all he could do to simply hold on to the shorter man. He jabbed the man's chin, then his shoulder, anger exploding in him, anger and instinct—he was fighting to save the kid. Dixon grabbed at the man's head, then saw his face in the shadows.

He was wrestling Saddam Hussein himself.

Dixon's shock was all the Iraqi needed. He rammed his head into BJ's chest, slamming against his ribs. Jolted by the pain, Dixon reeled on the ground; in the next second the man leaped back with something in his hand.

He'd grabbed the other grenade BJ had taken from the dead Iraqi that afternoon.

The fake Saddam took three steps away. He pulled the pin, took another step, dropped the grenade.

Wong took one step forward.

The boy dropped to his knees, three inches from the grenade, covering it with his body, his short legs curled at his chest, his back to Dixon and Wong.

Time became light. It became sound, a piercing cry of anguish that resounded in the desert, drowning out the drone of the approaching airplane.

Dixon saw himself at his mother's deathbed again. He looked down at her, stared at her face. The dead were supposed to find peace, but her mouth had contorted in a last gasp of pain.

"Lieutenant. Lieutenant. Quickly. We must go."

Dixon opened his eyes to find Wong over him. He took a hard breath, felt his ribs flame. Wong disappeared; Dixon felt his head slip back, blackness beckoning.

Up, he told himself. Save the kid.

He opened his eyes again, took another breath. This time, the pain helped him focus.

Wong had pulled the suit over him.

"I have to save Budge," he said.

"The boy is dead. So is the Iraqi," said Wong. "Here, quickly. More Iraqis are coming from the west."

Something flared to his left. Dixon turned, thinking he would hear the gunfire, but instead he heard the cry again. He closed his eyes.

Wong dragged him toward the pole, pulled on the harness. Dixon felt as if he were a little kid being helped into a snowsuit.

"You're staying on the ground?" he asked Wong.

"I intended to before the Iraqi took matters in his own hands. But that is no longer necessary." Wong looped himself into the special suit, snapping the restraints. "The shock should be no greater than a parachute opening. Of course, it depends on which parachute we are referring to. In my experience—"

A howl drowned out Wong's words, dirt flying in Dixon's face. As he blinked his eyes closed, he realized the sound didn't come from the Hercules but bullets being fired a short distance away.

29

He could see it all. His eyes were as good as they'd been twenty years ago. But Colonel Knowlington wasn't just seeing with his eyes—he saw everything with his head, knew where it all was. He could feel himself flying, feel the Hog following as he banked five hundred feet above the ground, the big Hercules dipping back in his direction as it came back for the second pickup.

Dixon would be there. He knew he would.

Something moved in the open scrubland beyond the rendezvous point. Knowlington pushed his Hog to take care of it, knowing it was Iraqis, knowing he was going to nail them just before the Herk got there.

"Herky Bird, assets are taking fire," Skull said over the radio. "I'm clearing them out for you."

The MC-130 didn't respond, but it didn't matter. Knowlington had them—he could see every little god-damn thing, Shotgun in trail on the right wing, closing quickly to help; the bastards on the ground, flailing at his men; his guys, Wong and Dixon, waiting to get picked up;

the Hercules coming in cool and calm like she was landing at an airport in North Dakota.

He aimed the nose of the Hog at the pinpricks of light on the ground and lit the cannon.

30

For a moment, everything was pitch black and quiet, consumed by the flaring hum of a fire burning itself out.

Then Captain Lars Warren opened his eyes.

A dervish slashed in front of him, spitting blood from its mouth.

Someone shouted at him, screaming that he was a failure, a coward, that he'd blown it big-time, that he'd wimped and screwed up and what the hell right did he have being in the cockpit and who said he could fly a plane—who said he could lead or even live, dare to breathe in a combat zone where millions of better men had been killed and maimed?

His hands trembled. Sweat poured from every inch of his body. He was on line, he was right there, at the spot, the balloon materializing before him like a bubble floating up in a glass of champagne. The whiskers snared it and it smacked against the glass panel. It bounced in front of him, splattering and growing, covering the entire forward area of the plane, a shroud thrown over the entire plane. It was bigger than the earth itself. The only thing Lars could do was hold the plane as tightly as he could, keep his hands on the control column, shaking and all, hold the plane for an eternity, hold the plane at a hundred knots, ninety-eight, ninety-six, its back end wide open, men screaming all around him, bullets flying. It was impossible to do this—it was impossible just to breathe.

"We're good, Captain! We're good!" said the navigator. "Shit, yeah. Shit, yeah."

"Just steady," Lars said. "Just steady."

The men in the back humped their own bricks, grabbing the guide rope, winching, pulling their passengers aboard.

More shouts. Someone brought the engines up. The rear bay snapped closed.

"We're good back here," said the loadmaster over the plane's interphone or internal communications system. "We've got four happy passengers. Kick-ass, Captain. Kick-fucking-ass!"

Four passengers?

Shit—had he already done it twice?

Shit.

Four? Not three?

Had they done this twice already? He couldn't remember.

Twice?

"Four?" he said.

Someone was cheering. Lars felt a hand slap him on the shoulder—the flight engineer.

"Looking good," said the navigator. "Looking A-fucking-one-good. We are on course and heading home. Falcons arriving at two o'clock. There's our escort. Oh, Mama, this is great."

"We're secure," said Kelly, relaying information from the crew chief in the back who had supervised the pickup. "We have an extra passenger aboard—Lieutenant William Dixon, U.S. Air Force, assigned as a forward ground controller with Delta, lost two days ago. Kick-ass, we've rescued the dead. Dixon was KIA. Kick-ass. Kick-fuckin'-ass. The guy's a fuckin' hero and we pulled him out. Lazarus returns. Shit. Major DiRiggio says well done. He's conscious; medic says he's doing better. Great going, Captain. Kick-ass."

But sweat kept pouring from Lars's hands and they wouldn't stop shaking, even as he checked his course for home.

31

"They got them!" screamed Shotgun over the short-range radio. "They got them! That's what I'm *talking* about!"

"One," said Skull.

"Shit, yeah! Shit, yeah!" Shotgun shouted, his voice nearly drowned out by the blare of rock music.

That or one of his engines was going funky.

"Hell of a call sign," said Skull.

"You don't sound very enthusiastic," said Shotgun.

Skull could swear the comment had been accompanied by a slurp from a mug.

"Maybe I should get you to rig me up a stereo system," said Knowlington. "Or a refrigerator."

"Just drinking coffee," said Shotgun.

"All right. We have about zero-five to the closest spot the tanker can meet us," Knowlington told him.

Wolf had managed to vector the tanker further north than originally intended. A flight of F-15's providing air cover had already flown ahead, a welcoming committee for a job well done.

Or escorts for the SAR crew that would be needed if they botched the tank.

"Gonna leave me with two minutes of fuel," said Shotgun. "Plenty of time."

"Two minutes? You've been holding out on me," said Skull.

"Drop back and I'll drip some in your tanks."

"Just watch my butt," Skull told his wingman. "I shaved it for you and everything."

"See, Boss, *now* you're talking like a Hog driver."

"What I'm talking about," replied Knowlington.

WARMING THE SOUL

1

Wong's shoulder had been dislocated, but one of the Air Force medics had helped get it back into position. Oddly, the jarring had cured his headache, as well as removed the ringing in his ear.

Davis had lost considerable blood, but had been stabilized; the odds were fifty-fifty that he would make it. Salt was cursing up a storm, complaining about his ankle, which he had whacked against something as he was hauled in. But if the volume of his obscenities were a rough gauge of his prognosis, he'd be walking in the morning.

The plane's pilot was resting as well, apparently after suffering a heart attack. His pulse was erratic, but the crew said he actually seemed to have gotten much better.

Dixon sat on the floor of the plane, head back against a metal spar. Worn and battered from his ordeal, he sipped water from a plastic bottle.

"We should be landing shortly," Wong told the others. "There will be a helicopter waiting to take us home to King Fahd, where we will be debriefed."

"That can't fucking wait until tomorrow?" asked Salt.

"Command wants to know what we've seen ASAP," Wong said.

"Fuck them."

"A suggestion that has been proposed in the past," said Wong. "But one which they do not seem prepared to follow."

Wong had meant that as a joke, the first he had made since coming to the Gulf. But no one laughed, not even Sergeant Salt.

"We will tell them what we saw," said Wong, sighing. "I would imagine that Lieutenant Dixon's testimony will be most crucial."

"Testimony, geez." Salt laughed uproariously, the ripping sound rising above the roar of the Herk's engines.

Exasperated, Wong looked at Dixon. "Lieutenant?"

Dixon stared at the floor.

"We'll be taken in to Riyadh after we land," Wong said.

Dixon turned and looked at him as if he were staring across a distant field.

"The kid saved us," said BJ.

Wong got up and slid down on his knees in front of him to hear better.

"Budge saved us," Dixon repeated.

"True," said Wong. "As you saved him."

"He didn't know what he was doing."

"War is not a pretty thing," Wong said. "That's why we're here."

"He was just a kid."

Wong frowned. The thoughts of many wise men flickered through his head—Nietzeche, Kierkegaard, Plato, St. Paul. None seemed quite to fit. And so he said nothing.

2

Doberman sat at the edge of the couch, wedged there with his feet up on the cushion. He'd finished debriefing only a few minutes before; normally he'd have gone either straight to bed or over to the Cavern, a just-off-the-base den of iniquity and booze. But he was too wound, and too worried about the others, so he'd wandered over to Cineplex. More than two dozen other squadron members, officers and NCOS, milled around the crowded room, waiting for word of the Strawman mission. The television was playing something off the VCR—an old Godzilla movie someone had bootlegged. Every so often, they'd hit pause and check CNN. Not that they expected the news station to find out about the mission, but you never could tell.

Among the NCOs clustered near the food table was Technical Sergeant Becky Rosen, whom Doberman realized was looking particularly gorgeous tonight. She smiled at him as she walked nearby, said something along the lines of "Thanks for risking your neck up there."

He felt like a thirteen-year-old, unable to say anything

intelligent in response. He watched her walk away, imagining what she might look like in a dress.

Damn, he was horny.

"So what's Preston like?" asked Jeff "Truck" Lewis, leaning against the nearby chair with a glass of seltzer. Lewis, a black guy who'd grown up in New Jersey, was a captain who'd flown Hogs for about a year and a half. No one, including Jeff, was exactly sure where his nickname had come from.

"I don't know," Doberman told him.

"He flew wing for you, right?"

Doberman shrugged.

"I hear he's a jerk," offered Lewis.

"Who knows," said Glenon.

"He talks nice about Glenon," said Terry Morris. Morris was attached to the intelligence unit that shared some of the trailer office space with Devil Squadron. "He was raving about what a great pilot you were, Doberman."

"I'm not in any mood for you guys to pull my chain, okay?"

"No, it's what he said," insisted Morris. "Said you kicked butt. Some of the best flying he's ever seen."

"Probably wants Doberman to replace him in that fast-mover squadron he came from," said Lewis.

"Screw off."

"Hey, Dog, take it easy."

"You ain't Shotgun, Truck. Don't call me Dog."

Lewis whistled, but backed off.

"Godzilla's gonna eat them," said someone with a laugh, looking at the TV. "Use your slime, Rhodan."

"Okay, here it is," said Major Preston, appearing in the doorway. His hair was slicked back from a shower and he'd obviously just shaved. Doberman couldn't help shaking his head.

"Colonel Knowlington and Captain O'Rourke are spending the night at King Khalid," announced Hack. "Apparently they tanked with about five seconds to spare. But they're fine, planes are intact."

"They better be," said Sergeant Clyston. The pilots laughed, though it wasn't entirely clear he was kidding.

"What about Dixon?" shouted someone.

"Captain Wong and the two Delta troopers were successfully recovered by the MC-130," continued Preston. He held up his hands. He was grinning. "And they have Lieutenant Dixon, a bit tired and beat up, but okay."

No one said anything, the room suddenly still.

"Dixon's *alive*," said Preston.

"Yes! Yes!" shouted Morris, and everyone began cheering at once. Doberman couldn't believe it for a second—it was too much to hope for.

Dixon was alive. He was *alive*.

Yeah, shit, yeah.

He jumped up from the couch. Everyone was slapping high fives and hugging each other, as if they'd won the World Series or the Super Bowl.

Sergeant Clyston loomed before him.

"Way to go, Captain," said the Capo.

"Kick-ass," replied Doberman. He patted the sergeant's broad back, then turned.

Sergeant Rosen was smiling next to him. He hugged her, folding her body into his. Glenon was short, but Rosen was even shorter. And though he knew she was strong— had in fact seen her haul a hundred-pound toolbox and carry a knapsack without breaking a sweat—her body felt soft and light in his arms.

Light and soft and delicious.

He leaned over and kissed her. It was a long, long kiss, a dream thing, the kind of kiss you want on the perfect night. He held it, felt her lips against his, felt his heart fading into oblivion.

She pulled away gently. He pulled away, looking into her face.

Her slap nearly knocked him over.

Doberman stared at her as she walked quickly from the room. The celebration continued on around him.

Had he imagined the kiss? Or the slap?

"Captain, I got bad news," said Preston behind him. He

nudged him aside. "It's not really bad, I guess, just disappointing."

Doberman, still stunned, listened as Preston told him they hadn't gotten Saddam.

"The car we hit—the car you hit—it wasn't Saddam. It was an impostor, part of their ruse. You nailed it, though. You nailed it good. You're a hell of a shot, Glenon. You're a damn good pilot, one of the best I've ever seen. A hell of a lot better than me."

Without saying anything, Doberman turned and started after Rosen. A meaty hand grabbed him from behind. Doberman snapped around, expecting to see Preston and ready to floor him with a roundhouse.

But it was Clyston who'd grabbed him.

"No offense, Captain. But you're much better off letting her be. Honest."

The way the sergeant said it, the only thing Doberman could do was nod.

3

King Khalid, aka the Emerald City, was near the border
with Kuwait, right on the so-called neutral zone and well
within striking distance of Saddam's troops. As such, it
was officially a forward operating area, a place for war-
planes like the A-10 to use as temporary bases, a kind of
scratch in the earth.

On the other hand, it was a fairly large base in a sophisticated international settlement, home to a large U.S. Army
contingent and a massive helicopter force, to say nothing of
some of the friendliest Air Force ground crew dogs and Spec
Ops Do-it Dudes—Shotgun's term—in the world. So Colonel
Knowlington wasn't all that surprised by the warm welcome
they received when Devils One and Two touched down. He'd
already decided they'd get some sleep there; King Fahd was
a good hour's flight away, and Shotgun looked like he hadn't
slept in a month.

"Don't worry about me, Skip," Shotgun insisted after they
checked over their Hogs on the ground. "I know where I can

get some real joe here—there's a secret Dunkin' Donuts outpost on the other side of the sports dome."

The sports dome being a nearby mosque.

"Colonel Knowlington, I'm Captain Hobbes," said an Air Force officer, hopping from a Hummer as it pulled to a stop in the A-10 parking area. "I'm here to make sure you're comfortable."

"You debriefing us?" Skull asked.

"I'm just hospitality." Hobbes grinned. "Do have a couple of goofy-looking intelligence types interested in talking to you about the missiles you came up against. Guy from Cent-Com too, carrying around a clipboard. First I thought he was just doing inventory, but he kept asking pointed questions on what time you guys were supposed to land, so he may think you were trying to steal one of these planes. Couple of Delta types looking to add a squiggle or two to their maps, Spec Ops lieutenant with some adoption papers, I think, and a French general who says you saved his son. Can't tell if it's really his son, though. I'm not too good with French this time of day."

Skull and Shotgun boarded the Humvee without getting out of their flight gear. Their tour of the flight-support shop turned into an international jawboning session as the welcome wagon crowded in to help them out of their fancy dress. A French helicopter unit based at King Khalid had heard about Skull's persistence in rescuing their fellow countryman and was determined to show its appreciation. Their efforts were augmented by the French Army general and his entourage, who were convinced that Skull and Shotgun deserved either medals or the Eiffel Tower for their exploits—it was hard to hear, let alone translate, in the din. Besides the base contingent, a half-dozen RAF and U.S. intel officers crowded around to ask what it was like to fly against the SA-11's, a Hog driver from another squadron wandered in to find out what was shaking, a colonel came by to ask about a nephew doing maintenance in Devil Squadron, a Saudi sergeant who knew Shotgun from somewhere walked up to pay off an old debt—Knowlington and O'Rourke were the guests of honor at a ragtag UN meeting. As people continued to materialize, someone decided to move it first to an empty hangar, and then off base to a building commandeered by the French.

Somewhere along the way, someone put a foam cup in Knowlington's hand. He got halfway through before realizing it was a beer.

No. That was a lie. He realized it on the first sip. He realized it and felt the light tingle on his tongue. A voice in his head screamed to spit it out, but a louder voice just laughed and said, "Drink."

When he finished the cup, someone put another in his hand, and then another and another. He drank them all, the tingle melting into a steady hum, a pleasant, familiar vibration that warmed his brain and rubbed his back, loosened the knots in his shoulders, and asked why he had waited so damn long to feel so damn good again.

A Note to the Reader

The operations described in the book, while in some respects inspired by actual events, are all invented and should be treated as fiction. Officially, the U.S. and its allies did not target Saddam for capture or execution.

In a few instances, details relating to procedures that could conceivably assist an enemy have either been omitted or obscured. These did not materially affect the story. And of course, actions depicted in the book that are contrary to military law and procedures, not to mention good sense, are all fictional.

The STAR retrieval system does exist and works more or less in the manner described—though I for one would rather walk.

C-130's of various descriptions performed a wide variety of missions in the Gulf; while the plane began flying in the 1950s, it remains an important though often overlooked member of the service.

Al Kajuk is an invention.

French aircraft flew a total of 2,258 sorties during the war, roughly two percent of the total missions and fourth among coalition partners after the U.S., Britain, and Saudi Arabia. While several French aircraft sustained heavy battle damage, no French pilots were shot down during the war. Naturally, Hog drivers would have snagged their butts and hauled them home if they had been.

Some more boring statistics: The day before most of this story takes place, something on the order of forty percent of the sorties flown against Iraq were devoted to Scud-hunting. That represented a major revamping of priorities to go against a small though admittedly politically significant threat. If that's not an argument for providing a serious defense against ballistic missiles from rogue states and terrorists, Shotgun's a neat freak.

Speaking of Shotgun, if you're interested in adding to his "Hog Rules" listed at the front of the book, you can E-mail me at Thrllrdad@aol.com. I'll try and include additions in a future installment. As a matter of fact, you can E-mail there with comments and suggestions—not to mentions heads-ups, corrections, and whatsamattafuhyous. Attaboys are also welcome.

I can't promise to get back to everyone, but I'll try.

—Ferro